KU-004-931

POT OF GOLD

Recent Titles by Rowena Summers from Severn House

The Caldwell Series

TAKING HEART
DAISY'S WAR
THE CALDWELL GIRLS
DREAMS OF PEACE

The Hotel Saga

SHELTER FROM THE STORM
MONDAY'S CHILD

BLACKTHORN COTTAGE
LONG SHADOWS
DISTANT HORIZONS

The Family Saga

CHASING RAINBOWS
POT OF GOLD

POT OF GOLD

Rowena Summers

This first world edition published 2009
in Great Britain and 2010 in the USA by
SEVERN HOUSE PUBLISHERS LTD of
9–15 High Street, Sutton, Surrey, England, SM1 1DF.
Trade paperback edition published
in Great Britain and the USA 2010 by
SEVERN HOUSE PUBLISHERS LTD

Copyright © 2009 by Jean Saunders.

All rights reserved.
The moral right of the author has been asserted.

British Library Cataloguing in Publication Data

Summers, Rowena, 1932–
    Pot of Gold.
    1. Farm life – Fiction. 2. Inheritance and succession –
    Fiction. 3. General Strike, Great Britain, 1926 – Fiction.
    4. Domestic fiction.
    I. Title
    823.9'14–dc22

ISBN-13: 978-0-7278-6845-9   (cased)
ISBN-13: 978-1-84751-186-7   (trade paper)

NEATH PORT TALBOT LIBRARIES		
2300004171 0		
HJ	COM	24-Sep-2009
AF		£18.99

Except where
described for
publication a
is purely coir

All Severn Ho

Typeset by Palimpsest Book Production Ltd.,
Grangemouth, Stirlingshire, Scotland.
Printed and bound in Great Britain by
MPG Books Ltd., Bodmin, Cornwall.

One

Ireland, 1926

C herry Melchoir stood at the window of the long, sprawling farmhouse, watching the deft movements of her husband tethering his horse, and feeling the usual jump of her heart as she admired his strength in handling the large, sleek animal. Though, quite which of the two she was referring to in her mind, was something she wasn't too sure about. As she saw him hand the reins to his groom and give him some crisp orders for the day, she moved back from the window a little, not wanting Lance to think she had been waiting for his return as if she had nothing else to do to occupy herself. Not that she did really, she thought wryly. The life of a gentleman farmer's wife was far removed from the working girl she had been all her life, and the fact that she was here at all was something of a miracle. More than a year after their arrival, she still had to pinch herself every morning to believe that it was real.

Had she really married the man of her dreams and come to this beautiful little village in the fold of the hills where the blue misty mornings resembled something out of a child's fairy-tale story? Had she really left behind a life of being a kitchen skivvy to being mistress of all she surveyed, with everything organized so smoothly and swiftly by others that she had had no real say in it at all? And was it really the happy-ever-after ending she had so joyfully imagined it would be?

'Is there something troubling you, Mrs Melchoir?'

She heard the soft voice behind her and turned with a start, to smile at the young, fresh-faced Irish girl.

'Nothing at all, Maureen. I was just wondering what kind of a day it was going to be.'

The girl nodded sagely. 'Me old granny used to say that when she got the screws in her knees it was going to rain, but Mammy said that since she got them every day of her life and spent her days hobbling about like a leprechaun, we might as well always take it with a pinch of salt. It rains half the year here anyway, as you'll have discovered by now! That's why everything's so green.'

Cherry laughed at her rambling. 'You do talk nonsense sometimes, Maureen, but you do me a lot of good. Did I ever tell you how much you remind me of my friend Paula?'

'Frequently, missus,' the girl said with a grin. 'And would she be the friend who's coming to stay for a spell when Captain Melchoir is away for the horse-trading next month?'

'She's the one,' said Cherry, feeling such an unexpected burst of nostalgia at the mention of Paula's name it almost took her breath away.

She turned away quickly, before the canny young Irish maid who fancied she had a bit of her granny's second sight, detected the shine of tears in her eyes. Cherry knew she was just being foolish, anyway. She had everything she ever wanted, and with Paula coming to stay for a week or two, it would be like old times. Except that those old times would never come again, and there was no reason why she should ever want them to.

'You'll be wanting to show her around the area, I daresay,' Maureen went on, as relentlessly cheerful as ever. 'I could ask my brother Declan to take you sightseeing in his old jalopy if it wouldn't rock your friend about too much. He reckons most English folk like to see something of our quaint country ways.'

She couldn't quite resist the small barb in her voice, as if to remind Cherry that even if she was the mistress here, the English were the interlopers. Not that she really needed to remind Cherry, who could still feel like a stranger.

'It sounds lovely,' she said quickly. 'But it all depends on how Paula's feeling. She may prefer to have a quiet time since she's expecting a child in six months' time. She wouldn't want to be too jolted about.'

'Ah well, you'll know best when the time comes,' Maureen said easily. 'I'll get on with my work then, missus.'

It was just as well she disappeared, clattering away to do the upstairs, as she called it, before Lance came indoors to hear her calling Cherry 'missus'. No matter how he tried, he couldn't persuade the girl to use any other term, and it irked him every time he heard it.

He didn't care too much for Maureen and her gossiping, but one of her many brothers was one of the best grooms and horse-gentlers for miles around, and Lance knew he couldn't do without him. But in this corner of the world, it seemed that if you got one hired hand, you were expected to hire other family members too. It was just one more little thing that seemed to irk Lance these days, Cherry thought with a sigh. Despite his enjoyment with the horse-trading and working with the animals he loved, she never thought he was entirely happy. And no matter how she tried, she couldn't ignore the fact that if he wasn't happy, it was her fault.

But she smiled at him brightly as he came indoors out of the chill January wind, rubbing his hands together to warm them.

'I've had another letter from Paula,' she said at once, waving the envelope at him. Knowing how little he liked to be reminded of the past lives of his wife and her best friend, Cherry was just as determined not to forget her.

'Is she still set on coming for a visit?' Lance said. 'I'm not sure it's wise in her condition. What does the husband have to say about it?'

Cherry kept the smile fixed on her face. 'The husband, whom you know very well is called Harold, is pleased for her, and the doctor approves too. He says the country air will do her good.' She put her hand on his arm. 'Lance, you will make her welcome, won't you? It means a lot to me to see her again.'

He leaned forward and kissed her on the cheek. 'Don't worry, my love, I think I know how to behave when we have company. Of course she's welcome. Now, the farm manager will be here shortly to attend to business matters. Show him in to the study when he arrives, then please see that we're not disturbed.'

She watched him go, as upright and elegant as he had ever been when he was an army captain and in charge of men, and just as forceful. Now, she knew he would shut himself away in his study for hours on end with the farm manager, doing whatever business they had to attend to for the running of this busy and productive farm, and the horse-breeding that meant so much to Lance. Whatever he did, he threw himself into it whole-heartedly, even though it was far from the indolent life he had envisaged for himself when he left the army and settled down as the indulged son of wealthy Bristol landowners.

She pushed down the uneasy thought, and opened the letter from Paula to read it again. It was as bubbly and excited as Paula herself, and somehow it made Cherry feel old. Which was ridiculous, since she was still little more than a girl herself, but the days when she and Paula had dressed up to the nines to go dancing in Bristol and meet young bucks seemed like a distant dream now.

Despite the fact that they were both married, and Paula was expecting her first child now, through her letters at least her friend seemed to have retained all the fun of those times, while she . . . where had that young girl gone?

Before she could read the letter again, the cook came in from the kitchen to go through the list of menus for the week with her mistress. Monday mornings were always the same. Always the same rituals to go through, except that in the old days it would be she and Paula who were taking orders from the cook at Melchoir House in the fashionable part of Bristol.

It would be Cherry O'Neill, kitchen-maid, scurrying about doing others' bidding, not Cherry Melchoir putting on airs and graces, acting the part of a lady and approving the menus herself. Now it was other folk doing the menial tasks, while Cherry was twiddling her thumbs for much of the time, and trying not to admit to herself that the life of a lady was generally pretty boring.

She drew in her breath, not wanting the word to come into her head as she read through the menus the cook was showing her, and making small suggestions of her own. It hadn't taken her long to discover that the wife of a gentleman farmer was in a strange situation. She wasn't a lady on a big estate, but nor was she what she had always presumed to be a regular farmer's wife, mucking in and helping – which she admitted she would have much preferred. When they had come here to this parcel of land that had belonged to Lance's family for several generations, she had had no idea how very different it was all going to be, and that Lance firmly intended to cling on to his old status of son and heir to a country squire as much as possible, expecting her to play the part of his consort.

As if you were blooming royalty, she could almost hear Paula scoff.

'This all looks fine, Mrs Brady,' she finally told the cook, concentrating again on the menus. 'And I've told you my friend will be coming for a visit next month, haven't I?'

'That you have, Mrs Melchoir, and I'm sure we'll do our best to accommodate the young lady with whatever choices she requires. Ladies in her condition do sometimes have strange fancies when it comes to food, and I believe you did tell me she was in a delicate condition?'

'So I did,' Cherry said, unable to recall telling her any such thing, but it was uncanny how such snippets of news seemed to get around – thanks mainly to Maureen in all probability. 'I don't imagine there'll be any problem, though. Paula always had the stomach of an ox when it came to food.'

'Ah well, we'll see when the time comes,' the cook said, not wavering.

Cherry couldn't imagine Paula giving in to being in the kind of delicate condition that kept most high-bred ladies confined to their beds, either. Even though Paula had always seemed to be a maggoty little thing compared with Cherry's robust constitution and dramatic colouring, there was nothing weak about Paula. She lived in a cosy little rented house with her husband now, and Harold had his longed-for job on the railway while Paula played at keeping house, just as she had always wanted. Lucky, lucky Paula . . .

Cherry bit her lips, wondering what had got into her today. It must be the weather, which had turned bitterly cold ever since the turn of the year, frosting the ground every morning and dusting the far hills with snow. It was beautiful to look at, but treacherous for walking, and she admitted it wasn't the best time for Paula to come visiting. But the doctor had told her she shouldn't leave it any later than halfway through her pregnancy, and they did so want to see one another.

For a heart-stopping moment, Cherry wondered about their first meeting after all this time. She and Paula had been friends all their lives, working together and sharing all their secrets. But they had both moved on from those early carefree days, and things had changed for both of them. Who would ever have guessed that Cherry would have married the son and heir of the big estate where she and Paula were both kitchen-maids? Who would have guessed that Paula would have met the humble house painter

with the big ambitions of working on the railway, who had
achieved his dream?

Who could have foreseen that Cherry and Captain Lance
Melchoir would be married quietly under a cloud of deceit, and
been banished to Ireland in disgrace by his family? Or that it
would be Paula, mild-mannered, sweet Paula, who would be the
one to be carrying the child that Cherry craved, and for whom
it simply hadn't happened yet? And in this part of the world,
where babies seemed to be born every five minutes, she knew
she was viewed with some suspicion that a young and healthy
young woman like her hadn't conceived yet.

A shadow passed by the window and she forced herself out
of pointless reminiscing as she saw the portly shape of the farm
manager outside. She hurried to open the door to him.

'Top of the morning, Mrs Melchoir, and a nippy one it is, to
be sure, though it looks like rain later,' he said predictably. 'Is the
lord and master inside?'

'Yes, he is, Mr Gilligan, so go on into the study. I'd send you
in some coffee, but I'm told you're not to be disturbed,' she added
tartly.

The man laughed throatily, wiping the steam off his glasses in
the warm air of the farmhouse.

'Your man is a stickler for business, so he is, like all the Melchoirs
before him. His old uncle who passed away last year was just the
same before the dampness got to his lungs and finished him off.
But Captain Lance is fine and dapper, so I'm sure he'll have many
years ahead of him here.'

He strode off towards the study, leaving Cherry with a sinking
feeling at his words about having many years ahead here. It
had never been Lance's wish to come here at all, and it was
vastly different from his one-time life as an ex-army officer
and latter playboy. But with his affinity for horses, he seemed
to have taken to it all with his usual verve and determination,
give or take a few minor irritations, while there were times
when Cherry had never felt so lost and lonely, and it was
absolutely the worst way she had expected to feel after marrying
the love of her life.

Sometimes she longed for Bristol with a positive ache in her
heart. But Lance was as stubborn as his father, and she knew that

there was only one way that they would ever return now. It would only be on his father's death when Lance would become Lord Melchoir . . . and she would be Lady Melchoir, for pity's sake! What a turn up that would be! Or not. It was at that point that the thoughts always deserted her, for she could no more imagine herself being the lady of the house where she had once been a skivvy, than she could imagine flying to the moon. She couldn't even think about it without feeling her blood run cold, the way she was feeling now.

She was suddenly angry at herself for being so spineless. She had never been a wishy-washy person and she wasn't about to start now. She knew that Cook would be sending in some sandwiches for the men in the study in a couple of hours, even if coffee was not required, and dinner was always served in the evening like gentry, so she had the rest of the day to herself. She decided to go down to the village later that afternoon and buy a few special things to brighten up the room she would get ready for Paula.

At least she would do that herself, she thought determinedly, and she needed no lady's maid to show her how to straighten a bedspread or dust a few ornaments. Lord knew she had done enough of those in her time, and she was still having to get used to these idle moments. Later, she brushed her coppery hair until it shone, remembering the time she and Paula had come back to Melchoir House with the fashionable flappers' bobs that had so shocked the rest of the kitchen staff that day. She had kept it that way too, knowing it suited her features and showed her emerald-green eyes off to perfection. She smiled into her reflection, remembering what a good day that had been, and how startled a certain Lance Melchoir had been too, when he saw the new vision of Cherry O'Neill for the first time. Oh, he had chased her then all right. He had wanted her then . . . and he wanted her now.

Her heart gave a little lift as she put on her hat and coat and ran down the stairs and out of the house, shivering for a moment as the blast of cold air struck her face and made her eyes smart. Or perhaps it wasn't just the cold air. Perhaps it had more to do with the disappointment that there was no actual pot of gold at the end of the rainbow, and she should leave such stupid fancies to the leprechauns the country folk round about always teased the newcomers about.

She toyed over asking one of the stable boys to take her down to the village in the horse and cart, but she decided to walk. She was well used to walking, and had walked much farther than the mile or so to Donaghy village in the past, and she needed to get some air in her lungs, bitingly fresh though it was. It would help to dispel the gloomy thoughts she couldn't quite get rid of today.

When they first came here to Donaghy, straight after their marriage, it had been like an Indian summer. The abundant trees and hills were a brilliant, verdant green, due mostly to the amount of winter rain, as Maureen Tring had told her, but it was all so beautiful it had all but taken her breath away. She had thought she had come to heaven, especially seeing the large white farm-house that was to be her new home set against those hills. In Cherry's eyes, it resembled a mansion more than a farmhouse, like a glorious, shining white pearl, with smoke gently curling from the chimneys, and a well-ordered staff already there to welcome the new owners. The farm had been left as a caretaker establishment since the previous Melchoir owner had died, but with Lance's father hastily looking around for somewhere to send the newly-weds, out of reach of any whiff of scandal, Donaghy Farmstead had seemed like a godsend.

Cherry knew full well that they would never have been allowed to marry at all but for the pretence that Cherry was carrying Lance's child. A pretence that she had finally confessed to him wasn't true. The deceit had initially infuriated him beyond measure, as expected, but he had been as besotted with Cherry, his Cherry-ripe, as she had been with him. He had eventually allowed the lie to continue, knowing that his mother would never allow her grandchild, even the child of a kitchen-maid, to be brought up out of wedlock.

Oh yes, he had loved her then . . . and he did still, she thought, almost missing a step and rucking her ankle over a rocky patch of land. He did love her. It was just that in the everyday life they led now, he never seemed to find time to show her as much.

Besides which, he had never expected that when they finally wrote and told his parents that there was to be no child after all, his father would turn on him, accusing him of gross irresponsibility, and of merely bedding the kitchen-maid for his own amusement. And that if he had wanted her that much, he could keep her and enjoy the wilds of Ireland with her, and expect no further contact from his mother or himself except when absolutely necessary. For a while, Cherry knew full well that the shock had killed some of the feeling Lance had had for his new wife, and the knowledge that she was so much to blame for his estrangement from his family made Cherry feel constantly guilty. She knew that Lance wrote regularly to his parents, but he rarely had a reply. When he did, it was only a brief note from his father, and there was never a word from his unbending mother.

By the time the village came into view Cherry had got herself into a right old state, and she walked into the haberdashery shop run by George Gilligan's wife with something like relief at hearing the general noise and chatter going on inside. Unfortunately for her, it stopped the moment she walked inside. She was still an outsider here, despite having lived here for well over a year now, and she stuck her chin in the air and smiled at the half-dozen village women eyeing her with guarded expressions.

'Good morning to you all. It's a cold day today, isn't it?' she said.

She was careful not to mimic any of their Irish voices. She was so adept at taking on any accent she heard, which had so amused Lance when he'd first heard her taking off his mother . . . but it wouldn't do to do the same here, and risk these good people thinking she was patronizing them. Patronizing them, for goodness' sake! When her own background was lower than most of theirs!

There were varying murmurs of response to her greeting, and then the buxom shop owner spoke more brightly.

'You're out and about early, Mrs Melchoir. What can I do for you?'

'Oh, please see to these other ladies first,' Cherry said hastily. 'I'm quite happy to browse for a while. I just want a few things to brighten up a bedroom when my friend comes to visit.'

'That'll be the one you used to know back in Bristol, will it?'

'That's the one,' she replied airily to Mrs Gilligan's remark, feeling her face flush at the knowing question.

How much did the old trout know of hers and Paula's lives?

She was bound to keep up a front here for Lance's sake, and it was second nature for her voice to be that of a lady now, and she no longer had the broad Bristol vowels she had been born with. It was a far cry from performing her old party piece at Melchoir House when she had imitated Lady Melchoir's cut-glass voice merely for the jollification of all the old Bristol kitchen staff – and Lance himself, when he'd first heard it, she reminded herself again.

For a moment, she imagined these women with their quizzing eyes trying to get Paula into conversation, and gauging their surprise when they heard her speak. Paula had none of the finesse of a lady and never wanted it, but she was as good as any lady Cherry had ever known, she thought with a surge of loyalty. All the same there was bound to be some speculation as to why the lordly Captain Melchoir's wife was befriending someone of an obviously lesser status. And they could damn well speculate all they liked, Cherry thought fiercely.

She concentrated on fingering some of the goods on display, and the women gradually lost interest in her and carried on with whatever they were doing. Eventually she had chosen some small ornaments and hair tidies that would be a gift for Paula, and then the shelf of knitting patterns and wool caught her attention. She had fully intended to knit something for Paula's coming baby, and it was high time she started on it. But she hardly had time to look through several patterns of tiny matinee coats and vests that looked as if they would fit nothing larger than a doll, than one of the countrywomen had edged near.

'Are congratulations going to be in order soon, Mrs Melchoir?' the woman said archly. 'Me and Maud here were taking the liberty of wondering how long it was going to be, a fine-looking lady like yourself, and with such a handsome husband, if you'll pardon the intrusion.'

Cherry dropped the knitting patterns as if they were red hot. She knew she should be amused at their eager nosiness. She should be used to it by now, and she shouldn't take it so personally. But what other way was there to take it when such questions *were* damn well intruding into her private life? She spoke as evenly as she could, considering how ridiculously flustered she felt.

'My friend is expecting a baby, and I want to knit her something for it, but I think I'll leave it for another day and just take these purchases, thank you, Mrs Gilligan,' she said, moving forward to the counter.

She left the shop with the little parcel, well aware of the buzz of conversation behind her. No doubt they'd be deciding whether or not she was telling the truth now, and if it was really Cherry Melchoir who was expecting after all. Her eyes smarted, knowing how badly she wished it were so. Perhaps that was what was wrong with her today, knowing it had become obvious a week ago that it wasn't going to happen this month. But wishing didn't make it come true, and she took a deep breath and began the long walk back to the farm, wondering why it always seemed so much farther on the way back.

Before she was halfway there the skies had darkened. The rain had begun pelting down, slapping against her legs and blinding her eyes, so torrential that she could hardly see where she was going. There was no shelter in this stretch of land, and she had no choice but to hurry on as best she could, while her feet slithered and slid in the increasingly muddy ground. Her light shoes were sodden already, and she knew she was going to look like a drowned rat by the time she got home. It all added to a growing feeling of wretchedness, especially as the brown paper parcel with her purchases was starting to feel like a damp mass in her hands and threatening to disintegrate.

Walking with her head down, she didn't see the rider coming towards her from the direction of the farm, and she suddenly let out a small scream as a horse's hooves threw up clumps of mud over her skirts. The rider cursed loudly as he reined in the animal and tried to control the small cart behind it.

'Are you all right, Mrs Melchoir?' the man said as he recognized her. 'I didn't see you for all this damn rain, begging your pardon, Ma'am. I was going to the village for supplies, but get into the cart and I'll get you back to the farm.'

'Thank you, Ned. I got caught out in the rain and stupidly didn't take an umbrella,' she gasped, stating the obvious, and recognizing one of Maureen Tring's brothers who worked as one of their stable boys. Though *boy* was hardly a word to apply to such a brawny young man.

For some crazy reason, she imagined how Lady Melchoir would view the sight of her daughter-in-law arriving home in such a state in a horse and cart, driven by a muscly young Irish farm worker. But since Lady Melchoir had rarely given her the time of day, anyway, her opinions didn't count for much in Cherry's mind. She knew how sad Lance was, though, at the continued silence from his mother, and that saddened her too.

'Here we are then, Ma'am,' Ned said a short while later when the rain and the clatter of the horse's hooves had meant there was no need for talking, to Cherry's relief. She had been too busy hanging on to the sides of the cart to bother about much else. 'You'll be glad to dry off, I daresay.'

'I will indeed,' she murmured, fully aware of how her clothes were clinging to her now, and thankful that at least her top coat hid her curves, because Ned Tring was nothing if not a lusty young man who had his share of willing girls in the village, according to his sister, Maureen.

She stepped down from the cart with his help and sped indoors with her parcel, hoping that she could escape unseen to her bedroom and get respectable again. Thankfully, she saw that Mr Gilligan's car had gone, and she hoped that Lance had gone with him, to save her from the embarrassment of looking like a gypsy.

The faint hope disappeared as soon as she had one foot on the stairs, and met Lance coming out of his study. He gave her a startled look that seemed to take in her appearance from head to toe, before he burst out laughing.

'Good God, Cherry-ripe, what have you been doing to yourself?' he said, with a kind of huskiness in his voice that she couldn't fathom for a minute.

And then he was on the stairs beside her and his arms were going around her, despite the bedraggled state she was in.

'I think you need some help getting out of those wet clothes, and perhaps a bath to warm you,' he went on, and the gleam in his eyes was one that she recognized at once. She felt her heart begin to beat faster.

'Then I wonder if you would do the honour of helping me – Sir,' she said provocatively, despite the little catch in her voice. 'Would Sir be willing to run a lady's bath?'

She couldn't quite catch his muttered reply, but whatever it was, it didn't matter. Because by then they were heading up the stairs together, two at a time, tripping and laughing. And even though it was the middle of the afternoon, Cherry felt the familiar tingling excitement and love for him, knowing this would only end one way.

Two

Cherry stretched her limbs in indolent, feline movements. Even though it was the middle of the afternoon and still daylight, she felt as lazily relaxed as if she was just waking from a wonderful night's sleep, and the realization of why it was so was as intoxicating as wine. Lying in her husband's arms in their bed, she could feel Lance's warm breath against her shoulder as he half dozed, and her heart began to beat faster, knowing how passionate he could be, and how much she adored him.

The ending to this wretchedly miserable afternoon had been so unexpected, and Lance's imagination had been caught, all because she had been caught in the rain and appeared back at Donaghy Farmstead looking like a bedraggled hoyden ... and more like the kitchen-maid she had once been than the lady of the house.

He stirred slightly now, his hand involuntarily squeezing her breast where he cupped it, and she caught her breath at the sweet sensation. There were no intruding clothes between them, and she hadn't been remotely embarrassed as they had torn them off in their eagerness to be together. The sheer wantonness of making love in the afternoon had made their coupling all the more erotic. It was as seductive as that first time, all those months ago in the sweet-smelling hayloft of Melchoir House ...

She realized that Lance was fully awake and looking into her eyes now.

'Well, my Cherry-ripe,' he said in a soft voice, 'I think we should allow ourselves a few more afternoon delights now and then, don't you?'

'I do,' she whispered back, thrilled that he loved and wanted her. But she spoke almost shyly now, remembering how abandoned she had been, her own desire matching every bit of his.

He gave a teasing laugh and gave her rump a gentle smack, and the tender moments were gone. 'But now we had better get up and make ourselves respectable, or there will be food on the dinner table and nobody there to eat it. I'll leave you to your modesty, my love.'

He moved out of the bed, unashamed of his nakedness, and she watched his powerful muscles as he strode easily across to his dressing room to don his clothes. She leapt out after him, fingers fumbling as she struggled back into her own clothes, and unable to stop thinking that surely if their love-making was ever going to produce a child, it should be at times like these when it had been so spectacular and they were so much in tune with one another . . .

Half an hour later Captain Melchoir and his wife were sitting decorously in the sitting room and drinking a pre-dinner glass of sherry before being summoned into the dining room. And despite the gleam that was still undisguised in his eyes, Lance was telling her of the horse fair he would be attending soon, and Cherry couldn't help thinking how very different it all was from her time at Melchoir House in Bristol when it was only the toffs upstairs who would be so genteel.

'What are you smiling at?' he said indulgently, not missing the way the corners of her mouth were curving up now. 'I'd ask if you were going to miss me, but I'm sure you won't, with Paula coming to stay.'

'Of course I'll miss you, but I'm looking forward to seeing her so much, Lance. And if you really want to know, I was just thinking how changed my life is now from what it once was.'

'Changed for the better, I hope.'

'A million times better,' Cherry said fervently, because this was not the time to be reflecting on how much more carefree her life had been then, with none of the trappings of responsibility she had now. But she wouldn't change it.

Not in those million years . . .

'There was one thing, though,' she said more hesitantly. 'I don't quite know how to ask you, nor how you'll react.'

'Well, you'll never know unless you ask, so out with it.'

He was never going to be in a better mood, and it was something she had been toying with for some time.

'You know how Paula and I always used to love dancing, Lance.'

He laughed. 'Good God, she won't want to go dancing in her condition, will she? Besides, it's hardly seemly for two young married women to go dancing on their own, and I trust you weren't going to suggest it, Cherry!'

She rushed on. Even though he sounded so indulgent, she hoped she hadn't chosen the wrong moment after all. 'Of course not. That's not what I meant at all. But you and I have both enjoyed the local concerts, and I know Paula would enjoy them too. She won't have heard Irish music before, nor seen Irish dancing, and it would be such a treat if we could both go. I know there's one taking place at the end of next week. What do you say, Lance?'

She held her breath. The local people seemed pleased that the owners of Donaghy Farmstead weren't so snooty that they couldn't enjoy a night out at the usual raucous concerts the fiddlers and dancers put on. If they did but know it, they were like a breath of fresh air to Cherry, who didn't have a snooty bone in her, no matter what they might think.

'Let me think about it,' Lance was saying now. 'I'm not sure that it would be wise for the two of you to go alone, but if our neighbours are going, I'm sure they would accompany you. I'll see the Devlins about it, Cherry.'

She had to be content with that, even if it made her feel a little like a child who needed to be looked after. She acknowledged that Paula probably did though, in her condition, and she knew it was for the best. There were as many roughnecks out and about here as there ever had been in Bristol after a night out of merrymaking and drinking.

She gave a small shiver. Hadn't it been on just such a night after a dance when she and Paula had been frantically running through the streets to get away from two drunkards, when a certain Captain Melchoir had pulled up beside them in his sleek Rolls Royce motor and given them a lift back to Melchoir House? The night when Paula had also had a little too much cider, and Lance had offered to show Cherry the stables while her friend snoozed in the car . . .? And if it hadn't been for that, the impossible wouldn't have happened, and she wouldn't be here now, with the man she adored.

'Is that all right?' he said, when she hadn't answered.

'Of course it is,' she said softly. 'You do what you think best, Lance.'

★　★　★

He was at his best in taking command and making arrangements. He had been in charge of many men during his army years, and it was second nature to him now to be an organizer and make swift decisions. It was how he had summed up so quickly what he wanted to do when he discovered Cherry's deceit over the baby that never was, and decided that he wanted to marry her anyway.

It was up to Paula's husband Harold to get her to Fishguard and on to the ferry that would bring her to Rosslare. But from then on, Lance had taken charge of arrangements. Before he went off to the horse fair, he would take Cherry to the port to meet Paula and bring her here, and in one way Cherry almost wished he hadn't been so efficient. If Paula was going to be intimidated by him, it might have been better if one of Maureen's brothers had taken her to meet her friend, but Lance would hear none of it. The young woman was pregnant and a guest, and deserved to be met by her hosts in a proper fashion.

Cherry gave an involuntary giggle at the thought of Paula being an honoured guest, and Lance automatically smiled back.

'Now what? I swear I don't know what goes on in that head of yours sometimes, Cherry-ripe.'

'I was just thinking of the last time, in fact, the one and only time, you drove me and Paula anywhere,' she said softly.

His eyes sparkled, and if it hadn't been for the announcement that dinner was served, she didn't know what his reply might have been. She had to be content with his squeeze of her arm and the heady knowledge that what had begun this afternoon was probably going to be continued later that night.

Cherry wasn't the only one getting excited about her friend's forthcoming visit. Paula Farmer, née Davey, was still twittering over which clothes to pack and praying that she wasn't going to be seasick on the ferry across the Irish Sea. She wished, too, that Harold could take her all the way, but it just wasn't practical, and he couldn't afford to lose so much work when she was perfectly capable of travelling by herself. She was no longer the little mouse she had once been.

She smiled at her reflection in the cheap mirror of her dressing table in the cosy little house she and Harold now shared near

Temple Meads railway station, thinking how different she was
now from the pasty little friend Cherry had left behind. It was
all due to Harold, of course, she thought contentedly. She had
always been stronger than she looked, but he had definitely
brought out the best in her, and her married status had seen to
the rest. And now there was this little one to look forward to,
she thought, patting her gently swelling stomach. Life was better
than it had ever been, and soon she would be seeing Cherry
again and that was the icing on the cake.

She gave a small shiver, because along with Cherry there would
also be Captain Lance, and she had never felt comfortable in his
company. But she refused to let it bother her too much. Besides,
Cherry had told her Lance would be away somewhere with his
horse business while Paula was there, so that would work out
just fine. They could gossip to their hearts' content without
Captain Superior looking down his nose at her . . . and that was
the last time she must think about him in such a way, she told
herself severely. He'd agreed to this visit, so he must be all right
about having another one-time kitchen-maid coming to his new
home, although Harold had teased her by saying it was a bit of
a comedown for him with his high and mighty graces.

At which point, Paula had bashed him playfully in the ribs
and told him if he thought that about his own wife, he could
be forgetting any shenanigans that night, and it was enough to
make both of them forget anyone else but themselves! It still
amazed her how daringly free and easy she had become with
Harold, and it was all due to love, she thought happily.

But now the day of departure was here, and she was a bundle
of nerves again and filled with a mixture of emotions. She was
excited at seeing Cherry again, nervous at meeting Captain Lance
on a social level, apprehensive about the sea voyage, and sad at
leaving Harold behind. She clung to him on the quayside at
Fishguard, and promised to think about him every day.

'You just enjoy yourself,' he said, his voice rough-edged enough
to let her know that he was going to miss her too. 'I'll still be
here when you get back and you can tell me all about this
wonderful Irish countryside Cherry's told you so much about.'

'Whatever it's like, it won't be a patch on Bristol,' she said
loyally. 'But I'll do my best to enjoy it, Harold.'

They hugged once more and then she was stepping on to the ferry and thinking this was just about the most scary thing she had done since going into service at the Melchoir mansion in Clifton all those years ago. But that had been going into the unknown too, and she was older now, and had so much to look forward to . . . and nearly four hours later, having survived it all without any more queasiness than she normally felt each morning, she was eagerly scanning the coastline of Rosslare for a familiar face.

'There she is!' Cherry breathed to her husband as she saw Paula waving to her frantically. 'Oh, doesn't she look well!'

She felt an unexpected stab of envy. Even from this distance, she could see that Paula was nicely dressed and looked far from being Cherry's shadow as she had once been. Besides which, she was expecting a baby, and for Cherry that was the biggest envy of all. But she wasn't going to let it overshadow their visit, and she waved back joyfully and rushed towards the ferry steps as Paula alighted, loaded down with several bags over her arms.

They hugged quickly, exclaiming excitedly how good it was to see one another, and then Lance came forward to take Paula's bags efficiently out of her arms, almost without her noticing it.

'Welcome to Ireland, Paula,' he said with a smile. 'I'll take your bags and put them in the car while you and Cherry get reacquainted.'

'Thank you, Captain Lance,' she began, and he laughed.

'Oh, we don't want to have any of that formality. It's Lance, all right?'

'All right,' she mumbled. 'Captain Lance,' she added beneath her breath as he strode away to where his car was parked.

Cherry laughed as she hugged her arm. 'You'll have to get used to it, Paula. We're all equals now, amazing as it may seem.'

'It's blooming-well more than amazing, but as long as we're all happy, that's all that counts. And you are happy, aren't you? I can see it in your eyes.'

'Blissfully,' Cherry assured her.

'And I daresay it helps not having the dragon of a mother-in-law breathing fire at you,' Paula said.

Cherry giggled. 'It does that all right, but don't let Lance hear

you say anything about her. She's never forgiven him for marrying
me. I'm just glad she never gets in touch, though I know it hurts
him, even if he never mentions it. She's still his mother.'

She couldn't resist a small grimace as they neared the car where
Lance was waiting, remembering the stiff, starchy woman who
had looked at her with such disgust and accused her of seducing
her son. Cherry and Lance knew it had been the other way
around, but it was hardly something you could tell that dried-
up old trout. There was only one person to whom she could
ever say what she thought about her mother-in-law, and that
person was beside her now.

The grimace faded, and in an instant she knew how easy it
was going to be to revive the old, slapdash camaraderie she and
Paula had shared in their attic bedroom at Melchoir House. It
was a good thing Lance would be away for a time while they
let their hair down. She would miss him, of course she would,
but there were things you could say with a special friend that
you couldn't say to a husband, however much you loved him.

As if by mutual agreement, she sat in the front passenger
seat beside Lance as they drove back to Donaghy Farmstead,
since it would be all too emotive for her and Paula to sit
together in the back seat, remembering that other time. She
had no doubt that Paula would be remembering it too, since
that night had started the chain reaction leading them to
where they were now.

Glancing back at her friend, so confident now in her married
state, she saw Paula give her the slightest wink, and she had to
turn back quickly before she started giggling in a most un-
ladylike way. But for all the change in Paula's circumstances, Cherry
knew she was still nervous at being on a social level with Lance.
This was confirmed soon after they arrived at the farmstead, and
Lance told them he would leave them to get acquainted while
he went outside to see to his horses, and he would see them at
dinner.

Cherry took Paula upstairs to her room at once, and after
exclaiming at the sheer pleasure of being here, the other girl
flopped down on her bed, clearly tired after the long journey.

'You and Captain Lance look well set up here, Cherry,' she
said.

Cherry laughed. 'For goodness' sake, stop calling him Captain Lance, Paula. He's just Lance.'

'I know, and it's easy for you to say, but it's hard for me to think of him that way,' Paula said, wrinkling her nose.

'Well, you'll just have to try. Now you sit there while I unpack some of your things for you.'

Paula was happy enough to do as Cherry suggested. 'Well, at least you don't have people doing every little thing for you,' she said at last.

'Servants, you mean, same as we were.'

'We weren't even given the dignity of being called proper servants. We were just kitchen-maids, weren't we? We've both come a long way since then, Cherry, and you more than me.'

Cherry paused in hanging up one of Paula's dresses in the wardrobe. 'So we have, but I doubt that I'm any happier than you are. You've got something very special to look forward to, which I don't, yet.'

She put on a bright smile before Paula started questioning her further on that score.

'Anyway, before I forget to tell you, Lance has arranged with our neighbours, the Devlins, to take us to a concert on Saturday night. The Devlins are a nice, middle-aged couple, and you'll love Irish concerts, Paula, all the dancing and the fiddle playing. It's very noisy and a bit mad, but a lot of fun, considering we're pretty much out in the sticks.'

Paula's eyes were thoughtful. 'Do you miss the city?'

A wave of nostalgia, as keen as a knife, washed over Cherry then, but she replied briskly. 'Of course I do, but this is my home now, and we have to make the best of what we're given, don't we? And I have Lance, which makes up for everything,' she added softly.

Paula laughed now. 'You're still as besotted with him as ever, I see, so it all turned out all right in the end, didn't it? And at least you're miles away from the old trout's sharp tongue.'

'That's no way to talk about my mother-in-law, miss,' Cherry said with mock severity, and then she had dropped down on the bed beside Paula and they were both laughing as the image of Lance's fierce mother entered their heads.

'Do you ever go back to Melchoir House to see Cook and

the others?' she said, asking Paula the question she'd been dying to ask. It had been a part of her life for so long – of both their lives – that it was impossible to shut out all those years of servitude to the Melchoirs completely.

'Now and again,' Paula admitted. 'They always ask about you, of course, and I tell them what I can from your letters. It's strange to go back, though, Cherry, even though I'm so fond of them all, and it'll be even stranger for you when the time comes one day. Not that it'll be for years yet,' she said hastily. 'Lord Melchoir doesn't look like popping his clogs, so you're not likely to become Lady Melchoir the younger for a while.'

'Good God, don't even think about it!' Cherry said with a shudder. The thought of sharing that great mansion with Lance's mother still at the helm didn't bear thinking about.

'Anyway, maybe she'll go first, which will solve a few problems,' Paula said mischievously. 'I'm sure she won't be thrilled to have you back, having set her sights on having the Hon. Cynthia Hetherington as her daughter-in-law. You must have been a great disappointment to her, Cherry,' she said, still in that teasing voice that got them giggling again.

'By the way,' she went on, 'in answer to the second question you were probably going to ask, I haven't seen hide nor hair of your brother.'

Cherry's heart jumped. 'I wasn't going to ask, actually. I put him out of my life before we came here, and that's exactly where I want him to stay. I don't even want to think about him, so the subject's closed, Paula.'

'Sorry I mentioned it then!' she said.

Without warning she gave a huge yawn, and immediately clapped her hand over her mouth.

'Oh God, sorry about that. I'm not bored, just a bit tired. It's one of the side-effects of you-know-what,' she added, patting her stomach in explanation.

Cherry nodded affectionately. 'I should have realized, and anyway, we've got plenty of time to talk. I'll leave you to have a snooze and see you again at dinner, which will be in an hour or so. Don't worry, you won't miss it. You always had a hearty appetite, and I don't suppose that's changed,' she said with a grin. 'Or do you want a cup of tea and a biscuit to tide you over?'

'No thanks, I'll stick to regular meals, otherwise I'm just as likely to throw it all up again,' Paula said cheerfully. 'That's another little side-effect.'

Cherry left her to it and went swiftly downstairs, surprised to find her eyes smarting a little. It was wonderful to see her again, and it was so easy to slip right back into their old, easy friendship. Paula hadn't changed a bit . . . which was a complete lie of course. They had both changed out of all recognition from the two carefree young girls who had both started work at Melchoir House all those years ago. Outwardly, it was Cherry whose fortunes had changed the most, married to the son and heir of the big estate, and who would one day become Lady Melchoir herself. But it was Paula who was the lucky one, despite the side-effects she mentioned so cheerfully. Paula who was expecting the baby that Cherry yearned for so much. She hadn't even realized quite how much until she actually saw her friend again and the reality of it was staring her in the face. She swallowed hard and told herself not to be so stupid, because nothing was going to spoil the joy of this long-overdue visit.

Paula's eyes had closed almost as soon as Cherry left her, and she knew no more until she awoke with a start, conscious that someone else was in the room. Still in that odd half-world of not being quite sure where she was, she gave a little scream as she saw the stranger looking down at her.

'Saints preserve us, I didn't mean to alarm you so, Ma'am,' Maureen Tring said hastily. 'Mrs Melchoir asked me to bring you up a jug of hot water and towels, and to tell you that you're to come downstairs at your leisure for dinner. It'll be served in about half an hour, so is there anything I can do for you now? My name's Maureen, by the way, and I'm the housemaid here. Maid of all sorts, you might say, and mistress of none,' she added with a cheeky laugh.

Paula struggled to sit up, still taking in all that the girl with the funny accent was saying, and the even wilder feeling that she must have entered into a different world if somebody was waiting on *her* now!

'Are you feeling quite well, Ma'am?' the girl was saying anxiously now. 'Mrs Melchoir told us about your certain condition, and it must have been a tiring journey for you, coming all the way from England to Donaghy. It probably seems like the back of beyond, so it does.'

'I'm fine,' Paula said finally. 'It just took me a minute or two to remember where I was, that's all.'

'That's all right then, but you just ask me if there's anything at all that you need while you're staying here. I'm at your beck and call as you might say, so now I'll leave you to your ablutions and I'll see you later. You'll find your way to the dining room easily enough. Just follow the smell of food,' she added, chortling at her own joke.

Paula felt slightly mesmerized after Maureen had left her, still chattering to herself as she went downstairs. It was such a reversal of the way things used to be, when she would have been the one scurrying to do someone else's bidding, and here she was, being brought a jug of hot water and told that Maureen Tring, whoever she was, was at her beck and call!

She leapt out of bed and went across to the jug of hot water on the washstand, and poured it into the bowl, glad of the chance to refresh herself. Presumably, Maureen would come up here unobtrusively while she was at dinner and clear it all away . . . and suddenly, Paula felt like laughing out loud at the absurdity of it all. Cherry would be well used to it by now, and it would have been unthinkable that Captain Lance Melchoir would exist without servants to attend him, even in the back of beyond as Maureen called it. It was what he had been used to all his life, even in the army, and Cherry would be used to it too by now. While Paula was more than content to be the housewife, cooking and cleaning for her darling husband in their little railway house, and once the baby arrived to make their lives complete, she knew she would never want for anything more.

By the time she found her way to the dining room, guided by the succulent smell of food as Maureen had said, she realized how hungry she was. The ferry hadn't made her any queasier than she normally was of a morning, but she had been wise enough not to eat too much all day, and now she was more than ready for the rabbit stew that the cook had prepared. There would be a cook, of course, she thought drily, who was grandly titled a cook-housekeeper, she later learned.

Dinner might have been awkward, with her still feeling shy at eating at the same table as Captain Lance, but he was adept in putting people at their ease, and the first time she slipped up and called him Captain Lance, he admonished her teasingly.

'We'll have no more of this Captain lark, Paula, or I shall be obliged to call you Mrs Farmer every time I speak to you. Agreed?'

'Agreed,' she said, blushing furiously.

'Good. And you won't see very much of me,' he went on. 'I shall be off in the morning and I won't be back until the day before you leave, in good time to take you back to the ferry. But we don't want to talk about your leaving when you've only just arrived, so has Cherry told you about the concert next Saturday?'

'Yes, and it sounds lovely!'

'You'll like Mary and Liam Devlin, and don't be alarmed if they want to take you under their wing as soon as they see you. They lost a son in the war and their daughter-in-law died in childbirth soon afterwards, losing the baby as well. So they'll probably dote on you a bit.'

It was the only reference he made to her condition, but if his words left her open-mouthed at hearing such a tragic story, it was Cherry who reacted strongly.

'For heaven's sake, Lance, don't frighten Paula with stories about dying in childbirth. She's come for a holiday, not to be scared out of her wits.'

'I only said it to forewarn her, my dear. It's natural when people meet for the first time to ask about their family, and they still find it upsetting to have to explain it all. Being forewarned is being forearmed, isn't it?'

'It's all right, Cherry,' Paula put in quickly, seeing the small clash between them. 'It's good to know the facts in advance, and I'm not in the least scared about having the baby. It's a perfectly natural happening, after all.'

She hid a small shiver all the same, remembering the times that she had looked in other people's perambulators and admired their babies, while secretly studying the size of the babies' heads, and wondering how it was possible for them to be born without tearing the mother's body to shreds. But those thoughts were secret ones, and as long as they remained in her head, nobody knew of her fears but herself.

'After dinner, I'll show you some maps and photographs of the area,' Cherry went on. 'Lance has sorted them out for us, so that you'll have an idea of exactly where you are.'

'That's good, 'cos I could be in the middle of nowhere for all I know, and oh Lord, I hope that didn't sound ungrateful.'

Lance laughed. 'Don't worry, it's what we both thought when we first came here, but at least you've only got a week to suffer it.'

'Now I know you think I was being rude,' Paula said, flame-faced.

'He's only teasing you, Paula,' Cherry said. 'We wondered where we'd been sent to at first but in spring and summer the country-side is really beautiful, and it's a shame you're not seeing it at its best at this time of year.'

She almost said Paula would have to come again at some later date, but with a small ripple of something like a presentiment deep inside her, she knew there was no likelihood of it. She shook off the feeling, not wanting any such thoughts to cloud this visit. Instead, as Lance discreetly left them alone again after dinner, they pored over the maps and photographs he had left out for them. Paula agreed that County Wexford could certainly look far lovelier than it did right now in midwinter. At least here in the south of the country it wasn't cold enough for snow, and that was something to be grateful for. But after eating such a tasty meal she began to feel sleepy again, and she was glad to take Cherry's suggestion of an early night after her long journey, glad to snuggle down in the unfamiliar bed, resting her hands gently over her unborn child and to dream of Harold and their life together.

But Cherry's suggestion wasn't only for Paula's benefit. Tomorrow, Lance would be going away for the week, and she wanted to spend every last minute with him. As she too cuddled down in the bed she shared with him, she felt his arms go around her, and she was caught tightly in his embrace.

'Will you miss me now that you've got your little mousy friend to keep you company, Cherry-ripe?' he whispered.

'I'll miss you every moment,' she whispered back.

He pulled her even closer, his hands caressing her, and his voice was filled with emotion when he spoke.

'I never expected how seeing the two of you together again

would remind me so much of certain other times, and how damn lucky we are to have got what we wanted more than anything in the world. So if you're going to miss me so much, I'd better give you something extra-special to remember me by,' he said huskily, and seconds later he was covering her body with his own and feathering her face with kisses.

Three

The visit was definitely going well. The old country saying that after three days visitors, like fish, began to smell, simply didn't apply when two old friends had so much to talk about and to remember, plus new horizons to discover. Paula was filling Cherry's head with so many memories of her life in Bristol that it made her sometimes long to be there, which she knew was only to be expected. And if Paula was clearly envious of the easy life that Cherry now had, compared to their old lives as kitchen-maids, that was understandable too. None of it marred the pleasure they both felt in being together again, nor the fact that in reality each was perfectly content with their own lives.

In the first three days they had walked to the village several times and browsed the quaint little shops, and unavoidably over-heard plenty of gossip to make them smile. The Irish were great talkers, and if they liked to indulge in gossip about anything and everybody, it only made the time pass more cheerily. They had also had a short visit from Liam and Mary Devlin, confirming that they would be happy to collect the two young ladies early on Saturday evening to take them to the concert in the nearby town.

By the time it arrived Cherry and Paula excitedly dressed up for the evening, much as they had done when they used to go dancing in what their old cook had always called the 'fleshpots of Bristol'.

'You look exactly the same as you always did, Cherry,' Paula said admiringly. 'No wonder the lusty Captain couldn't keep his hands off you – or anything else!'

Cherry laughed. 'I'm sure the same thing could be said about your Harold. There wasn't much doubt he had fallen for you when he came with the team of painters and decorators to spring-clean Melchoir House.'

'It all seems such a long time ago now,' Paula said. 'And when the family had got back from their visit to London to see the

Exhibition, all hell broke loose on account of your brother's anonymous letters, didn't it?'

Cherry shivered. 'I don't want to think about that. He did a wicked thing sending letters to Lance and his father saying that Lance had got one of their kitchen-maids pregnant and demanding money to keep his mouth shut, but maybe if he hadn't, Lance and I would never have got married at all.'

'Pull the other one. He was always potty about you.'

Cherry was suddenly terse. 'Well, not that potty. You may go around with stars in your eyes, Paula, but you know damned well his parents intended that he would marry somebody of his own class, and that certainly wasn't me.'

'At his age, I should think he could marry whoever he wanted to,' Paula snapped back. 'I never thought of him as a mummy's boy.'

'Nobody could ever accuse him of that! When it was import- ant for him to do so, he stood up to them both. He stood up for me! He was even prepared to fight with my brother, and nobody could accuse him of being a coward. My God, Brian wa a bare-knuckle fighter, and nobody would willingly get tangl up with the likes of him.'

'Well, I know that, and I wasn't suggesting any such thin

They glared at one another, realizing how quickly their banter had descended into something more serious. In an i Cherry knew that the undeniable truths had always simmering beneath the surface, even between herself and and it had taken Paula's visit to bring them so harshly consciousness again. Was she living in a fool's paradis time, pretending that what had happened in those te would never have any effect on their lives together?

Maybe it was also fool's luck that it hadn't done

Paula gave a hooting laugh. 'Blooming heck, C just like old times, isn't it? You've even forgotten t posh voice. It's gone back to normal now, and y like the Cherry I used to know when you could living daylights out of me with words!'

Listening to her, Cherry felt a kind of horr house, or in the village, knew of her past. Th had been no more than a kitchen-maid, work

the snooty Melchoirs in Bristol. All they knew was that she was the attractive young wife of Captain Lance Melchoir, and would naturally assume that she was equal in class to himself. It would be shaming for Lance if the truth ever came out that they were virtually banished here as a condition of their marriage.

She put a trembling hand on Paula's arm. She spoke quietly, and her voice had unconsciously assumed the accent that now came so effortlessly to her.

'We're not the same people we once were, Paula, and it's important for Lance that nobody here ever knows what happened. You do see that, don't you?'

'Of course I do, and you know I didn't mean to upset you,' Paula said almost tearfully. 'I've always looked up to you, Cherry, you know that.'

'Don't be daft. Just be my friend, that's all I ask.'

'Perhaps I'd better try to talk proper too,' she went on, trying to make light of it, and putting on a totally unrealistic accent.

'God, no!' Cherry said with a grin. 'If that's an example, you'd only make a hash of it and people would see right through you. Besides, you're perfect just the way you are. Now, are we going to this concert or aren't we?'

They gave one another a quick hug and made their way downstairs to await the arrival of the Devlins, unaware that someone had been hovering outside on the landing and had overheard just enough of this extraordinary conversation to sense a mystery.

'I tell you, things up at Donaghy Farmstead ain't all as clear-cut as they seem,' Maureen Tring said excitedly to her mother and brothers when she next went home on her afternoon off. 'I couldn't hear too much of what they was saying, on account of the bedroom door being tight shut, but I reckon the Captain married beneath him. The young lady who's come to visit don't talk half as posh as my lady, anyway, and they seem to be as close as clams all right.'

'You're away with the fairies and making nonsense of it as usual, girl,' her mother said briskly. 'You've got a good job there with the Melchoirs, so don't you go spreading any such rumours about, or you'll find yourself slung out on your ear quicker'n winking.'

'Mammy's right,' her brother Declan said lazily. 'With three of us employed up there, you don't want to be rocking no boats, our Maureen. Whatever you think you heard, you'd best keep it to yourself.'

'Yes, but what if it's true?' Maureen persisted, put-out that none of them seemed to be taking it seriously, when she'd come home agog with news. 'What if the high and mighty Mrs Melchoir was once no more than a servant, and no better than me?'

'What if she was? It ain't what she is now,' Declan snapped. 'And if it's all a bit of nonsense and it gets back to you for spreading it, you can be sure Captain Melchoir won't just chuck you and Charlie and Ned out, he'll make sure that nobody for miles around employs any of us. He's got a lot of influence around here, so just you remember that. Better still, you'd better forget you ever heard anything – or imagined that you did. It's a good tale, but that's all it is.'

'Our Maureen always did go about romancing about things, and liked to think of herself as fortunate as being Cinderella one day,' her mother chuckled. 'I reckon she's shifted the story on to that nice Mrs Melchoir now.'

'No I haven't,' Maureen said resentfully. 'I know what I heard but I can see the sense in what you say, so I'll not go on about it.'

Besides which, if she was being completely honest, she was beginning to doubt it herself now. It was true that the friend from England didn't seem anything like as posh as her employers. But they might have befriended her at one time and were generous enough to offer her a wee holiday. Considering that folk around here liked the Captain and his wife, and that they were good employers, she decided it was for the best to do as her family said, and keep her trap shut. If they didn't believe her, how could she expect anybody else to do so? Otherwise, it might well be Maureen Tring who'd be getting a touch of the cold shoulder from her neighbours.

Unaware that any of their conversation had been overheard, Cherry and Paula were enjoying a night out at the small theatre in Donaghy town, and Paula was as animated as Cherry had ever seen her. Never having heard the Irish fiddlers or seen Irish dancing before, she was thrilled by their agility and skill.

'It was a joy to see it all through your eyes, my dear,' Mary Devlin said smilingly to Paula when they were on their way home again. 'We take it for granted when we see it all the time, but when it's all new to somebody, we can realize how special it is. Don't you have anything of the same in England?'

'Well, we have morris dancing, if you like that sort of thing, with blokes waving handkerchiefs about and with bells tied on their legs as they prance about,' Paula added with a giggle.

'I've heard about that,' Mary said, while Liam couldn't resist a loud guffaw from the driving seat, remarking that it was a mighty-odd thing for a bunch of grown men to be doing.

'But it's good fun to watch, and it goes back into ancient times.' Cherry defended it, not prepared to let a national tradition be mocked.

'Me and Cherry have seen it quite a few times on the Downs in Bristol, and we've always enjoyed it,' Paula agreed. 'I daresay it's as quaint to outsiders as your little leprechauns.'

In the back seat of the car Cherry dug her in the ribs, knowing how Paula was in danger of getting heated, and not wanting to offend their neighbours by any stupid remarks about the little people. Paula would be going home in a few days, while Cherry had to live here for the foreseeable future. Even so, the mere mention of the morris dancers on Durdham Downs had sent a wave of nostalgia through her that took her by surprise.

Thankfully, Liam Devlin wasn't in the least offended. 'Oh, to be sure, they're a quaint-enough tale unless a body has seen them,' he said mysteriously.

'Have you seen them, Mr Devlin?' Paula said eagerly.

His wife broke in. 'Now then, Liam, don't go filling the young lady's head with your fairy-tale nonsense, or she'll not sleep tonight.'

She changed the conversation at once, asking Paula about the coming baby and if she hoped for a boy or a girl, and telling her to be sure to wish on a new moon for what she wanted and that her wish would surely be answered.

'Now who's away with the fairies?' Cherry whispered as they reached the farm and said goodbye to the Devlins.

'Well, he did make it sound as if he'd seen a leprechaun, didn't he?'

Cherry laughed. 'If you lived around here, you'd realize that there are plenty of chaps who'd make it a plausible enough tale if it got him a pint of ale in the local pub. Maureen's brothers are experts when it comes to teasing strangers, so be glad you're not an ale drinker or you'd soon be out of pocket. I'd rather have a cup of cocoa before we go to bed. What do you say?'

Paula gave an unexpected yawn and her eyelids were already drooping now that the excitement of the evening was over.

'I don't think I could even manage that before I fall asleep, so I'll go straight to bed if you don't mind. But thanks for arranging tonight, Cherry, and I'm going to try to remember every bit of it to tell Harold when I get home.'

Without waiting for an answer she moved towards the stairs and Cherry watched her go with an odd twist of sadness. Once, even though they would have been working from dawn until dusk, they would have been chattering long into the night. Had she really expected it to be the same? Everything here was so new to Paula, and it was wonderful for them to be together again, but nothing was the way it had once been. There was a distance between them now that they could never cross. It was far deeper than the Irish Sea, and it would have been even more evident if Lance hadn't been away, to emphasize that Cherry Melchoir was no longer Cherry O'Neill with the hateful brother.

And it was just as obvious that although Paula was enjoying the visit, she was also longing to see her Harold again. Just as Cherry was longing to see Lance as always when he had been away, she reminded herself. And with that thought, she ignored any thought of cocoa and went to bed.

'You know, you could have telephoned Harold while you were here,' she said casually to Paula the next morning when the girl seemed to be a little deflated after the night before. 'We do have the telephone, and Lance always phones to tell me he's arrived somewhere. I'm sure Harold could have arranged to be near one at a certain time. Didn't you think of it?'

Paula shook her head. 'I wouldn't have known what to say.'

'Don't be daft. You'd say the same things you'd say if he was in the room with you. Haven't you ever used one before?'

'We don't live in the same kind of world as you, Cherry,' Paula said crossly. 'I'd go all doolally the minute I heard his voice.'

It was one more thing to make Cherry realize how different their lives had become. But she remembered the time when she had discovered Lance was in hospital, and had wanted to call his father to let him know where he was. She had been all fingers and thumbs then too, not knowing the telephone number of Melchoir House, nor even how to ask the operator for it.

'You know I'd have done it for you, Paula,' she said gently now. 'I'd do anything for you, same as I always did.'

Paula cleared her throat. 'I know, and it's the same for me and I'm being a pig for sounding so blooming jealous. I'm glad you got everything you wanted, Cherry, and you know that, don't you?'

'Of course I do, even if I haven't quite got everything yet.'

She hadn't meant to say it, but Paula was cute enough to catch on at once.

'It'll happen, Cherry, especially if your Lance is still as lusty as he used to be,' she said with a giggle.

'But what if it doesn't? What if my wickedness in pretending to be pregnant when I wasn't, has somehow stopped it ever happening?'

She hadn't meant to say that either, but it was out in the open now.

'Well, if you're asking my opinion, I think that's another fairy tale, and you're just being daft to let it worry you.'

'I know, but I want it so much, Paula, and I know Lance does too. He'd love to call his father and tell him he's going to be a grandfather. They've got to accept me now, and it would help to heal the breach between them.'

She avoided mentioning Lance's mother, knowing the last thing she would want was for Lady Melchoir to get her hands on her baby and try to mould it. But providing they still lived here, it was unlikely they would have to see her mother-in-law at all, unless she deigned to come for a brief visit.

She hadn't realized she had given a deep sigh until she felt Paula's hand clasp hers for a moment.

'Cheer up,' Paula said. 'You sit here while I go and ask Cook to make us a drink of something.'

'I should be doing that. You're the guest, remember?'

Paula snorted. 'Rats. The day I can't find my way around a kitchen is the day I'll hang up my pinny. Besides, I'd like the chance to poke around it a bit and I need a bit of exercise. Is that all right with you, my lady?'

Cherry laughed. 'Of course it is.'

She watched her go with a huge rush of affection. They had been through so much together over the years, and whatever else happened, wars or famine or earthquake, they would always be friends. The brief cloud vanished and as Maureen appeared to ask what she wanted her to do next, she smiled at the girl and made a quick decision.

'My friend and I will be going down to the village this afternoon, but would you ask your brother Declan if he'd meet us with his car outside Gilligan's shop at about four o'clock to save us walking back?'

'Of course, Ma'am. Anything you say, Ma'am. We're all at your disposal, so we are.'

Cherry looked at her sharply, unable to fathom why she was sounding mildly sarcastic.

'Is anything wrong, Maureen? It's nothing to do with your family, I hope? If your mother still has that nasty cough, please tell Cook she should let you take home a jug of onion broth for her tea,' she said. 'And make sure there's enough for the little ones as well,' she added generously.

To her surprise Maureen went a deep red. 'You're a very kind lady, Mrs Melchoir, and I know my mammy will be grateful, so I'll tell Cook right away.'

She almost fled to the kitchen, where Cook and the visitor were having a good old chuckle over what the young lady called this newfangled Irish recipe that she said she was going to try out on her husband when she got home to see if it would put hairs on his chest. They were in such easy cahoots together that it instantly confirmed what Maureen had surmised.

This one wasn't unused to kitchen life, and even if the other one was the same, she was a generous employer and gave her and

her brothers a good living here, and whatever the circumstances
of their knowing one another, it was no business of hers, and
best forgotten.

All too soon the visit was coming to an end. The last few days
flew by, and the night before Paula was due to leave, Lance arrived
home with the news that he had purchased two good breeding
mares from the fair, a comment that had Paula flushing with
embarrassment and Cherry hastening to ask teasingly if he had
thought to bring his wife anything from his expedition.

'Don't worry, I haven't forgotten you, my love, and I know
how you like your trinkets, but it can wait until later.'

'Should I leave you two alone?' Paula said with a smile. 'I
wouldn't want to spoil a touching reunion and I know how
impatient Cherry can be!'

'You stay where you are, Paula,' Cherry told her. 'I may be
impatient, but hopefully the anticipation will be worth the
wait.'

'Well, I'm not staying downstairs long after dinner,' Paula said.
'I want to pack my things ready for the journey tomorrow, and
I need to get a good night's sleep beforehand.'

'Very sensible,' Lance said.

They still weren't completely comfortable with each other,
thought Cherry, and because of the past they were never likely
to be. It made it all the more generous of him to allow Paula to
come here to stay which he knew Cherry had so badly wanted.
And she couldn't deny that she was glad Paula wanted to retire
early to give them time to themselves, even if she suspected that
part of the reason was the reticence she always felt when Lance
was around.

But the minute the meal was over and they were left alone in
the drawing room where the firelight warmed them both, they
sat close together on the sofa, and she forgot all about Paula and
everyone else. Whenever he went away he always brought something back for her, sometimes a pretty little trinket that cost very
little, and sometimes it was something more costly. Tonight was
no exception, as Lance drew out a jeweller's box from his pocket.

'As soon as I saw this I knew I had to buy it for my lady with
the most beautiful green eyes. I don't forget that crossing the

water was more than just a journey for us both, and this little token is a reminder of how much you mean to me,' he said simply.

Cherry felt her heart beat faster at the look on his face, and she opened the box quickly. Inside was an exquisite brooch in the shape of a dolphin, studded with emeralds. It glittered in the firelight and she loved it. She loved *him.*

'It's beautiful,' she breathed. 'Thank you, Lance.'

He kissed the nape of her neck. 'Thank *you* for sharing my life. And since we've been apart for a whole seven days, and Paula has been discreet enough to leave us alone, I think it's time we retired too, don't you?'

They drove Paula to the port at Rosslare the next day, on a miserable, windy morning with occasional flurries of stinging rain.

'You don't know how lucky you were to have a week of relatively calm weather,' Cherry told her. 'This is nothing to the storms we sometimes get, even here in the south. Be sure to wrap up warm on the ferry, Paula, and stay below, even if you're feeling queasy. You don't want to risk catching cold.'

'Don't worry. I'll be careful.'

Lance broke in with an amused smile. 'Was Cherry always this fussy about your welfare, Paula?'

She laughed awkwardly, still not too sure of him, and guiltily glad that she hadn't had to spend a whole week in his company.

'We always took care of each other, didn't we, Cherry? Whenever one of us was in danger of doing something foolish, the other one took charge. It wasn't always the same person, mind, and the other one didn't usually take a lot of notice, anyway.'

She found herself babbling, since this topic was too reminiscent of the time she had tried so hard to make Cherry admit to Lance that she wasn't expecting his baby. If she had done so, this whole chain of events would never have happened. And if it hadn't, her best friend might never have found the happiness she had now with the love of her life. So sometimes, even what seemed like the worst of things could turn out for the best, she thought desperately.

But if Cherry had any inkling of the way Paula's mind was working she didn't show it. Instead, she said that she intended to start knitting the baby's shawl they had agreed on right away, and she would send it to Paula as soon as it was finished.

'Knowing how fast I knit, it's a good thing I've got six months to do it, or the baby would be walking before you got it!' she said with a wry smile.

Images of the baby seemed to flash in front of her eyes then like a moving picture. She didn't want the images, but she could almost see the child being cradled in Paula's arms as a newborn, then sitting up and laughing, showing its first baby teeth, and later crawling, walking . . .

'We're here,' Lance said, breaking into her thoughts to her wild relief.

Not that she wanted Paula to go, and it had been such a joy to renew their old friendship but she realized, too, that her presence had disturbed her in a way she hadn't expected. Reminding her that Paula and Harold were anticipating the happiest event of their marriage, while she was still waiting, still frustrated. And now she had done the daftest thing in promising to knit her a shawl. Why couldn't she just have said a simple pair of bootees, for God's sake!

But there was no more time to wonder why she did anything any more. The ferry was waiting for passengers to board, and then there were hugs and kisses and promises to write, and waving Paula goodbye and trying to hide the weak tears at losing a friend all over again.

'Come on, old girl, buck up,' she heard Lance say briskly. 'It's not as if you're never going to see her again, is it? If she wants to come again, she'll probably be bringing her husband and a screaming baby as well, and you'll be wishing for some peace and quiet.'

He only meant to tease her, but he was totally unprepared for the way her eyes suddenly blazed with fury as they walked back to the car.

'Well, that remark makes me feel about a hundred years old, and I'm not your old girl! Sometimes you can be so insensitive that I wonder if you've got any idea at all about what goes on in my head, Lance,' she raged.

'Good God, I should think I do after all these years! You've had a good time with your old friend and imagined yourselves being young girls again, I daresay. But you're not the same person any more, Cherry, and now she's gone back to her real life, and you have to get back to yours. I'll remind you that as my wife we have a certain reputation in this community, which means no brawling in public, if you please.'

His arrogance almost took her breath away. At that moment he was his mother all over again, looking down his nose at everyone around him. She knew in her heart that it wasn't true, but it was all she could see right then.

'If I'm such a disappointment to you, I wonder why you ever wanted to marry me at all,' she said heatedly.

'I wonder that myself sometimes,' he said, wrenching open the passenger door of the car for her, and almost bundling her inside.

They drove back to Donaghy in chilly silence, and when they reached the village she asked him to wait while she went into Gilligan's shop.

'Don't be too long then. I've business to attend to regarding the two new brood mares since I won't be stabling them at the farm.'

It was almost the first thing he had told her about his week's dealings. Last night they had been too occupied in being together, and now they might have been a world apart.

She went into Gilligan's shop with her head held high. It was empty of customers at present, since the rain was coming in more steadily now. The owner smiled at her companionably.

'What can I do for you today, Mrs Melchoir? Come to browse, have you? I can't say there's much pleasure in doing anything else in such weather.'

'My husband's waiting for me, so I don't really have time for browsing, Mrs Gilligan. If you can find me a pattern for a baby's shawl and supply me with the wool and needles, that will do fine.'

'Ah well, I can do that for you, my dear. It's to be a gift for your little friend, I daresay,' she said knowingly.

Naturally. Why would anyone assume it was going to be for her! By now she had probably been dubbed as poor Captain Melchoir's barren wife, since most folk around here seemed to drop babies by the dozen, as easily as shelling peas, as Maureen Tring had told her cheerfully when reporting on another expected babe in the village.

She left the shop armed with her package, her ears ringing with Mrs Gilligan's tales of who was and who wasn't expecting, as if the mere fact of someone buying wool and a baby pattern was enough to stir their interest in every other female in the same condition. It was enough to make Cherry want to scream, and her mood had plunged considerably by the time they reached the farm, and Lance had departed to his study and left her alone.

Four

Cherry couldn't bear to remain at loggerheads with Lance. They had been through too much to let something like a trivial tiff and bruised feelings spoil their relationship. She knew they had a certain standing in the community, and she wasn't going to let him down. If it put her in the role of submitting to his wishes, so be it. In service, she had been doing that all her life, and it had never meant a loss of personal pride. Besides, being Lance's wife was what she had always longed to be, and that included whatever went with it.

She frequently admitted that an idle life was completely different from anything she had ever known, and it had taken time to get used to it. She had always had to be busy, but she had a new purpose now. She had a shawl to make for Paula's baby, and she refused to let jealousy rule her head as she diligently set about trying to work through the complicated instructions.

A wet and windy January gave way to a frosty February and then came the first glimmerings of spring in early March as the first primroses showed their delicate yellow faces in hedgerows and gardens. And still the shawl wasn't making much headway.

Lance couldn't resist a smile as he watched his wife getting to grips with the intricate pattern one evening, just about able to resist letting the cuss words slip out of her mouth as her fingers sweated over the needles.

'You're not exactly an expert knitter, are you, Cherry-ripe?' he said finally, using the pet name for her that she still loved to hear him say.

'I thought I was capable enough, but this is a bit more complicated than I expected. I really wanted to do something special for Paula, and it seems to be going all wrong,' she said, her eyes beginning to smart as she unpicked yet another row of dropped stitches. 'By the time it's finished – if it ever gets that far – it will be a grey shawl instead of a white one.'

'Why don't you leave it for tonight?' he suggested. 'There's no point in getting so frustrated with it that you ruin it. You could always ask Maureen to sort it out for you. I'm sure she's had plenty of experience with such things.'

'Servant girls don't have time to waste on knitting,' she replied smartly.

He didn't rise to the bait. 'I'm sure they don't, but with her brothers' wives having so many children, I'm sure she's made things for them, so why don't you ask her for help if you get stuck?'

Cherry sighed, knowing she had been ridiculously quick to think he was comparing her with Maureen. 'I might, but I'll leave it for tonight, anyway.'

'Good. Come and sit by me on the sofa and I'll ring the bell for Cook to bring us some cocoa to calm you down before bedtime.'

As he spoke the shrill of the telephone from his study made them jump.

'Well, that was spooky,' Cherry said with a grin. 'You mentioned ringing the bell and then the telephone rang. You don't have a secret admirer, do you?'

Lance frowned. 'Hardly. I don't know who it can be at this hour. I've asked my contacts not to call me after nine o'clock in the evening.'

Cherry hadn't realized it was so late. She had been concentrating so hard on the blessed shawl that the time had flown by since they had had their dinner.

She rang the bell herself for Cook to bring them their cocoa. Her head was starting to ache, and an early night would be all to the good. Lance seemed to be gone a very long time answering the call, and she guessed that he wasn't going to be in a very good mood at the end of it.

The two cups of cocoa were already starting to get cold by the time he returned to the drawing room and Cherry was about to order some more when she saw his ashen face. Her first thought was that something had happened to one of his horses, and she prayed that it wasn't his beloved Noble, his favourite that had come with them from England, or that one of the costly brood mares had had a fall and had to be put down.

'What's happened?' she said, her heart starting to beat rapidly.

He didn't say anything for a moment, and then he went straight to the sideboard and poured himself a glass of brandy from a decanter. He drank it so quickly she knew it had to be something really serious. She was even more alarmed when he poured himself another glass and downed that too.

Cherry stood up, her legs shaky with a presentiment about something she didn't yet understand. 'Lance, you're frightening me now. I know it must be something terrible, so can't you tell me?'

He put down the brandy glass and came across to her, taking her hands in both of his in such a tight grip that it hurt.

'That was the family solicitor,' he said harshly. 'My father had a massive heart attack while he was out alone yesterday and there was nothing anyone could do to save him. By the time he was discovered, he was already dead.'

'Oh, my God,' Cherry breathed, hardly able to take it in. The loss of a horse, however valuable, was nothing compared with this. The thoughts whirled around in her head, knowing how shocked Lance must be feeling, never having really made amends with his parents over their enforced marriage. And now he would never get the chance – not with his father, anyway.

Her heart lurched, and she tried not to think how that cold and bitter woman must also be feeling. But whatever Cherry's own feelings towards her, she was still Lance's mother, and she had just lost her husband. Presumably she had been too upset to telephone her son herself, which was why it had been left to the family solicitor. She wouldn't let herself consider the thought that that was the way the upper classes did things.

'Lance, I'm so sorry,' she whispered, already feeling, from the frozen look on his face, as though he had gone a million miles away from her now. 'You'll want to see your mother as soon as possible, of course.'

He seemed to bring her face into focus then.

'Of course. We'll leave on the ferry tomorrow morning,' he said curtly.

'We?' she echoed, her stomach churning.

'Naturally we must both go. There will be funeral arrangements to be made, and as my wife you'll be expected to be there to give my mother the support she needs at this time.'

'Good God, the last person she'll want to see is me!' Cherry said, aghast.

He continued speaking in the cold, distant way that he seemed to have adopted now, which she guessed was a foil to hide his real feelings, the way the upper classes did. The hated phrase was in her head again before she could stop it.

'You don't seem to have comprehended what all this means, do you, Cherry? My father is dead,' he emphasized.

'I know, and I've said how sorry I am,' she said, her lips shaking. 'I don't know what more I can say, but of course you know I'll do whatever you want,' she added unhappily, knowing she had to do this for him, however much she was going to hate being in the same house as that woman for an hour, let alone any longer.

He had held on to her hands for so long that her fingers began to feel numb, but now he let them go abruptly.

'My father is dead,' he said it again, as if he had to keep repeating it to believe it, and then he continued as if he was explaining things to a child. 'What you don't seem to understand is that from the moment of his death, I inherited the title and everything that goes with it. I became Lord Melchoir, and it's my duty to return to England and run the estate.'

Cherry gasped. 'But what about everything we've built up here? We've grown to love this place. At least, I thought we had, or was it all a sham?'

She knew she shouldn't have said such a thing at this time, because where his face had been so white it burned with anger now. She ached to hold him close and let him sob out his pain, but it wasn't his way.

It wasn't the toffs' way, as she and Paula would have once said. Keeping their emotions in check, putting on brave faces and stiff upper lips and all that rot, was what they did best. Again, she wished the hated thoughts didn't keep entering her head.

'You must have known that our time here was only temporary,' he went on. 'It doesn't pay to get too attached to anywhere when you know that one day you'll have to leave it.'

'I never even thought about it,' she said shakily.

She should have done so, of course. If she had been born with half his wit and intelligence, she should have known. She felt acute anger at the way he seemed to belittle her now. In her mind they had spent an idyllic time here, give or take a few unavoidable differences, but now those differences were so marked as to become almost insurmountable. But the thought of going back to that mausoleum of a place, which was how Cherry thought of Melchoir House now, ignoring its elegance and charm, was just appalling.

'Well, think about something else you seem to be overlooking,' Lance went on harshly. 'As my wife, you are now Lady Melchoir.'

Not bad for a former kitchen-maid, is it?

He didn't say the words, and maybe he never intended them, but it was all she could think of at that moment. Unconsciously, her chin lifted, and even though he was so distant, she had to say what was in her heart.

'It's true that it was something else I never thought about, nor wanted, but if it has to be, then I promise I will never let you down, Lance.'

She would have liked to add that she had meant every word of their marriage vows too, but he must know that. He had wanted her so much then, and she had been crazy with love for him. But if she dared to say those words, she was afraid he might remember them all too well – and not in a good way.

For richer or poorer didn't quite come into it now. She was about to be richer than she had ever dreamed of. The servant had become a lady, and all because of a wanton fling in a sweet-smelling hayloft all that time ago.

Not bad for a former kitchen-maid, is it?

She smothered a sob. 'I'll take these cold cups of cocoa back to the kitchen, Lance, and bring us some more,' she said, defying him to make any comment about her intention to do the menial task herself. 'If you want to add some more brandy to yours, it's up to you, but I need something to warm me after this sad news. I always respected your father, whatever you may think, and I'm truly sorry.'

She didn't wait for any reply. She simply fled to the kitchen with the two cups and saucers, and told Cook they had forgotten them and would like two more. If the woman read anything into her wild, distracted eyes and shaking hands, she didn't comment, but merely did as Cherry asked, putting the drinks on a tray and adding a small plate of biscuits.

She went back to the drawing room with a feeling of dread in her heart. The reality of it all was sinking in now, and there was no way she could get out of the inevitable, short of doing something terrible and disappearing out of Lance's life altogether. And what good would that do? It would humiliate him, and send her back to what she was before, a girl looking for work anywhere she could get it. And it would have to be anywhere away from here, where she was well known now.

Even a lingering nostalgia for Bristol didn't compensate for this, but in the end, she knew there was no choice to be made. A wife's place was beside her husband, providing that was where he wanted her to be.

She put the tray on the table and looked at him, her eyes brimming with tears, but willing herself not to shed them. But it was obvious he had had a few moments alone to think, and to her utter relief he held out his arms to her.

'I'm sorry,' he said thickly. 'And if you don't think it will be a wrench for me to leave all this, any more than it is for you, then you don't know me at all.'

She rushed into his embrace as they sank on to the sofa together, and she became aware that for all his former calm his body was heaving now, and in moments he was sobbing uncontrollably against her. And now she was the strong one, holding him, murmuring words of whatever comfort she could find, and knowing that all of it was futile, for when somebody close to a person died, there was no comfort anywhere.

It was only in her sleepless hours of the night, when Lance lay exhausted beside her, that she began to think of the other implications of what the change in their lives would mean. They had finally managed to talk more sensibly about what had happened, and it was midnight before they came to bed, by which time it had been decided that they would go back to Bristol for the funeral and for the meetings with the solicitor and the Will reading.

Once that was over they would return here to tie everything up, as he called it, ready for the permanent move back to Bristol. There was no question but that his inheritance would be as his father had always intended and that he and Cherry would take their rightful places as the owners of Melchoir House.

What then? Her heart jumped every time she thought about it. Because there wasn't just the imperious Lady Elspeth Melchoir to deal with. There was the staff as well. How could she possibly be comfortable there, where she had been a kitchen-maid for so long, and have to start lording it over her immediate superiors, their old cook and Gerard, the butler cum chauffeur, and the housemaids?

And presumably there would be several more girls in the kitchen now, taking over the duties that she and Paula had once held. How could she face them – and more to the point, how would they want to face *her*? There might even be a revolt against the new order and they would all walk out . . .

Lance stirred in his sleep and gave a small moan as unwelcome dreams disturbed him. Cherry put her arm around him and snuggled into his back, feeling him relax slightly at her touch. Her eyes filled with tears, knowing she had been the unwitting cause of everything that had gone wrong in his life, but as if he was somehow miraculously reading all the turbulent thoughts in her mind right then, he turned into her, his lips close to her flustered cheek.

'No matter what else happens, we've still got each other, Cherry-ripe,' he murmured almost incoherently, and still half-asleep. 'We can face anything together, you and I.'

She kissed him gently, hoping with all her heart that he was going to remember those words in the days to come.

He was brisk and efficient the next morning, having spent some time on the telephone, and then informing the staff that they would be away for a couple of weeks, while Cherry organized the clothes packing.

Flitting around her like an annoying little fly that wouldn't go away, Maureen Tring was agog with curiosity, but Lance had decided that as yet they shouldn't reveal the reason for their leaving, other than they wanted to visit the family, which only made their sudden departure all the more intriguing and full of speculation.

'I daresay you'll be seeing that nice friend of yours while you're back in Bristol,' Maureen prompted, wanting to help, and being told smartly that Cherry preferred to do the packing herself. 'How long does she have to go now, Ma'am? A few more months yet, isn't it?'

Cherry started at her words. Paula had been the last person on her mind in these last frantic hours, but of course she would want to see her, she thought with a flood of relief. Paula would be the one sane person she would definitely want to see. Paula would have no truck with addressing her as Lady Melchoir, either. But she kept her fingers firmly crossed as she thought it.

'I'm not quite sure,' she muttered in answer to Maureen's question. 'About four months, I think.'

Maureen nodded sagely. With all the babies that had been born in her own large family, she considered herself something of an expert in such matters.

'She'll have got over the morning sickness by now then, and be in the bloom of it, as my old granny used to say.'

'Just take these bags downstairs for me, Maureen, and stop chattering. There's still plenty to do before we set off for the ferry this morning,' Cherry said testily, not wanting to hear the girl's observations of Paula's progress.

'All right,' the girl replied, fully intending to report to her mammy that evening that there was definitely something going on up at the farm, with the two of them so red-eyed and short-tempered with everybody.

But the mention of Paula had sent a small feeling of relief to Cherry's mind. She hadn't seen the little house where Paula and Harold lived, although she knew its whereabouts in Bristol, and she imagined sitting down and having a cup of tea and a laugh with Paula, and the very thought of it was like a refuge.

She kept the thought in her head all the time the taxi took them to the Rosslare–Fishguard ferry. She hadn't even asked how they would get from there to Bristol, but she might have known that Lance would have arranged everything, and her heart thumped as she saw the Melchoirs' familiar sleek limousine waiting for them on the quay. It thumped even more uncomfortably as she saw Mr Gerard standing beside it in his chauffeur's attire, adorned with a respectful black mourning band around his sleeve.

He tipped his cap to Lance, and it seemed to Cherry that he avoided looking at her – or it may have been simply because she was so sensitive to the staff's reaction to her new status, as he took their bags to stow them in the spacious boot. She could never have helped, since she was all fingers and thumbs, just knowing she had every right to travel in this car from now on.

'Welcome home, my Lord, and Madam, although I'm very sorry it has to be such sad circumstances,' the chauffeur said.

'Thank you, Gerard,' Lance said briskly. 'Now, don't let's hang about here. I want to get home as soon as possible to see my mother.'

'Of course, Sir.'

It was true. He wouldn't look at her. As Lance sat beside her in the back seat of the limousine, Cherry burned with embarrassment and a growing indignity. It wasn't her fault the old boy had died and they had to come back here when they had been enjoying a good life in Ireland. And there was no way she would let this pompous oaf of a butler cum chauffeur ignore her, either.

She leaned forward and spoke directly to him. Without thinking, her voice had assumed a little of her old Bristol accent.

'Lord Melchoir's death must have been a shock to you all, Mr Gerard. I know how fond we all were of him.'

She heard Lance's intake of breath and knew he wouldn't be pleased at her interference, especially as her words had virtually implied that she was still *one of them*. She didn't care. The fact that she had forced Gerard into replying was good enough.

'It was a shock, as you say, Madam, and Cook has taken it particularly hard, having served the family for so many years.'

'Please give her my regards, and tell her I'll have a few words with her as soon as I can,' Cherry promised.

The man merely nodded, and then she realized that Lance was closing the glass partition that separated the driver from the passengers in the back seat. He turned to her, his face furious.

'What the hell do you think you're doing?' he said in a low angry voice.

'I'm suggesting that I have a few words with old friends over what has happened,' she said unsteadily. 'Your father's death obviously affects you and your mother most of all, but there are people who have been in the Melchoir service for many years who will also be mourning the loss of a good man.'

'And which of these people do you associate yourself with? I notice you put my mother and I together without including yourself in our family.'

Cherry bit her lip and tried to stop it trembling. 'I'm not sure that your mother will see my inclusion in the family in the same way, and you must see how difficult this is going to be for me.'

He turned his head away from her as the car covered the miles to watch the ever-changing countryside in all its early spring beauty, without really seeing any of it. His voice was full of pain when he spoke, saying what she already knew only too well.

'And you must see that while I'm in a state of mourning my father I can't think of anything else but the implications for the future. The first thing is the meeting with my mother, who I'm sure is devastated by what's happened, and then there is the funeral to get through. Those are the things that matter most to me right now, not how you are going to face your former workmates.'

If it hadn't been that she could hear the suffering in his voice, she would have lashed out at him for his cruelty. But she did hear it, and she forgave him for his harsh words, just as she had always forgiven him. Did that make her weak? If so, it was love that made her so. She knew Lance must be feeling endless remorse and guilt over the estrangement from his father all this time, but Cherry too felt as if her whole world had turned upside down, and the future that had seemed so wonderful, was beset with doubts now. Any wife would be devastated by her husband's death, but the thought of that stiff woman revealing a vestige of her feelings to anyone else was something she couldn't quite imagine, no matter how hard she tried.

But she desperately wanted to give Lance some small sense of reassurance, whether he wanted it or not, and she dared to put her hand in his. For a moment she thought he was going to snatch it away, but then she felt his unspoken response, and he let her hand lie in his for the rest of the journey home.

The limousine covered the miles smoothly and swiftly, and Cherry felt her throat tighten as the ancient city that had once been so familiar to them both eventually came into view. Far below was the curve of the Avon river carving its way through the city, the water at full tide bluer than usual in the sunlight and hiding its treacherous mud banks on either side, and spanned by the graceful

Clifton suspension bridge that Brunel had engineered and never lived to see completed. And there was the glorious Durdham Downs, the surprisingly vast expanse of shady green in a crowded city, where people exercised their dogs, and ladies and gentlemen perambulated. The Downs had a great history, staging events of all kinds in its distant past, from circuses and annual fairs and flower shows to such outlawed events as cock-baiting and bare-knuckle boxing . . .

Cherry drew in her breath. Bare-knuckle boxing still went on, and her brother was well known in such circles as Knuckles O'Neill. Such a stupid name, she had always thought scathingly, but it described what he did all too well. And despite her anxiety in coming back to Melchoir House and all that it implied, he was still the one person above all others that she definitely didn't want to see. She hadn't had any news of him at all since before her marriage, and she never wanted to see him again after he had tried so despicably to extort money out of Lance and his father.

'Are you all right?' Lance said, and she realized her grip on his hand had involuntarily tightened.

'Yes,' she mumbled. 'Still getting cold feet, that's all.'

'Don't worry, you've still got me,' he said.

She hoped it would always be so. Among her many other doubts about coming back under such life-changing circum-stances, was the shameful one she hadn't really allowed to enter her head too seriously. But as they got ever nearer to the mansion and estate that now belonged to Lance – and unbelievably to herself – was the knowledge that not too far away was another estate belonging to the family of the Honourable Cynthia Hetherington.

There had never been any doubt in her mind that this was the lady Lance's family had wanted him to marry – the far more suitable lady with the same class and background as himself. The Hon. Cynthia's family, and others like them, were the kind of people who would certainly turn up at Lord Melchoir's funeral, and with whom she would be expected to socialize from now on.

And oh God, the more she thought about it, the more petri-fied she became, and the more she seemed to shrivel into herself at the ludicrous idea of being on equal terms with them all – which she definitely was not, and never would be. She knew she had begun breathing much too fast, and her terror must have been all too evident on her face, because she suddenly became aware that Lance had put his arm around her and was holding her closer to him.

'I do know how difficult this is going to be for you, Cherry,' he said, 'but you must have known it would happen someday, and I need you to help me get through the next days and weeks.'

She felt choked at his words, and she nodded wordlessly. The truth was she had simply blotted out the knowledge that someday they would have to return to Bristol. They had left under such a cloud of resentment and anger from his parents, and now his father was dead, and he had never had the chance to make amends, she thought again.

His mother would be as stony-hearted as ever, absolutely hating the fact that a former kitchen-maid was now to be on a level with herself. More than that, in fact, since the little upstart was the wife of the new Lord Melchoir, and as such the former lady would have to take second place. Cherry *knew* all that and she knew that Lance sympathized with her worries. But he couldn't truly understand her fears, because they had never been part of his life. He hadn't risen from rags to riches in the way she had. The riches had always been there for him, and nobody would ever begrudge him his new status. While she . . . she had it all to learn, and she wasn't at all sure that she was capable of it.

'Whatever we have to face, we'll face it together,' Lance went on quietly, unaware of just how much turmoil was still going on inside her. 'We did it before, and we can do it again. Can't we, Cherry-ripe?'

It was that name that did it. That sweet, silly name for her that nobody used but him. One minute she was lost in a panic, and the next she had swayed right into his arms, regardless of the chauffeur in the front seat and what he might see or think.

'Of course we can,' she said huskily.

It was a brave sentiment, and she sincerely meant to try her best to live up to it. She was no chicken, and she had enough pride to hold her head up high as the limousine swept up the final part of the journey and came to a halt outside the elaborate frontage of the Melchoir mansion.

As Gerard stepped out of the car and came around to open the rear doors for them, Lance squeezed her hand tightly.

'Welcome home, my lady,' he whispered in her ear, but his voice was not quite as steady as before as they registered that the curtains were drawn across every window to indicate that this was a house in mourning, and the daylight wouldn't be allowed in until the funeral was over. There could have been no more obvious fact to remind Cherry of why they were here.

Five

A housemaid Cherry hadn't seen before came forward to take the bags from Gerard's hands and gave a small nervous bob to the new Lord Melchoir and his wife. Cherry's heart thudded as she and Lance followed her up the broad, winding staircase to Lance's old bedroom that she would now share. It was a room she had only ever seen before when the house was having its spring clean while the family had gone to London several years ago to see the Empire Exhibition. It was also ridiculously large for two people, compared with the cramped little attic room she and Paula had once shared here.

But she mustn't think of that any more, or she would be a bag of nerves before she had even seen another person in the house. This was where she belonged now, she told herself, and she had every right to be here.

Before she had a chance to think of anything more, Lance left her to go and see his mother, saying he would be back in a little while.

'Should I unpack for you then, Madam?' the maid said, her eyes wide with curiosity, and obviously knowing every single detail of who Cherry was, and more to the point, who she had been. Kitchen gossip wouldn't have been slow to inform any new members of staff.

'That won't be necessary, and I prefer to unpack myself,' she said quickly, ignoring what Lance might have thought. 'What's your name, by the way?'

'It's Jenny, Madam.'

'Well, Jenny, will you please tell Cook that I will look forward to seeing her again as soon as it's convenient for me to do so?'

The girl nodded and fled out of the room, clearly nonplussed by this remark. When she got downstairs again, she reported every bit of the brief conversation to Cook and the rest of the kitchen staff.

'She's not a bit like I thought she'd be, either. She's not as snooty as the old girl upstairs, o' course, but she talks like a toff and she dresses ever so nice, and her hair's such a lovely colour and so smart.'

Cook spoke sharply. 'You mind your manners, my girl, and don't go referring to Lady Melchoir as the old girl upstairs or you'll have Mr Gerard after your guts for garters.'

Jenny pulled a face behind her back, which got the other maids sniggering.

'Is she still Lady Melchoir now that our Cherry's taken over, Cook?' Lucy, one of the housemaids, put in.

Her reply was a clip round the ear from Cook.

'You can all just stop being so stupid. Of course Lady Melchoir's still Lady Melchoir, and if Captain Lance's wife now has the same title, on account of what's happened, we'll just have to get used to it until we're told any different, won't we? The poor old gentleman's hardly cold in his coffin yet, so don't start surmising what's what before we're told the new order of things.'

'It's true though ain't it, Cook?' Lucy added. 'We can't go calling Cherry "Cherry" when we see her, not now she's gone up in the world, can we?'

'I doubt that we'll see much of her at all, and don't forget they've come back for a sad reason and not for any social occasion, especially not to chew the fat with the likes of us when they're only here to bury poor Lord Melchoir. It'll be a sad day for all of us when that happens, but I reckon they'll be off back to Ireland once it's all over.'

She gave a loud sniff and wiped her eyes with her apron, and then told the maids to scurry around as the butler came into the kitchen wearing his everyday attire now. He had obviously overheard Cook's words and spoke briskly to her.

'The young Lady Melchoir sends her regards to you, Cook, and says she'll have a few words with you as soon as it's convenient for her to do so,' he said without any expression to betray his feelings.

'Told you so,' Jenny muttered in an aside to the other maids.

'Well, thank you for the message, Mr Gerard,' Cook said, more taken aback than she let on. 'She was always a polite young lady and it's only good manners for her not to forget her old friends, which is no more than I expected,' she added, suppressing her earlier remarks.

She ignored the mutterings of the maids and told them sharply to get on with preparing vegetables and their other duties, since there would be two more for dinner that evening – and for as long as the young couple were here.

'Do you really think they'll go back to Ireland?' she asked Gerard once the others were out of hearing.

The man shrugged. 'They haven't brought a large wardrobe with them, so I think this is a fairly short stay. But after that, well, I reckon the Captain will expect to take up the reins here, no matter how many ructions it may cause between the other two.'

He didn't need to explain any further, and Cook merely nodded sagely, wishing she could be a fly on the wall when the two Lady Melchoirs first set eyes on one another.

Lance had always known it would be a difficult meeting with his mother. They hadn't seen one another since the day he and Cherry had set sail for Ireland nearly two years ago after their quiet wedding. None of their old acquaintances had been invited, the reason being circulated was that Lance had needed to take up occupancy of the farmstead as soon as possible. Whether or not any of them believed such a feeble excuse, Lance neither knew nor cared.

His mother had never been a demonstrative woman, and dressed all in black now, she looked anything but welcoming as he entered the drawing room from where she had watched the approach of the limousine a little earlier. He walked quickly forward and pressed his lips to her cold cheek. She gave away none of her emotions, any more than he had expected she would.

He had commanded many men in the army and coped with desperate and dangerous situations, but this was completely different. Even writing to grieving relatives when one of his men had been killed and sometimes inventing a gallantry not all of them had displayed for the relatives' peace of mind, was as nothing to facing his own mother after all this time. It wasn't only Cherry who had nerves, he thought grimly. He sat on a chair close to his mother, searching for any sign of pleasure at seeing him. She didn't say a word, and he racked his brain for the right thing to say. But in the end there was only one thing he could say.

'Mother, you know how distressed I am to come home in these circumstances,' he said in a low voice. 'You must know that I'd have given anything to be here for both of you when Father died.'

She inclined her head. 'Of course I know it, but you made your bed and you have to lie in it.'

It was a cruel and thoughtless remark, but he kept his temper in check, telling himself that for all her coldness, she must be grieving deeply inside. But he had already decided it was best to state his plans frankly and at once.

'I want to pay my respects to Father as soon as possible, and also to make my peace with him in my own way. I will instruct Gerard to take me to the Chapel of Rest this evening. I intended to go there alone, but I would like it if you would accompany me,' he said.

When she didn't reply, he went on, deliberately bringing his wife's name to the fore. 'I also want to say that Cherry and I will be here for two weeks. After that we will go back to Donaghy to arrange everything there, and then we will return to Melchoir House to take up our new positions.'

His mother's eyes flashed with the first sign of animation since he had arrived, and she stood up stiffly. 'Your new *positions*? I have no quibble with your new title, Lance, since you are my son and it is the right order of things, but you cannot expect me to receive that person in the same way.'

Lance stood up too, his eyes as hard as hers. 'You can, and you will. Cherry is my wife, Mother, and she is also correctly to be known as Lady Melchoir, and there is nothing you can do about it.'

'And what title do you have in mind for me, may I ask?' Elspeth said.

'The same as you always had, of course, unless you prefer to be known as Lady Elspeth. Nothing has changed there, Mother,' he said more gently.

'On the contrary! Everything in my world has changed, not least the fact that I have lost my husband, and nothing will ever be the same for me again.'

At that moment he glimpsed the raw vulnerability in her eyes, and whether she wanted it or not, he moved towards her and hugged her close to him. He felt her lean against him for the merest time, and he knew how difficult this was going to be for her.

'I really would appreciate it if you would come with me to the Chapel of Rest tonight,' he repeated. 'I think it would be appropriate for the two of us to be there together, if you feel up to it.'

If he was shutting Cherry out from having to make such a visit, he knew she would be relieved rather than affronted, and it was right and proper for him and his mother to go there together. To his relief he heard her give a heavy sigh.

'Yes, please see to it, Lance, but I don't wish to join you for dinner this evening. I will have mine sent to my room tonight and I will receive your wife later, after we return.'

She hadn't lost the knack of making a gracious comment and a downright slur to Cherry in the same remark, but he knew Cherry would be relieved about that too. They had had a long journey and they were both tired, their nerves on edge. Tomorrow would have been soon enough for Cherry to be summoned to the presence, which was the only way he could think of it. But if his mother said she would see her later this evening, so be it.

'Well, thank the Lord for small mercies!' she said when he told her of the evening arrangements. 'I can't tell you how much I was dreading sitting opposite her at the dining table, Lance. Though I'd much rather have waited until tomorrow to see her. I won't know what the hell to say to her and I couldn't bear to have seen your father laid out, either. I never did care for public viewing of dead bodies, thank you very much.'

She had been a bundle of nerves ever since he had left her to see his mother, and in her relief she heard herself babbling, her accent slipping, and she saw him frown at her insensitive remark. She spoke quickly again.

'Oh God, I'm sorry, that was an awful thing to say. I'm so het up about being here and over all that's happened, and I'm not thinking straight any more.'

'Well, you had better start thinking straight,' he said, more coldly than she had heard him talk to her before. 'We have a lot to get through in these next weeks, and the last thing I want is for you and Mother to be at loggerheads while we're here.

A daughter-in-law should be a great support to her at this time, and when it comes to the funeral, we have to be seen to be a united family.'

She couldn't look at him, and she kept her eyes lowered for fear she would betray the emotions inside her now that would have outraged him. She wanted to laugh out loud at such ludicrous remarks, and that would have been disastrous. She was damn sure his mother was never going to think of her privately as her daughter-in-law, but in public this was how the upper classes behaved. It was all for show. Nothing else mattered.

'*Cherry?*' Lance said sharply, when she didn't answer.

'Don't worry, I won't let you down,' she said in a choked voice. 'I'll play my part, providing your mother will play hers.'

She couldn't resist the small barb, but he chose to ignore it and told her they should get ready for dinner. She realized she was hungry, though she hadn't expected to be able to eat much with Lady Elspeth looking on disapprovingly. But that was removed now, and she ate more heartily than Lance did.

She was thankful when the meal was over and he and his mother left for the Chapel of Rest. Hopefully when he came back he would feel a mite more relaxed, having done all he could to make whatever kind of peace he felt he could with his father. And once the limousine had left to go to the city, she was left in limbo and not quite knowing what to do with herself.

What did she normally do after a meal at Melchoir House? In the past she would have waited for the dirty dishes to be brought to the kitchen and she and Paula would start on the mammoth task of washing up, scrubbing pots and pans, putting things away on shelves and in cupboards, and being nagged by Cook to stop chattering and wasting time if they ever wanted to get to bed that night. She hid a small sob. They had been hectic, scrambling days, doing everything they were told to escape the wrath of Cook, and they had also been close-knit, friendly days where people could say what they thought without having to watch their Ps and Qs every damn minute.

Being here was so different now. So horribly, weirdly different. Even Lance was already different. She felt a sense of panic rise up inside, feeling a sudden urge to run away and hide, and not to be a part of this strange new world into which she was now a part. How could she ever have thought she could fit into Lance's world? How could she ever face all his friends and try to make meaningless small talk with them in the way the toffs did?

A tap on the bedroom door made her jump, and she croaked out a request for someone to enter. The maid called Jenny came inside, making the same nervous little bob she had done before.

'Is there anything else you need, Madam? Cook wondered if you would like a drink of some kind.'

'No, thank you, Jenny.'

'I'll be back later to turn down the bed for you then,' the girl went on.

She turned and left quickly, leaving Cherry staring at the door. She was perfectly capable of turning down a bed sheet by herself, but presumably this was what she had to look forward to now. For the first time in her life she thought what a waste of time and money it was to hire people to cater for the pampered life. Despite having had Maureen Tring fussing about the farm, life had been far more relaxed in Ireland, but for a girl who had scrimped all her life Cherry still felt embarrassed that such simple things were going to be done for her, and she was helpless to do anything about it but accept it.

She felt a stab of impatience at herself. What was she thinking of to get so jittery? She was here now – and unwittingly she echoed Lady Elspeth's words to Lance. *She had made her bed and she had to lie in it* – and she was sharing it with the man she loved. But she was nobody's puppet, and without another moment's thought she went out of the bedroom and along the corridor, to speed through the house and down the stairs to more familiar territory. The people inside the spacious kitchen looked up from what they were doing, startled to hear footsteps approaching. It was like a stage set, Cherry thought, with everyone frozen for a moment and not knowing quite what to say or do, except for the new young kitchen-maids who giggled and whispered together.

'Shut up, you idiots. It's *her*,' Cherry heard Jenny say in a hoarse whisper as she dug them in the ribs.

Cook recovered first.

'It's good to see you looking so well, Madam,' she said awkwardly.

Cherry gave a nervous laugh. 'Good God, Cook, I never thought to hear you calling me Madam! It was always more likely to be you lazy so-and-so, from what I remember!'

She groaned inwardly, knowing she shouldn't be saying such things to give the younger ones such ammunition for gossip. Lance would be horrified, but she knew only too well how the kitchen staff liked to gossip about their betters, considering how she and Paula had done it a thousand times, but she had never expected to be one of the toffs upstairs, and she still didn't.

'Is there something I can do for you?' Cook went on, clearly not sure how to address her at all now.

Cherry came to a decision. Damn it, these people – the ones she used to know, anyway – had been her friends and work-mates, and she'd be blowed if she was going to be treated any differently now. She sat down at the big scrubbed table where she had prepared so many vegetables over the years until her fingers were raw, and asked directly if there was any tea going.

'I'll take a decent cup of tea any day rather than a mouthful of coffee in those potty little cups they use upstairs,' she went on.

'Coming up then,' Cook said more heartily. 'And you skivvies can get on about your business, while me and the Madam have a chinwag.'

As they scurried off to do her bidding, not daring to argue, Cherry felt her eyes grow moist. It seemed such a little time ago that she would have been doing the same thing, and here she was now, in a different world. She gave a soft sigh as Cook poured her a cup of tea from the large brown teapot, and sat down at the opposite side of the table. The woman spoke shrewdly as Cherry took the first sip of Cook's well-remembered strong brew.

'I'm not sure it's right for you and me to be sitting together, now that you're Lady Melchoir, but something tells me that all's not quite as it should be.'

'Why wouldn't it be, Cook? Don't you think I've got every-thing I ever wanted?' Cherry said with a small smile. She added teasingly: 'Even coming down here, and seeing how you order those girls about, reminds me of that!'

Cook snorted. 'Money ain't everything and you know it, and

I'm not apologizing for saying as much, for all your fine clothes and status now. If you didn't want a bit of straight talking, you'd have stayed upstairs.'

She was right, damn it. But the truth was, Cherry didn't know what she did want. She didn't belong to the life upstairs, not really, and she didn't belong downstairs any more either. She drank more of the tea, trying to stop her mouth wobbling. God, it wouldn't do for the new Lady Melchoir to start blubbing over Cook, especially if any of the skivvies were hovering close enough to hear what was going on. She couldn't get the hated name for them out of her head now.

She gathered up her dignity, remembering where she was, and that she owed it to Lance to remember who she was too.

'Well, I just wanted to say hello and to say that I know you'll all be grieving over Lord Melchoir's death. It must have been a shock to all of you.'

For the first time, the older woman's face crumbled a little. 'Oh aye, it was a shock all right. He were a good man, and well liked by all of us. It must have been a nasty shock to you and the Captain, over there in Ireland, I'm sure. He'd have been feeling extra bad at not being here at the time.'

And whose fault was that?

'Of course he did. He and his mother have gone to pay their respects to him now,' Cherry said numbly.

The message was stark. Either she hadn't wanted to go with them or they hadn't invited her. Whichever Cook chose to think, she suddenly got up and came around the table to put her arm around Cherry's shoulder for a second.

'You were always the brightest of my girls,' she said roughly, 'and if I know you, you won't falter now. If you can't face 'em, then put on an act, the way you always did. That will see you through, Cherry. And that's the last time I can afford to be so free with you unless you come to see me in private.'

As Cherry took in all that she said, she felt a sliver of comfort from it. She wasn't entirely alone in this great mausoleum of a house. She had Lance . . . and she had an ally here if she ever needed one. The strange word entered her head before she had time to think. She drained her cup of tea and gave Cook a small hug before she went back to the rooms that were now her right

and proper domain, and waited for Lance to return home from
his sad mission.

'So what do you intend to do now?' Lady Elspeth said to her
son.

They had spent half an hour with Lance's father, and returned
to her private sitting room now, where Lance poured them both
a large glass of brandy. If he was drinking too much of the stuff
these days, he didn't care. He had to do something to get him
through these nightmare days. He should go to his wife, but
for all his mother's iron control, he felt that she needed his
company most right now. He had seen more than a glimpse of
her grief at the Chapel of Rest, but she would never let it show
in public.

'What do you mean?' he asked her now. 'I'm here for a couple
of weeks, and then I will wind up everything in Ireland and
return. What more can I say?'

'What of the girl?'

Lance felt his anger start to rise and tried to control it.

'If you mean my wife, you know very well her name is Cherry,
and I ask you to please use it and give her the respect she deserves.'

'She deceived you and all of us, Lance, and I don't know how
you can forget that. Pretending to be with child when she wasn't
was a despicable thing to do, and what one might have expected
from a person of her class. That you were gullible and foolhardy
enough to carry on with the deceit long enough to marry her
without telling your father and me it was all a lie is something
I can never forgive.'

'I married Cherry because I loved her, and I still love her.
Can't you understand that? At least Father knew it.'

She brushed aside his comment. Her face was red with fury
at having to speak to him in this way, but she hadn't finished yet.

'Men will believe whatever they want to believe from a pretty
girl, but there's no need to continue with the charade any longer.
You have a position to uphold now, Lance, and divorce is no
disgrace these days. It can be arranged as quietly and quickly as
the marriage.'

He was so outraged at this that he felt ready to explode. His
hands were clenched so tightly his nails dug into his palms like

needles, and if they hadn't done so he thought he might be in danger of throttling her.

'You are the most insensitive woman on this earth, Mother. I will never divorce Cherry and she will continue to be my wife until the day I die, and I expect – no, I *demand* – that you honour her.'

'Then you'll be disappointed,' Elspeth said frigidly. 'No gentleman would ever demean his mother by asking her to honour a former kitchen-maid.'

Lance's voice was icily calm now.

'I do not ask you anything in those terms. I ask you to honour your daughter-in-law, as any parent would. No matter what you think, the relationship between us all is irrefutable, and I expect all our friends to accept it too.'

'Then you expect too much,' she snapped.

Then, without warning, she wilted, and she brushed a shaking hand across her forehead. 'I'm an old woman, Lance, and you make me ill. But I've said my piece now, and for the sake of peace and propriety I suppose I will have to pretend that all is well. I will never forget how the girl wormed her way into our family, nor how you went along with the deceit, but I can see from your attitude that it is too late to do anything about it.'

Lance looked at her guardedly, wondering if she intended to feign illness in order not to see Cherry at all. If that was the case, he had no intention of letting it happen.

'Then the sooner you and Cherry meet, the better,' he went on determinedly. 'I'll fetch her directly, and we'll have a nightcap together while we discuss the funeral arrangements. She has every right to be included, Mother.'

She responded with the slightest inclination of her head, and he left her to inform Cherry that she was wanted. In every way, he added to himself.

'Right now?' she asked. 'I thought we were leaving it until tomorrow!'

'There's no point in putting it off if you've been sitting here all evening worrying about when you're going to face her.'

'I've been doing no such thing. I went downstairs to say hello to Cook,' she said, before she could stop herself.

'Good God, Cherry, that was hardly the wisest thing to do!'

'I don't see why not. I worked in the kitchens for years, so why shouldn't I say hello to her ? She'd soon have thought I was getting above myself if I totally ignored her.'

'You have to remember that you're not one of them any longer, Cherry. You can't just pop down for a chat any time you feel like it, and you can't drift between two lives any more.'

He tried hard to keep calm, but after the scene with his mother, and now this, it was beginning to alarm him.

'Well, I hope you're not going to stop me seeing Paula,' she said defiantly. 'You were happy enough for her to come and visit us in Ireland, even though you weren't around for very long, and I certainly mean to go and see her as soon as I can. She'll have heard about your father's death by now, of course, and she'll know we've come back. I'm not turning my back on her, no matter what you say.'

'I'm not asking you to do so. Just be circumspect about it, that's all.'

'I would, if I knew what the stupid word meant!' she said, swallowing. 'I've always done my best to be what you want me to be, Lance, but I can't lose myself completely. You didn't fall in love with me because I was some high and mighty chinless wonder, did you?'

Her words brought a smile to his lips. 'I certainly did not! I fell in love with a warm and passionate woman, and there's nothing I want to change about that. I also know you can be anything you want to be. I remember the first time I heard you mimicking my mother for the benefit of your workmates.'

She smiled too, remembering. She had thought he'd be horrified, but he had enjoyed the performance as much as Cook and the others. She remembered too, the first time he had insisted she should meet his parents, and she had gone upstairs with her knees knocking, and then startled them both by using the upper class accent she could mimic so well. Cook always said she could pass for a lady any day, and there was no day like the present. She took a deep breath.

'All right, then. If I have to go and meet the dragon in her den, let's get on with it,' she said.

Lance smiled with relief, but he added a word of caution.

'She's still in mourning, Cherry, so if she speaks harshly towards you, please remember that and be tolerant.'

'I'll just be surprised if she speaks to me at all,' Cherry answered drily.

But she would do it for him, if not for his mother. After all, she and Lance had the rest of their lives to be together, and who knew how many more years his mother might have? She wouldn't be so heartless as to wish for anything awful to happen to Lady Elspeth, but in the correct order of things, parents were supposed to die before their children. Lord Melchoir had proved that, and she couldn't help a guilty tinge of relief at knowing that the bad feeling between Lance's mother and herself couldn't last for ever.

Six

Her heart was beating fast as they went into Lady Elspeth's sitting room, and Cherry saw that Lance's mother was as stiff and starchy as ever. She sat bolt upright in an armchair, giving nothing to its luxurious comfort. Dressed all in black and looking so formal, despite being in her own surroundings, she seemed smaller than Cherry remembered, and she gave no indication that two people had entered the room.

Cherry had expected this to be a difficult meeting, but without warning she felt the most enormous sense of pity for the woman, who couldn't seem to express her emotions the way other people did. Whether it was due to her own upbringing, or the way the toffs usually behaved, at that moment Cherry could only see a woman who was suffering. She was still trying to come to terms with the shock of losing her husband and she seemed to be so terribly alone.

Before Lance had any idea what his wife was going to do, any more than she did herself, Cherry had sped across the room and knelt down beside his mother, taking her cold hands in her own.

'I'm so very sorry to have come home under such sad circumstances, Lady Elspeth,' she said, her voice shaking. 'I know you could never think of me as a daughter, and I will try to keep out of your way as much as possible. I have no mother of my own, but please believe that I would always try to be all that a daughter should be for you.'

She had no idea where the words came from, and she felt her stomach churning even as she said them, knowing how audacious they must sound. What a fool she was to put herself in such a position for ridicule! If this woman had had her way, she would have been sent packing long ago. It was only Lord Melchoir's grudging intervention over the child she was supposed to be carrying, that had swayed her to agreeing to her son's marriage to a kitchen-maid, since getting rid of Cherry O'Neill would also be losing her grandchild for ever. Now that they had been apart for nearly two years, she might have realized she had been in danger of losing her son as well.

Cherry stood up clumsily, letting go of Lady Elspeth's hands and turning to look desperately at Lance, and wishing that at least one of them would say something. But she could see by his face that he was too stunned by what had just happened to say anything for a few seconds. Then, before she could move, she heard Lady Elspeth speak without any expression.

'In this life we all have our roles to play. Some of us would choose to have it otherwise, but at this particular time it's important to show a united face in public, no matter how we feel in private. I acknowledge that you are my son's wife, but I have never had a daughter and I don't have one now. That is all I wish to say, and now I am very tired, and I wish to retire.'

'Then we will see you in the morning, Mother,' Lance said, his voice hard, and clearly not intending to prolong this inter-view. 'Now that Cherry has humbled herself unnecessarily, I hope you will think about what she has said and how generous she is being in offering you her affection. And I would remind you of one more thing. If we are to put on this united public face as you call it, my wife's name is Cherry. I ask that you remember it, and use it.'

Without another word, he put his arm around Cherry and ushered her out of his mother's sitting room. They walked quickly along the landing to their bedroom, where she sank tremblingly on to the bed, her head in her hands.

'How could I have said such daft things to her, Lance?' she almost wept. 'She'll never think of me as a daughter – any more than I could ever think of her as my mother, if you really want to know! Never, never, *never!*'

She felt his arms go around her, holding her tight, and she sobbed against him. All this time, all this journey home, she real-ized now, had been leading up to her dread of this first meeting with his mother. She had meant to be so dignified, so proud, proving herself worthy of Lance. And what had she done? Made herself out to be a simpleton, begging for scraps, and had had them tossed back in her face.

'You were magnificent, my Cherry-ripe.'

Unbelievingly, she heard the tenderness in his voice, and she gradually stopped shaking and looked up into his face.

'That's not what I'd have called it – and it's certainly not what your mother thought!' she whispered.

'I think my mother was too flabbergasted to think too much at all, but no doubt she'll be considering it now. I know you were completely sincere, and she would have seen that too. But I always said you should be on the stage, sweetheart, and if the words had been written for you, no actress could have carried them off better.'

'I'm not sure whether that makes me feel flattered or upset now,' she mumbled.

'Then be comforted, and just carry on being your own sweet self and remember how much I love you. And let me remind you in somewhere far more comfortable than a hayloft.'

She caught her breath as he pushed her gently back on to the bed, knowing where all this was leading. And that was unbelievable too, since he hadn't made love to her since hearing of his father's death, and rightly so. Was this the right time, even now, when his father hadn't yet been laid to rest? But now they were here, they were home where they belonged, they were young and in love, and any such objections quickly vanished. She wound her arms around him, wanting him with an urgency that matched his, and gladly put the rest of the world out of her mind.

No matter how much Lance applauded her, it would have been foolish to think that after one outburst on her part, Lady Elspeth would warm towards her. They met only when they were obliged to, and Cherry was aware that she carefully avoided addressing her by name. By now the funeral had been arranged for one week's time, and between now and then, Lance was always busy, and visitors called constantly to pay their respects and offer condolences to his mother. He was also often on the telephone to Ireland, or on estate business, so that Cherry was often left twiddling her thumbs with nothing to do. She decided she would visit Paula at the first opportunity.

'You can ask Gerard to drive you if I'm not using the motor myself,' Lance said not very enthusiastically when she told him. She shook her head.

'I don't think so, thank you! I don't want him breathing fire at me from the driver's seat. I'll catch the bus halfway and then I'll walk the rest of it, since it's time I reacquainted myself with my city. I'll go this afternoon as the weather's so mild. Paula and I used to walk miles in the old days,' she reminded him, perhaps tactlessly, since so many of their walks across the Downs and into the city would be on Cook's errands.

She thought he might have something to say about her wanting to catch the bus, but hearing the defiance in her voice he made no comment. In any case, she had made up her mind. It would be good to have a laugh and a joke with Paula again, and she was keen to know how her friend's pregnancy was progressing. Her face softened at the thought of Paula being a mother. She would be wonderful, thought Cherry, and felt again the stab of envy that for all the wealth and status that marriage to Lance Melchoir had brought her, she still didn't have the one thing she most desired, a child of her own.

She put such thoughts out of her head as she set out early that afternoon to cross the Downs on a remarkably calm and sunny day for March, but after a short bus-ride she preferred to walk the rest of the way on such a good day, and she was soon enveloped in the crowded buildings of the city she knew so well. The countryside was lovely, she conceded, but for a girl who had grown up in a town, there was nothing to match the pungent smells and the heat and the traffic of a city, especially combined with the whiffs of the river and the ships that brought goods from faraway places. She felt a lift to her heart, just being here.

Beyond Temple Meads railway station – another marvel accredited to their great engineer, Brunel – she found her way to the little street with the railway cottages, and knocked on the door of Paula's house with excited anticipation. The door opened, and Paula's face was a picture as she saw her visitor.

'My God, I thought I was seeing a ghost,' she squeaked. 'We don't expect to get many titled ladies coming down our street!'

'Don't be daft, Paula. It's me, Cherry, not Lady Muck!'

For a second she wondered if Paula was going to be all snotty towards her, just because she'd come into the title. It hadn't even

occurred to her that it could be so. Not Paula, who she had
known all her life . . . then she saw her friend grin.

'So it is. You'd better come in then, my lady.'

'Well, I will, providing you're going to stop calling me that.
I've come for a cup of tea and a chinwag, not to be mocked for
something I couldn't help,' she said, her spirits suddenly deflating.

'Oh come on, you dope, I'm only kidding. How's the old girl,
anyway? Everybody heard about Lord M's death. It was in the
paper already.'

It would have been, of course. Lord Francis Melchoir was
well known in the city, and there would probably have been a
proper obituary about him already prepared in advance. Toffs
did that.

Cherry followed her friend into the cosy little sitting room.
Compared with Melchoir House, there was hardly room to
swing a cat, but she doubted that Paula would worry about
that since she had her Harold and the coming baby to look
forward to.

'You're looking well,' she commented, nodding towards Paula's
bump.

'He's keeping me awake at night with his kicking now,' Paula
said proudly. 'I don't mind, though, and Harold thinks he's going
to be a footballer, anyway. Sit down, Cherry, and I'll put the kettle
on and you can tell me how you're getting on with her ladyship. I bet she don't like the new way of things.'

'She don't like it at all, but there's not much she can do
about it.'

'Are you back for good now?'

'No. We've got to go back to Donaghy for Lance to clear
things up there, but he won't want to stay long now. He'll
have to sell most of his horses, except for Noble, but Lance
is the kind of chap that when things have to change, he simply
changes with them. It comes from having to make quick decisions
in the Army, I suppose, but it's better than moping for ever,
isn't it?'

She wasn't sure who she was trying to convince, herself or
Paula. She took the cup of tea Paula gave her, and dunked her
biscuit in it, which was something she could never do in Lady
Elspeth's presence, she thought fleetingly.

'I suppose you'd rather stay in Donaghy,' Paula said.

'I thought I would, and I don't fancy sharing a place with her ladyship, but now that I'm back, and especially now that I've had a walk through the city, and seen you again, I know this is where I really want to be,' she said, almost to her own surprise.

'Good for you, girl,' Paula said. 'And how's the lovely Captain? Was he very cut-up to hear about his father?'

'Of course he was. It was a hell of a shock, coming out of the blue like that. It had to happen sometime, but it wasn't something we ever thought about. If we'd had a baby before now it might have softened his parents towards us.'

She hadn't meant to say it, knowing Paula might feel awkward at being the one to produce the first one between them. But Paula was as practical as ever.

'It'll happen when you're least worrying about it, and not just for the old girl's benefit, either. Have another cup of tea and tell me how they're all getting on up there.'

She was like a breath of fresh air as always, and by the time she left to go back to the upper part of the city, Cherry felt a lot chirpier. She even abandoned the thought of catching a bus back, and it was only when she reached the Downs that she realized how foolish that had been, since her feet were starting to ache like mad. She sat down thankfully on one of the benches that were placed at intervals on the Downs, and she took off her shoes and wriggled her toes to ease them a little.

There were plenty of other people about, but they were all going about their business, and nobody was going to take any notice of her. There were kids throwing sticks for a dog to fetch, and several Nannies pushing perambulators and gossiping, and a small group of well-dressed young men and women taking the air. Cherry averted her eyes from all of them, and concentrated on getting her aching feet sorted out before the final walk home.

It was only when a shadow crossed her vision that she was obliged to look up. The sun was in her eyes and she squinted at the person standing near her, wondering what she wanted. Then she moved slightly, and Cherry's heart jolted.

'It's Cherry, isn't it? I thought it was you sitting there and looking so forlorn,' the cultured voice said. 'I had to come and say hello, and of course, I'm aware of what has brought you and Lance back. So sad.'

Her mouth almost too dry to speak, Cherry hastily slid her feet back into her shoes, and nodded. 'You've caught me, Miss Hetherington,' she croaked.

The other girl laughed softly. 'Oh, for goodness' sake, call me Cynthia. Or Cyn, if you like. It's what Lance usually calls me.'

'I'm not sure that would be right,' Cherry burst out before she could stop herself. *She was an Honourable, for God's sake! And not only that, she was the so-suitable young lady the Melchoirs wanted Lance to marry.*

'Why on earth not? Lance is one of my oldest friends, and you're Lance's wife, so that makes you my friend too. And forgive me if I'm wrong, my dear, but I suspect you may be glad of a friendly face on the day of the funeral, and perhaps afterwards too.'

Cherry wanted to say that she already had a friend, but what use was pride now, when she knew Cynthia Hetherington was so right?

'You suspect correctly,' she said huskily.

'And I suppose Lance is up to his eyes in business and you're feeling even more lost,' the girl persisted.

'Do you have a crystal ball or something?'

Cynthia laughed. 'No, but I know the way of things. Look, it would hardly be the done thing for us to get out and about too much before the funeral, but once it's over why don't we meet at Smithy's Tea Rooms sometime for tea and cakes, my treat? We should get to know one another, and you know where Smithy's is, don't you?'

'Yes. Well – thank you,' Cherry said awkwardly, her head spinning, and not quite sure what to say to this.

'Good. We'll arrange it afterwards. Now I must go and join my friends, and you should go home and soak those poor feet. And keep your chin up, darling. It can only get better.'

After she had gone, Cherry stared after her, wondering if she had just dreamed the last ten minutes. Had she really just agreed to go to Smithy's Tea Rooms sometime to take tea and cakes with the Honourable Cynthia Hetherington? She felt like laughing

at the thought. She had only ever been inside the posh establishment in the past to collect a cake order, when the rest of the
kitchen staff had collected together to give Cook a surprise
birthday treat that she hadn't made herself!

Paula would say she was really going up in the world now. And
so she was. And so she had to be, if she didn't want to be an
embarrassment to Lance. She stood up, squaring her shoulders and
walking back to Melchoir House as if she was a lady and her
perishing feet weren't still giving her gyp.

She found Lance deep in paperwork in what had been his
father's study. He looked impatient at being disturbed, but when
she told him she had met Cynthia and what she had suggested,
he nodded approvingly.

'That's so typical of Cynthia. I knew you'd like her when you
got to know her, Cherry. She's a great girl.'

'I didn't say I like her,' she said guardedly, trying not to feel
jealous at his enthusiasm. 'I don't really know her, and she might
even forget about it. I don't suppose you put her up to this, did
you?'

Suspicious at the thought, she had to ask, knowing she would
be humiliated if it was true. But she could tell by his face that
he'd known nothing about it, and that the meeting on the Downs
was as accidental as it had seemed.

'Of course not. I haven't seen her yet. But I'm glad you've
got something to think about while we're here because I know
I've been neglecting you. In fact I've been on the telephone
all afternoon arranging for Noble to be sent home. He'll be
unsettled after the journey so I must be here tomorrow when
he arrives, and the sooner he's back in his old surroundings
the better.'

If there was anything that underlined that their future destiny
was here, it was Lance's decision to bring his favourite horse
home as soon as possible. He wasn't even waiting until he and
Cherry went back to Ireland to arrange it. Noble would be
stabled back at Melchoir House with all possible speed. Even
with his father's funeral imminent, he still had his horse's welfare
in mind.

'Does that suit you?' Lance said when she didn't comment.

'Whatever you say. I was just thinking, that's all.'

'I sometimes wonder just what does go on in that head of yours, Cherry-ripe,' he said with a sigh.

She felt her face flush. 'I think my feelings are pretty open. You should know how I feel about you, anyway.'

He smiled. 'That's the most important thing, and if I seem constantly distracted lately, it's because I'm having to deal with too many things at once.'

He hadn't been too distracted to make love to her when she had least expected it, she thought with a little glow, and as long as he loved her she could forgive him anything. And right now, she could see he was itching to get back to his paperwork.

'I'm going to give my feet a rest,' she told him, relieving him of any need to be fussing around her, 'and then I'll find something else to do until I see you at dinner time.'

She knew she had said the right thing by the relief on his face, and she left the study quickly. She really must get on with knitting the baby's shawl, she thought, especially having seen some of the little garments Paula had already made herself. She went into their bedroom and propped herself up on the bed to rest her feet, determined to tackle the shawl again.

Half an hour later she was getting heated with frustration. Every young girl was taught to knit, so why couldn't she get it right? The lowliest skivvy would do better than this. She could just imagine that the Hon. Cynthia Hetherington was an expert, and even Lady Elspeth would have mastered the skill in her youth, though she would hardly occupy herself with such a task nowadays – unless it was for her own grandchild, of course. Maybe then she would even be willing to create something personal . . .

Cherry drew in her breath. Was this a way to enlist her mother-in-law's attention, by asking for help? And did she dare?

Before she had time to think, she stuffed the half-made shawl into her knitting bag, slid off the bed and put her shoes back on, wincing a little as she did so, and hurried along the landing to Lady Elspeth's sitting room. She might not be there, she thought, almost hopefully, but she'd never know by standing outside. She tapped on the door and heard a voice bid her enter.

Lady Elspeth was sitting by the fireplace. A writing pad lay open on her lap, a pen held listlessly in her hand, but she gazed unseeingly into the distance, apparently lost in her own thoughts. Nervously, Cherry prayed that she wouldn't see this as too much of an unwanted intrusion.

'Yes? Is there something you wanted?' she was finally asked.

It wasn't the best of welcomes, but if she was ever to break through the iciness between them, Cherry could think of no other way than this. She stayed where she was by the door, her palms damp, already wondering why she had ever had such a stupid idea. But she had to say her piece now.

'I'm trying to knit a baby's shawl for my friend, Lady Elspeth, and I'm getting into a terrible mess with the stitches. I was wondering if you could help me,' she said, her voice fading away at the end as she saw the uncompromising look on the older woman's face, tinged with surprise. 'I'm obviously taking too much of a liberty in asking you,' she rushed on, and then stopped as Lady Elspeth put up a restraining hand.

'I can't do anything while you stand over there. You'd better come and sit down and show me the problem,' she said.

Her heart beating fast, Cherry crossed the room to sit gingerly on the chair on the opposite side of the fireplace and took out the shawl from her bag.

'It's the pattern that's got me flummoxed,' she mumbled. 'I thought I could master it but it's more complicated than I expected.'

'Let me see.'

Cherry handed it over and waited while her handiwork was examined.

'Well, I can see where you're going wrong,' Lady Elspeth said at last. 'It's easy enough to put right, and show you how to correct it. You're making it for a friend, you say. Is it someone in Ireland?'

Oh God. Cherry found herself speaking jerkily.

'No, Ma'am, it's for my friend Paula who used to work here. She left when she got married, and she came to visit us in Donaghy in January. She's expecting a baby in May, and the way I'm going with this shawl I know I've taken on far too much, and I wonder if I'll ever finish it. It'll certainly need a good wash before any baby could be wrapped in it.'

She realized Lady Elspeth's hands had paused while she was babbling about Paula. She'd probably done it now. Her mother-in-law had seemed to be making a small effort to be civil, and if only

she could have said the shawl was for an acquaintance in Donaghy . . .
if only she could have been quick-witted enough to invent such a
friend instead of mentioning the former kitchen-maid . . . but she
was an inherently honest person, and she couldn't lie about Paula.

'Well, you've got enough time to finish it,' Lady Elspeth said
more crisply. 'I've put it right for now, and I'm sure if you exercise
a little extra patience at reading the pattern correctly, you won't
have any more trouble.'

In other words, she was dismissed.

'Thank you,' she gasped, and she thrust everything back into
her knitting bag and rushed towards the door.

'Ladies don't run, Cherry,' she heard the stern voice admonish
her.

She nodded quickly and got on the other side of the door as
fast as she could. Once back in her own room, she felt slightly
hysterical. She had braved the dragon's den by herself, and in that
last moment, she had been given the smallest instruction on how
to behave like a lady, and been called by her name. She couldn't
ever imagine Lance's mother truly unbending towards her, and
nor could she imagine ever feeling close to her, but it was a start.

'You did what?' Lance asked her in astonishment as he got ready
for dinner.

She sat on the edge of the bed, having already changed into
a dark-green frock and a discreet row of beads, rather than wearing
the dreary black she knew she would have to don for the funeral.

'I asked your mother for some help with my knitting,' she
repeated. 'She showed me where I was going wrong, and when
she told me off, she actually used my name.'

She had begun to speak triumphantly, knowing he'd be pleased
that Cherry had approached his mother independently. Then, to
her horror she felt an enormous lump in her throat and the tears
spilled over.

'Well, it's nothing to cry about, is it?' he teased. 'I know it must
have been an effort for you to ask for her help, and I'm proud
of you, sweetheart. The first step is always the hardest.'

She shook her head vigorously. 'You don't understand. I'm not
crying because of that. It's just that I suddenly realized what I'm
missing, and what I've been missing all these years.'

He still looked mystified. Were all men so stupid and short-sighted, Cherry raged, even one as intelligent as Lance?

As she slid off the bed he put his arms around her.

'Why don't you tell me what you've been missing all these years then?' he said quietly. It took a few seconds before she could get the words out.

'My mother,' she croaked. 'I miss my mother.'

She leaned into him, not able to say anything more, and not wanting him to say anything. What was there to say? Certainly nothing as cringe-making as to suggest that Lady Elspeth could ever take her mother's place. The past couldn't be changed, but she didn't know any rule that said you couldn't be sad about it, or regret it, or long for things to be different. She gave a deep, shuddering breath and blinked the tears away, forcing herself to be strong.

'It's all right, I'm not going to blubber all night,' she said. 'I haven't felt such a sense of loss about my mother for years, and it was just a bad moment, that's all. It's being here, and being sad about your father, and knowing what's ahead of me. But I'll get over it, Lance. I will.'

He stroked her hair and kissed her so gently that she felt an overwhelming surge of love for him.

'We all have to face losing people at sometime in our lives, but you'll always have me, my darling.'

He did understand, and his words gave her comfort, even though she knew there were no guarantees about anything in this life.

'We'd better show our faces in the dining room then, or your mother will wonder what we're doing up here. After all,' she added cheekily, trying to lighten the atmosphere, 'isn't it some-thing to my credit that I'm even ready to share a meal with the dragon lady?'

Lance smiled, clearly relieved that she sounded more like her old self.

'You be careful, Cherry-ripe, or one of these days you're going to slip up and let her know what name you've given her.'

But maybe they had both begun to respect one another a tiny bit more after today's meeting, thought Cherry. It was a surprising thought, but one that was also reassuring. She wasn't sure that

Lady Elspeth had felt any real softening towards her, but maybe she was finally prepared to meet Cherry halfway for the sake of her son.

More likely for the sake of that outward public show she was on about, Cherry could almost hear Paula say derisively.

Seven

Someone else's attention had been caught by the recent obituary announcement in the *Bristol Evening Post*. Brian 'Knuckles' O'Neill was back in Bristol after a haphazard tour around the country at various local fairs and private events where he could earn a modest wage at bare-knuckle fighting. Despite the evening chill, he was settling down on a waterfront bench to eat his fish and chip supper. He spread out the newspaper wrapping, feeling his nostrils twitch at the enticing smell of vinegar that arose from the food, and then noticed the name on the newsprint that was almost obliterated by cooking grease.

'Well, *bugger me!*' he said out loud, causing a few fellow down-and-outs near by to look up and snigger.

'What's caught your eye now, you sly old sod?' one of his drinking companions slurred.

Brian snapped back. 'Nothing that's any concern of yours, just that I might be coming into money one of these fine days, and sooner'n I thought.'

The other one hooted. 'Oh ah, and I'm the king of Spain.'

Brian tossed him a rude gesture and wrapped up his fish and chips hastily, to march away from the waterfront and the jeers of the down-and-outs. He needed to go somewhere quieter to spread out the newspaper properly before it got completely unreadable, and well away from any interruptions while he considered what to do with the unexpected information that had come his way.

He went back to his lodgings and let himself in quietly with the spare key, well aware that he owed a considerable amount of rent, and that he was only here under sufferance on his manager's say-so. The place stank anyway, even to him, well used to unsavoury lodgings and other seedy places to lay his head.

But none of that mattered tonight. Once before, he had realized that his sister could be the goose that laid the golden egg . . . or at least, the poncey bloke who'd got her in the family way. Even when it had all gone wrong, and there was to be no baby at all, he'd still found out the information that the toff had married her anyway and whisked her off to some godforsaken place in Ireland. And now, according to what he could read in the soggy newsprint, the old boy was dead, and the young one had come into the title. Which meant that his snot-nosed sister was now Her Ladyship, be buggered, and presumably they'd be lording it in the big house up in Clifton like the rest of the toffs.

He steadied his giddy thoughts, because it needed thinking about before he rushed in like a bull at a gate as usual. They had parted on such evil terms, and she'd screamed at him that she never wanted to see him again after his attempts to extort money from the Melchoirs had failed so miserably. But blood was blood, and now that she was in the money, she couldn't be so heartless as to let a struggling brother starve.

By the time he'd finished every morsel of his fish and chips, and swilled it down with a bottle of beer, he had convinced himself that he was the hard-done-by sibling, and that Cherry owed him something.

But he had to bide his time. The old boy wasn't planted yet, and they'd be all at sixes and sevens until he was. There was no doubt that the young one would inherit the title and everything that went with it, though, so Cherry hadn't been so daft after all, pretending to be having a kid when she wasn't. It had all turned out good for her in the end, he thought with a scowl, remembering how she had leathered into him.

He tried to think how he could find out more. The Melchoir cook had always had a soft spot for him and often gave him a meal when he'd popped up there on the pretext of seeing how Cherry was doing, but that was long ago now and he hadn't been there in ages. Maybe he wouldn't be so welcome now that his sister was no longer one of them. His eyes narrowed. He'd seen that friend of hers once or twice in the market lately, the one Cherry worked with when they were as thick as thieves. Paula, that was it. She was wearing a wedding ring now and was looking a bit more buxom than before, so it seemed as if she was up the duff too. And it was a sure bet that Cherry would have gone to see her the minute she got back to Bristol. He only had to watch and wait, catch the friend unawares and give her a bit of the old sweet talk, and find out what was going on.

He leaned back in his chair, already sozzled from the amount of beer he'd drunk that night. But the drink never befuddled his mind completely when it came to making devious plans. There wasn't much work in the offing at present and the spring travelling fairs were still a month or so away, but there were always other ways to make a few quid, so all in all, it hadn't been a bad couple of hours. He raised his half-empty beer bottle silently to his sister and finished it off before sinking into a stupor exactly where he was.

It was the day of Lord Francis Melchoir's funeral. Cherry had never felt so nervous in her life, apart from the day she had been obliged to face the Melchoirs and falsely confess that she was expecting Lance's child. That had sent terror to her heart, if you like, and she had firmly expected to be thrown out of the house. But she hadn't reckoned on the twist of family pride, nor the love of the man she had adored for so long. Even when she had told Lance there was to be no baby, once he had got over his wrath he hadn't deserted her, and the lie had continued.

But today had produced a different kind of terror. Today she would be driven in the limousine along with Lance and his mother to church for the burial service and then to the churchyard to see Lord Francis properly buried. Afterwards, all the toffs who had gathered in the church and at the graveside, would come back to Melchoir House for what she and Paula would have referred to as the bunfight.

She looked at herself in the dressing-table mirror as she was finally ready, her white face and the brightness of her hair almost an affront against the stark black hat and outfit she wore now as befitting the new Lady Melchoir. She swallowed hard, aware of the panic already rising inside her, and she and Lance hadn't even left the sanctuary of their bedroom yet.

She felt his hands on her slim shoulders.

'Once this day is over things will be easier, you'll see,' he said quietly.

She leaned back against him, her eyes large and scared. Even without the circumstances that had brought them back to Bristol, the visit would have been an ordeal for her, but she had coped as best she could. She felt as though she had been holding everything together until now. But now the day she had dreaded was here, and she wasn't sure how she was going to get through it.

'How will things be easier? Can you promise me that? Don't you think all those posh friends of yours will be looking at me and whispering about me?'

Unconsciously, her voice rose, but instead of reassuring her, she felt Lance's hands move from her shoulders as he turned away.

'No, I don't. I think most of the people who attend my father's funeral today will be there to honour the man they all knew and liked. I don't think the main reason for their attendance will be to stare at you.'

It might have been a harsh censure, but somehow it wasn't, and, too late, Cherry knew how selfish she was being. Until that moment she had never quite realized how alike he and his mother were in keeping their feelings in check when the need arose. His voice had been lacking in emotion, but for all that she could sense the pain he was going through. She turned and put her arms around his tense body, holding him tight. She must be brave for him. If there was ever any time in her life to use her supposed acting skills, it was now when she had to put her own feelings aside and play the role she had assumed when she became his wife, and be everything he expected of her.

'Forgive me,' she whispered. 'I won't let you down, Lance.'

He kissed her swiftly and then said it was time they joined his mother and others who had already arrived to join the small procession to the church once the hearse containing Lord Melchoir's body was brought to the house.

She smothered the last flicker of nerves and told him she was ready. It was an added ordeal to know that people were arriving here instead of waiting for them at the church, but it was probably better to face a few of them beforehand.

Once in the drawing room where the maids were handing round small glasses of sherry to the guests, she saw Cynthia Hetherington with her parents and other family friends. Should she speak to her? Would the other girl even acknowledge her? While she was still wondering what to do, Cynthia spoke quickly to her parents and came across to Cherry and squeezed her hand.

'Chin up, darling, and remember that you'll be no more than a five-minute wonder. And by the way, you look stunning. Lance is a lucky fellow, and most of the chaps I know will be envying him.'

She could have said nothing more calming, and Cherry took a long deep breath as she was quickly introduced to the other people in the room as Cynthia seemed determined not to leave her alone.

'Why are you doing all this for me?' she said under her breath a little later.

'Why not? I told you that Lance is my friend, and that makes you my friend too. Take a tip from me, Cherry, and don't look a gift horse in the mouth.'

'I won't, even if I'm not too sure what that means,' Cherry said, with the first real smile of the day.

There was little time for any more talk when Gerard appeared to say that the cortège had arrived. It was all very formal, and yet in a way the dignity and control of these people made it easier for Cherry. She was involved, and yet she could still feel partly detached because of the way they behaved, with none of the ranting and wailing that she had observed in the few funerals she had been to in the past. It didn't mean that they didn't care, simply that they reacted differently. She felt that in an odd way this day was helping her to understand them more.

It was a different feeling when they went downstairs to where the rest of the staff were lining up to pay their silent respects as the family and guests filed out to the waiting cars. Behind the hearse stood the Melchoir limousine, in which the family would be going to church, and as Gerard opened the doors, she saw to her horror that Lance sat in the front beside him, while she and Lady Elspeth were obliged to sit in the rear seats together. She had expected Lance to be with her at all times. While they had all been in the drawing room, Lady Elspeth had not needed to speak to her, even if she had wanted to, having been surrounded and supported by old friends, but now it was just the two of them.

Cherry licked her dry lips, frantically trying to think of something to say, when she felt her mother-in-law's gloved hand cover hers for a brief moment.

'I have seen too many of these occasions in my lifetime, and they never get any easier, my dear, whether the departed is close to you or not. Part of you wants to record every moment in your mind, and another part desperately wants to think of anything else, rather than what is actually happening. Isn't that the case?'

'Yes,' Cherry whispered, thinking how strange it was that this woman should understand so exactly what had been going on in her own mind.

'So today we must all play our part. We grieve and we mourn, but most of it happens in private, Cherry. That's the way things are done.'

Was this a private little piece of instruction on how to be a lady? If so, it was the oddest time to show any softening towards her unwanted daughter-in-law, and Cherry was too astonished to reply, and merely nodded as Lady Elspeth's hand was removed from her own. For the first time, she wondered just how much crying Lance's mother had done in private in order to present a brave face to the world.

'I won't let you down,' she murmured for the second time that day. She wasn't even sure if the other woman heard her, but from that moment on, she determined to be the wife that a good husband would want her to be.

Lord Francis Melchoir had been a well-known figure in Bristol for many years, and as expected, the church was full. To Cherry the service seemed endless, but at last it was over and it was time for the interment. She had glimpsed Paula and Harold at the back of the church, and managed to give her a wan smile before taking her place in the front pew. As the group of family and friends circled the graveside, with others standing respectfully beyond, Lance physically supported his mother, with Cherry at her other side.

None of them had noticed another figure standing behind the trees and watching everything with cynical and calculating eyes. Brian O'Neill marvelled at the way his snot-nosed sister seemed to melt so effortlessly into the group of toffs saying bye-bye to the old boy. She'd certainly come up in the world, he thought with a scowl, while he was still scratching for a living, and something needed to be done about it.

The vicar's intoning seemed to have finished around the graveside and some of the onlookers began to drift away, and he became aware that he was being stared at himself. Paula

murmured something to her husband and strode across to where
he was standing.

'What are you doing, lurking about? You're not wanted here,'
she said in a harder voice than he remembered from the little
squirt. Though not so little now, he observed, again noting the
bump beneath her coat.

'Who are you to tell me where I can and can't go?' he sneered.

'I'm Cherry's friend, as you very well know, and she was more
than thankful to see the last of you when she went to Ireland.'

'Pity she didn't stay there then, but I daresay all that's changed
now that she's Lady Muck.'

Paula clamped her lips together. If he thought he was getting
any information out of her he could think again. Harold was
hovering behind her now, and she turned without another word
and clung to his arm as they walked away. She couldn't deny that
her heart was pounding though, knowing what a rat the man
could be, and wondering how she'd had the temerity to stand
up to him the way she had. The old Paula would never have
done so.

She felt Harold squeeze her arm more tightly to his side.

'Are you going to tell me what that was all about, love? That
was Cherry's brother, wasn't it? She won't have wanted to see
him here today.'

'Nor any other day,' Paula muttered.

She shivered, wishing she hadn't seen him either. His presence
had always meant trouble for Cherry, despite the way that Cook
at Melchoir House had seemed to take a bit of a shine to him
and was always ready to give him a piece of pie and a cup of
cocoa whenever he dropped in. The other maids too, had seen
him as a bit of a glamour figure, rough and ready . . . and just as
ready to do the dirty on Cherry and Lance now if he got the
chance, Paula thought worriedly. She should warn her . . . but not
today.

With an anxious glance back, she realized that Brian had disappeared. Hopefully gone back to some hole in the ground where
he belonged, she thought. The groups around the grave were
dispersing too, back to their fine limousines and the spread that
Cook and the maids would have got ready for them. It would
all be so dignified upstairs. And instead of scurrying about and

taking frantic orders from Cook to see that nothing went wrong for the bigwigs, Cherry would be in the midst of it all, the lady of the manor . . .

'Ghosts walking over your grave, my love?' Harold said, as they began the long trek home.

'Not really. I was just thinking that I wouldn't change my life for Cherry's in a million years,' she said honestly, feeling a rush of love for him as always. 'For all her wealth and fancy clothes now, I've got everything I ever wanted.'

He laughed. 'Then it's a good thing you're never likely to, I reckon. You know you'll always be a lady to me, Paula, but pigs will fly the day I turn into Lord Harold Farmer!'

With linked arms, and cheerfully shaking off the gloom of the afternoon, to which they had felt obliged to attend, they hurried through the streets of the city, only stopping to buy a couple of iced buns as a treat for their tea. It was easy enough not to be concerned with the way other folk lived when they were so content with their own, thought Paula happily.

'I was proud of you today, Cherry,' Lance told her much later that afternoon.

The curtains had been drawn back by then, letting in much-welcomed daylight to the gloom of the house, and the last of the guests had finally gone home, by which time his mother had gone to her bedroom to rest before dinner.

'I don't know about that,' Cherry said, feeling more exhausted than she had ever done in her life before. 'All I wanted was to feel that I didn't let you down in front of all your friends.'

'*Our* friends,' he replied. 'And I'm really glad that you and Cyn seemed to have hit it off.'

Cherry gave him the ghost of a smile. 'She did rather look after me like a mother hen, didn't she? As if to say she was my friend, so everyone else had to be as well. It was nice of her to do that.'

'You underestimate yourself, my sweet. You're not the same girl who caught my eye in the kitchen garden any more, with your wild hair and your flashing eyes. You're a sleek, elegant young lady now, and anyone can see that.'

For some reason his words didn't make her feel any better.

She wasn't sure what was wrong with her today. The whole day so far was one that she had been dreading, and now that the worst was over, she was totally unsettled.

She made an effort to talk more lightly. 'Well, since we're meeting at Smithy's for tea and cakes next week, if you remember, at least I'm not jealous of Cynthia any more, like I once was. In those days I certainly never expected to be the one you'd marry, not in a million years. Especially when your parents had earmarked her for you!'

Lance laughed, running his fingers around the curve of her chin. She might still be unsettled at the trauma of this day, but he seemed to have recovered completely, she thought, with a touch of resentment. But the look in his eyes made her heart beat faster all the same.

'She had no chance when my heart was already given elsewhere, my Cherry-ripe,' he said. 'But now we must plan on what to do next.'

She had long discovered that he had a quicksilver brain, and as always, his mood changed swiftly to what circumstances demanded, and she could see that he was already thinking ahead.

'In what way?' she asked.

'Well, since Father's Will was read a few days ago and everything was in satisfactory order, there's no question of our remaining in Ireland any longer than necessary, so we must arrange to return there immediately, settle up everything there, and come home for good.'

'So soon?' Cherry echoed.

To her, things seemed to be happening with the speed of a whirlwind. The old Lord was dead, and the new one wasn't wasting any time to step into his shoes. It would have been ghoulish had she not known how Lance had truly grieved for his father, and deeply regretted all the bad feeling between them.

Lance took hold of her hands. 'There's no point in prolonging something that's inevitable, Cherry. Besides, much as you enjoyed our life in Ireland, I suspect that your heart will always be here. Your roots are here, the same as mine. You'll be able to see your friend Paula now and again, and don't forget that Mother will need us now.'

Until his last words, she had been comforted by all he was saying, but the thought that Lady Elspeth was going to need her in any way was almost laughable. She had certainly unbent towards Cherry in these last few days, and she must still be in a vulnerable state of mind for all her rigid self-control, but how long was it going to be before she began resenting the little upstart who had snared her precious son?

'You do understand what I'm saying, don't you, Cherry?' Lance's voice was sharper when she didn't immediately reply.

'Of course I do. I'm not daft!'

His beloved horse had already been sent home, and if that wasn't the clearest indication that Lance's place was here, she couldn't think of one.

She drew a deep breath. 'You won't mind if I go and see Paula again before we leave, will you? I'd like to let her know what's going on.'

She dared him to say it wasn't suitable for a lady to go visiting people in railway houses too often. He didn't, of course, and she was briefly ashamed of herself for thinking he would be that much of a snob. But she had no intention of deserting her old friend, she thought fiercely, even if the new one had invited her for tea and cakes to the elegant Smithy's restaurant. But since Lance made no demur, and things were obviously going to move swiftly, she decided there was no time like the present. She didn't want to turn up unannounced again, but she knew Paula would be at the market and she would certainly find her there.

'Unless you think I should offer to keep your mother company,' she added reluctantly as the thought struck her.

Relieved, she saw Lance shake his head. 'She needs to be left alone for a while. She has a lot of correspondence to attend to and said she doesn't want to be disturbed. It will be time enough for us all to meet at dinner this evening.'

They were a strange family, thought Cherry, even though she knew she hadn't done much to bring them together. Rather the reverse, of course. But at a time of grief and mourning, families usually wanted to be together to give one another support. But not this one. Each continued with their own pursuits. She supposed it was the way with the upper classes, but it was sad all the same.

Down at the busy fruit and vegetable market, with the variety of sweet and pungent smells of the wares on sale, rubbing shoulders with housewives and maids buying produce for their households, she began to feel more like her old self than at any time since coming home. She mustn't feel too much like it though, she thought guiltily. She was not going to be doing such menial tasks for the family when she and Lance returned here for good. That would be left to the kitchen-maids.

She had been jostled about by people for less than half an hour when she spotted Paula with her shopping bag over her arm, and looking every bit the proud expectant mother. Cherry smothered the twist of envy and called her name.

'Blimey, what are you doing down here amongst all this lot?' Paula said at once. 'I thought you'd be off hobnobbing with them other young ladies I saw you with at the funeral by now. You really looked the part, I must say.'

Cherry ignored the hint of defensiveness in her voice.

'I wanted to see you before I go back to Ireland. Everything's being done in such a rush that I felt the need to take my time and do something normal.'

'What, like getting crushed to death by this mob?' Paula said, but her face had relaxed into a smile now. 'You can help me find the best bargains here if you like and come back with me for a cup of tea. Is that normal enough for you?'

It sounded wonderful. Smithy's might be a posh establishment where it was good to be seen, but there was nothing like sitting down with a friend in the cosy atmosphere of her own home. It was almost like being back in the Melchoir kitchen and having Cook bellowing at them to get a move on, whether it scalded their mouths or not.

With all the bustle and noise going on around them it was a good thing Paula couldn't hear her indrawn breath, nor guess that for just that one moment she was really missing their old life. How crazy was that!

It was as well that she couldn't guess at the thoughts running around Paula's head too, as her friend wondered whether or not to tell her that Brian was back on the scene, and had been snooping about at the funeral. Knowing what a rotter he was, and how badly the two of them had parted, Paula wisely decided to keep that bit of information to herself.

But by the time Cherry returned to Melchoir House later, she was feeling more cheerful. There was nothing she could do to change things, so she might as well accept them for what they were. She could even feel more tolerant towards Lady Elspeth at dinner that evening, even though the lady said very little directly to her. Cherry was determined not to let it annoy or upset her. They were going to live in the same house for the foreseeable future, and there was nothing her mother-in-law could do about that, so they might as well get on with it.

With that in mind, she smiled nervously at Lady Elspeth as they came to the end of their meal, and tried to make conversation with her.

'Have I mentioned that I shall be meeting Cynthia Hetherington soon for tea at Smithy's, Lady Elspeth?'

'You haven't, but I'm sure you'll enjoy the experience,' she was told.

It wasn't exactly an enthusiastic reply, but Cherry was determined to let her know that she wasn't being ostracized by society because of her former employment. Aware of the small silence between them that followed, Lance spoke sharply.

'Cyn's taken quite a shine to Cherry, Mother. I'm pleased to see that they're becoming friends.'

'Well, she was always a kind girl for taking people under her wing,' his mother said.

There was no doubting now that she was implying that Cynthia looked on Cherry as a charity case, but as she saw the flash of anger in Lance's eyes, Cherry refused to let it bother her.

'Then I'm even more pleased to have her as my friend,' she said sweetly. 'It's not everyone who thinks of others in the same light and it's all credit to her good nature. And speaking of that, I'm so grateful to you for helping me with my knitting, Lady Elspeth. The baby's shawl is progressing nicely now.'

She had the satisfaction of seeing the older woman's cheeks go a touch pinker than before, but suddenly she was tired of trying to score points against her. The woman had just lost her husband, and however much she tried to hide it, she must be churning inside.

'It's not so difficult providing you follow the instructions precisely, is it?' Cherry added. 'But it really does help to have someone showing you the ropes.'

It would help in many ways, she thought keenly, if only this unbending woman would realize she had a ready-made family still here, and didn't resent her son's choice of wife so much. In her new role, Cherry knew she had so much to learn, and what better teacher would there be than her mother-in-law? But maybe that was just too much to ask.

She was thankful when Lance said they had better retire as they were off early the next morning for the journey back to Ireland.

'Goodnight, Mother,' he said, bending to kiss her cold cheek.

'Night 'night, and don't let the bed bugs bite . . .

Cherry didn't dare say it, but she would dearly have liked to, just to see the reaction. *But it was up to her now. It was up to her now.*

She found the thought hammering around in her head, and before she stopped to think how it would be received, she too, bent and touched her lips to Lady Elspeth's cheek.

'Sleep well,' she said softly.

Eight

A few days later the Melchoir cook looked up in surprise as she heard whistling outside the kitchen door. It sounded vaguely familiar but she couldn't place it for a moment. She wasn't expecting any deliveries in the late afternoon, and if it was a caller sniffing around one of the kitchen-maids she'd soon give them short shrift. In any case, she didn't welcome visitors at this hour, when she had sent her girls off on other pursuits and had a welcome half-hour on her own. Then the door opened and a rugged face appeared.

'Well, bless my soul, where have you sprung from?' she exclaimed. 'I thought you'd done a disappearing act long ago!'

Brian O'Neill gave a forced laugh. 'Not me, Cook. I'm like the bad penny always turning up when you least expect me.'

'Yes, well, I'm not so sure that you should be here at all,' she went on guardedly. 'Things are different now.'

His brain wasn't totally addled by all the punches he'd taken in his life, and he was quick-witted enough to take her lead and pretend that he knew nothing of what had been happening here recently.

'Well, I've been away for a while, so aren't you even going to offer me a cup of tea and a piece of your seed cake?' he wheedled. 'Then you can tell me how things are different.'

She looked at him with narrowed eyes. He could be a charmer when he wanted to, and he could usually get around her, but he was a fly one all right, and how that sweet girl Cherry ever came to have a crafty brother like him, she couldn't imagine.

'Sit you down then, and I'll put you in the picture,' she said at last, glad that she was on her own without any simpering maids hanging about.

Brian relaxed, knowing he could worm anything out of the old trout with a few arch bits of flattery.

'So what's the news then?' he said, once he had a large mug of steaming tea put in front of him and a large slice of seed cake.

'You know that old Lord Melchoir died recently, I suppose?'

Brian feigned shocked surprise. 'Good God, no. I told you I've been away and I've only just got back. I thought I might have a word with Cherry to see if she's forgiven me for the wrong I did her yet,' he added piously.

Cook snorted. 'You'd have to wait a long time for that, my lad. We all know what you got up to with your wicked black-mail demands for money, and I haven't forgiven you either.'

'I don't blame you, and I'm truly sorry,' he said, his voice full of contrition. 'But I was desperate, Cook, and I've regretted it ever since.'

He was desperate now if the truth be told, but he tried to gloss over that. His eyes never flickered as Cook watched him suspiciously.

'Well, you can't see her now anyway,' she said finally. 'She's been living in Ireland with her husband for these past two years. They've gone back there now, and I don't know when they'll be back.'

And even if she did, she wasn't going to tell him. The last thing young Cherry, the new Lady Melchoir, would want, would be to have him on the doorstep. He might charm some of the girls, but he was a thug all the same.

'She got somebody to marry her then,' Brian sniggered. 'Who was it?'

He knew damn well who it was, but he wasn't letting on about that either. He wanted to hear it from the old trout's lips. Her eyes widened now.

'You mean you don't know that your sister's now the new Lady Melchoir? She and Captain Lance got married and left the country to go and live in Ireland after all the fuss, but now that the old gentleman's died, Captain Lance is the new Lord Melchoir.'

'Bloody hell, begging your pardon, Cook! But this is a turn-up and no mistake. I never expected our Cherry to end up as the mistress of this place, nor for the posh geyser to marry her.'

'You'd better mind your words, my lad,' Cook said more sharply. 'You're speaking about my lady now, and whatever she was in the past, she deserves all our respect.'

'In the past, she was still my sister, and still is,' Brian retorted. 'Blood's thicker than water and nothing can change that.'

Before he knew what was happening, Cook had whisked his plate away from in front of him. Her voice was steely now.

'Don't think you can come here and make more trouble, young man. The old Lord Melchoir had plenty of influence in this city, and his son commands the same. Lady Melchoir won't want to see you, and I'll thank you not to come near my kitchen again if you know what's good for you. And if you're thinking of trying to wheedle your way back into her good books, don't waste your time. She and Lord Melchoir have gone back to Ireland to settle things there, and they'll be back in their own good time and not before.'

He got up clumsily. 'Don't worry. There's more than one way of getting on in this world, and better places to live in than this.'

He blundered out of the kitchen, pushing roughly past the two kitchen-maids returning from the market, their arms full of bags of groceries.

'Who was that ruffian!' one of them exclaimed angrily. 'He nearly knocked us over.'

'Never you mind,' said Cook smartly. 'He's nobody you'd want to know, and you won't be seeing him here again.'

'Pity,' the bolder one of the two said with a giggle. 'He was quite nice looking in a gypsy sort of way.'

'And I'll box your ears if I hear you talking such nonsense again,' Cook almost shouted. 'You two are here to work, not to flirt with every roughneck who stops by for a warm and a bite.'

The girls scuttled about their business at once, seeing that Cook was more put out than she admitted, even to herself, at seeing Brian O'Neill again. She would have been even more so if she could have followed the working of his devious mind as he strode back down the hill towards the city.

So Cherry and the toff had left Bristol already, but he reckoned it wouldn't be for too long. He wasn't so befuddled that he couldn't reason that they'd soon be back to lord it over the estate for good. And that meant that Cherry now had money to spare. Money that he could desperately do with. There hadn't been so much call for his services lately, and he'd started gambling recklessly, with the result that he was now seriously in debt to a number of bookies, here in Bristol and elsewhere. It wouldn't be long before they caught up with him, and if he had the wherewithal the safest thing would be for him to get out of the country.

One way or another, he decided that Cherry was going to be the goose that laid his golden egg. She owed it to him to see that he didn't want. But he'd need to lie low until she was back here again, and it wouldn't be too difficult to find out when that happened. He could keep watch on the Melchoir estate, and he could always ask that pale friend of hers that she used to work with. Paula would know – but he wouldn't put it past her to report him to the authorities if she thought he was out to ruin his sister. It would also be favourable to do a moonlight from his present lodgings, and that was his first priority.

Back on Irish soil again, Cherry's stomach was still churning from the ferry journey to Rosslare, following the momentous events of the past days. Even now, she could hardly believe how everything had happened so quickly. She was still in a daze and wishing she could turn back the clock to when she and Lance had been merely the proud landowners of the modest whitewashed farm in Donaghy, instead of lords of the manor back in Bristol. She loved this place with a fervour, since it was the first real home of her own, and she had never realized it so much until now when she had to leave it.

But there was no escape from Lance's destiny, and which she now shared. Nor would he want to escape it. It was only Cherry whose nerves had taken a severe knocking, knowing what was expected of her now. Even the afternoon tea at Smithy's restaurant to which Cynthia Hetherington had invited her, had turned out to be something of a minor instruction hour on how to behave as a lady. It had all been done in the gentlest way, but it had left Cherry in no doubt of the task ahead of her.

There was no doubt, either, that the people of Donaghy were viewing them differently now. She wanted to shriek that she was the same girl she had always been. Deep inside, she was still Cherry O'Neill who loved to go dancing with Paula or to the flicks on a Saturday night, and wasn't averse to a bit of a mild flirtation with the Bristol lads.

All that was gone for ever now. Besides, she reminded herself, a mild flirtation with a Bristol lad could never compare with the wild and hopeless love she had felt for Captain Lance Melchoir, never expecting in a million years that it would be returned. She wished she knew what was wrong with her now. She had everything she ever wanted, and she was assured of Lance's love.

At least, she had been, when they had been virtually banished to Donaghy through her deceit in pretending to be pregnant with Lance's baby when she wasn't. He too, had perpetuated the lie in order to force his parents to agree to their marriage. It had all been romantic and exciting then, the heir to a fortune and the kitchen-maid. It was the stuff of fairy tales, but now . . . ?

No matter how much she tried, Cherry couldn't ignore the doubts creeping into her mind. Lance was the only son of Lord Francis and Lady Elspeth Melchoir, and he had been indulged all his life by doting parents. That indulgence had been stretched to the limit when Lance had confessed that he loved Cherry O'Neill, and that he intended to marry her.

Unconsciously, she echoed Cook's words. *Things were different now.*

Would Lance be regretting his rashness in marrying a servant, rather than looking for a wife in his own class? People who said the class system had faltered after the end of the Great War were talking out of their hats. Servants knew that only too well, even if the toffs pretended to take a more liberal attitude.

'Cherry, you've been staring at that menu for the last half-hour,' she heard Lance say impatiently. 'It can't be that difficult to let Cook know what meals we want for the next week.'

She jumped at his voice. What did she care what they ate? Her stomach was still upset from the journey here and she was in no mood to issue orders to anyone. If she had her way she would simply go to bed and curl up and sleep for the foreseeable future. She began to wonder what on earth was the matter with her. It was so unlike her to be so feeble and she didn't like the feeling.

'I can't think properly,' she said thickly. 'I'm sure Cook can make the right decisions.'

'But it's not Cook's job,' he said. 'It's yours, my love, and it's something you will have to get used to when we go home again – unless you want to hand it over to my mother,' he added with a smile.

Why not? Why the bloody hell not! Lady Elspeth would surely love to be still holding some of the household reins . . . but she realized at once that Lance was not being serious, and that he would think her failing in her duty if she didn't do things properly.

'Of course not, and I'll attend to this at once,' she said quickly. 'But I'm terribly tired, Lance, and once I've seen to this, would you mind if I have an early night?'

'Not at all. I need to speak to Gilligan about the horses, and since Mother and I have decided to put this place up for sale I shall have a busy day tomorrow with the agents, so I shan't be long in joining you.'

'Very well.' She kept her eyes lowered, not letting him guess at her feelings at knowing the discussion about the farm had been made between him and his mother, without any input from her. Obviously, she didn't count.

She felt his hands on her shoulders as he came around the table and placed a gentle kiss on the top of her head.

'I know it's all so bewildering. There's so much legal business still to attend to, and sometimes my head is in the clouds as much as yours, but I promise you that very soon now everything will be ironed out, and we'll be the same as we always were.'

'I just wish I could help,' she murmured. 'I feel so useless.'

'You're never that, and you can always start packing a few personal knick-knacks that you want to take back to Bristol. We won't stay here any longer than necessary, and just as long as you're with me, that's all I ask, my Cherry-ripe.'

He squeezed her shoulders again and then he was gone to attend to his business matters, leaving her with weak tears in her eyes for the pet name he had used that meant so much to her. Then she sat upright and took a deep breath, asking herself if she was going to be a mouse or a helpmeet to him. And the first thing she could do, the most simple thing of all, was to write out the menus for the week, especially his favourites.

Next day, while Cherry tried to make lists of what should go home to Bristol with them and what should stay behind as part of the fittings and furnishings for the new owners, Maureen Tring dusted and flitted about the parlour, almost tearful at the thought of Cherry leaving for good, but barely able to control the curiosity that was nagging her.

'Sure and I've become that fond of you, Ma'am, even if 'tis not really my place to say so,' she said. 'It'll be hard to break in some new owners, that's if they want me, of course.'

'I don't mind you saying it at all,' Cherry said warmly. 'I'm fond of you too, and it will be quite a wrench to leave after two years. I've really loved it here, and I'll be sure to give you a good reference.'

'I'll be grateful for that, Ma'am, but you'll be the grand lady now, won't you? When you're in your big house in Bristol, I mean,' the girl said with an envious sigh. 'It must be lovely to be called a real lady of quality and have people look up to you.'

'I suppose so, but however you look on the outside, you can never really change what you are inside, can you? And if you want to stay true to yourself, no one should ever try,' she added.

'And what would that be, Ma'am? What you are on the inside, I mean?' Maureen said with studied casualness.

Cherry heard warning bells in her head. The folk here had no idea of the circumstances that had brought her and Lance to Donaghy, and he had been very firm in insisting that it should be kept private. The very last thing she wanted to reveal to Maureen Tring and her gossipy family was that Lance Melchoir had married a kitchen-maid. If that bit of news wasn't enough, the speculation about just *why* he had done so, would let them very quickly put two and two together.

She gave a forced laugh. 'You talk too much, Maureen! Why, for all you know, I might have been born a princess and come down in the world! Maybe I was one of those foreign princesses down on their luck and looking for a handsome husband to whisk me away from it all!'

'Well, I'd say you could easily pass for a foreign princess, Ma'am. Maybe you were one of them Russian ones I once heard about,' Maureen said, cocking her head on one side and appraising Cherry as keenly as if she was inspecting her through a microscope.

'Of course I wasn't,' Cherry said crossly, realizing how nearly she had let herself be trapped. 'I was just teasing, that's all, and you shouldn't let yourself get carried away by such tales, Maureen.

And all this nonsense is stopping you from getting on with your work, so look lively, there's a good girl.'

It made her think, though, of how careful she needed to be. It would humiliate Lance so much if there was the faintest whisper over the circumstances of their marriage. It made her realize how soon they needed to get away from here after all, and start the new life that was to be hers for the rest of her life.

She clung to Lance in the warmth of their bed that night, and he held her closer in some surprise at the sudden show of affection. Not that it was so unusual, but he could sense that there was something more behind it than the mere wish to be loved.

'What is it, Cherry-ripe?' he said gently, pressing his lips softly against her cheek. 'I can always tell when something's troubling you, especially when you ate so little of Cook's excellent dinner this evening. I think she's hoping to persuade us to stay,' he added with a laugh.

'She couldn't do that though, could she?' Cherry said. 'We do have to go, don't we, Lance?'

She couldn't help the touch of anxiety in her voice. She could hardly understand herself. She had wanted to get away from Bristol after their marriage, if only to avoid any embarrassment for Lance and his parents. Yes, she had loved it here. But with his father's death everything had changed, and despite the new regime at Melchoir House, which wasn't going to be easy for her, she couldn't wait to get back there now.

'I'm afraid we do, my love,' he said with a frown, misunderstanding her. 'We always knew this day had to happen. We can't live the life of country gentlemen farmers for ever, however much we might wish it, and I can't turn my back on my responsibilities.'

'Oh, Lance, don't be so pompous!' she said before she could stop herself. 'I'm not asking you to do any such thing. If you must know, I'll be happy to be back in Bristol for good, however difficult it might be for me, especially with your mother breathing down my neck like a fiery dragon.'

She suddenly realized with relief that he was laughing at her. Thank goodness! He might have turned quite the other way at hearing his mother referred to as a fiery dragon. Her lips twitched in response.

'Nobody but my Cherry-ripe would dare to call my queenly mother a fiery dragon, and I shall probably never be able to look at her in quite the same way again,' he said, chuckling.

'I thought you'd be offended,' she said. 'Why aren't you? I doubt that any of your upper-class thin Lizzies would have said such a thing to you!'

'Well, maybe that's why I was never attracted to any of them enough to marry them. They were always too busy trying to impress me, while you, my little witch, you never bothered to mind your words, did you? If a thing needed to be said, you said it.'

'And that doesn't worry you? Even when your posh friends are wondering why in the dickens you married someone like me?'

He hugged her close beneath the bedclothes, and she could feel the hardness of his body responding to her.

'Envying me my luck, more like,' he said huskily.

Cherry's heart beat faster as she felt his hands roam over her body. Since his father's death, a natural sense of loss and decorum had put a certain barrier to their normal closeness, especially at Melchoir House, but here they had always felt freer and more at ease, and she knew that nothing was going to stop them now. She wound her arms around his neck, abandoning any inhibitions that might be found in the well-brought-up girls in his usual circle.

'I do love you, Lance,' she whispered against his neck.

'No more than I love you, my darling,' he whispered back, and then as his body covered hers the sweet and familiar sensations enveloped her.

Things moved swiftly from then on. There was no reason for them to stay any longer than necessary, and Lance was anxious to get back to Bristol and assume his rightful position. The farm and land had already been put in the hands of a reliable agency, with the proviso that everyone already working for them would be retained by new owners if it was their wish.

'It certainly will be, unless the new owners turn out to be monsters,' Lance said candidly. 'The staff here have a good living, and will want to stay where they're familiar with the place.'

So less than a month later the new Lord and Lady Melchoir

were on their way back to Bristol, having sent all their belongings ahead of them, and having bid a fond farewell to staff and villagers and close acquaintances alike. Cherry's head was in a whirl from the speed with which it had all been arranged. But that was Lance. His quicksilver mind and strict army training could always see what had to be done, and to do it swiftly. She admired him intensely for that. It echoed something in her own mind, even if the thoughts were far less precise than Lance would have said them. But it amounted to the same thing. If something couldn't be changed, then you had to adapt to the new way of things and get on with it.

It was April now, and the countryside was starting to blossom into spring. The Irish Sea wasn't as choppy as the time they had crossed it for Lord Melchoir's funeral, but still unstable enough for Cherry to feel queasy and thankful when they reached dry land to find Mr Gerard waiting for them with the limousine at Fishguard. He greeted them deferentially, and with more warmth in his eyes for Cherry now, and she felt relieved to think that perhaps she wasn't such a pariah now that her old workmates had got used to the new regime.

And she would soon be able to see Paula again, she thought, with a little rush of pleasure. Maybe not quite as often as she liked, but there was no reason why she couldn't invite Paula to the house for afternoon tea, or just to have a gossip. It was her house now, she thought defiantly. In any case, when her baby arrived Paula would be eager to come to Melchoir House to show him or her off to the kitchen staff. Her eyes glazed a little, imagining what that would be like . . .

'Where have you gone?' Lance said softly to her from the opposite side of the car. 'You've been breathing heavily for the last few minutes. Are you feeling quite well?'

She nodded. How could she tell him, that for those few moments, she had been filled with the most intense sense of envy, so real that she had almost imagined she was holding Paula's baby in her arms and breathing in the sweet musky scent of him – or her. It had been that real . . .

'I'm fine,' she said huskily. 'It's just the aftermath of the sea crossing, that's all. Even on a fine day, I'm not such a good sailor, am I?'

'Well, it's the last time we have to do it, and I'm sure you'll settle down once we reach home,' he reassured her.

Just as long as she didn't disgrace herself by throwing up in the car, she thought, with a sudden crazy urge to do just that!

She swallowed hard and forced the feeling down, concentrating on looking out of the car window as the miles sped by. Forcing all thoughts of babies out of her mind, and wondering instead what the reception was going to be like from her mother-in-law now that she and Lance were back for good. There had certainly been a slight softening towards her after the funeral, but she didn't know how long that was going to last. Vulnerability and Lady Elspeth didn't go hand in hand very often, and any chink in her armour was likely to be short-lived.

But she was determined to do all she could to make life smooth for Lance, and to smother her own feelings if his mother was openly rude to her, or worse still, ignored her completely. It was her new resolve, and she knew it would be what Lance wanted and expected of her. She snuggled closer to him in the back seat of the car, uncaring whether it was seemly of a lady or not.

She soon realized that she wouldn't see so much of him on a daily basis. It wasn't as though he went out to work every day like most people. He didn't have to clock on for the daily grind by a stern employer, or work halfway around the clock like she and Paula had sometimes seemed to do, but running a large estate always kept him busy and at somebody else's beck and call. She never knew exactly what he did, but whatever it was, there was always time to give his horse a good run every day. Whatever else went by the board, Noble always got his attention from his master.

'Don't you resent that?' Paula asked her curiously, when Cherry had made the trip down to Paula's railway house after they had been back in Bristol for a couple of weeks and commented on his love for the horse.

'Of course not. Anyway, you can't have forgotten when Lance was in hospital after that blow on his head and had lost his memory. The only thing he could remember was the name of his horse, and the nurses thought he was a Mr Noble.' She laughed nervously at the memory. 'It was only when I picked up on it that I guessed who he was and alerted his father. No, I owe Noble something, so I would never resent Lance's attachment to him.'

'I haven't forgotten that it was your brother who bashed him, either,' Paula reminded her.

'That was never proved.' Even as she said it, Cherry wondered why she even bothered to defend him, when she knew very well, proof or not, that Brian O'Neill had put Lance in hospital that night.

After a few moments' deliberation Paula made up her mind.

'Oh well, you can keep your head under the sand if you like, Cherry, but I ought to tell you that I've seen him recently.'

'*What?* Where?' Cherry said at once.

'It was at Lord Melchoir's funeral,' Paula said unhappily, wishing she had kept her mouth shut from the way Cherry's face had lost its colour now. 'He was hovering about behind the trees. He'd probably have found out the old boy had died from the newspaper report.'

'Well, he'd better keep out of my way,' Cherry said viciously. 'I told him I never want to see him again and I meant it.'

'He's still your brother, though,' Paula muttered. 'If he's down and out, he'll come to you, now that you're in the money. He'll say you owe it to him.'

'He won't get any! Lance will see to that.'

Her stomach revolted though, knowing how Brian despised all toffs, and remembering how Lance and his father had totally ignored his demands for money when he'd tried to blackmail them. Brian never forgot a grudge, and her own demands that he stayed out of her life for good sounded puny now. But she took a deep breath and tried to put him out of her mind, for now at least.

'Never mind him. How are you and Harold getting on? You certainly look blooming,' she went on, with an effort to be cheerful.

To her surprise, Paula's face puckered. 'Oh, we're all right. Well, better than all right, if you know what I mean! But Harold's getting a bit worried about all this miners' business.'

Cherry stared at her. Nobody with any sense in their noddles could be unaware of the way the miners were being treated, expected to take a cut in their wages, which were pitiful enough already. The newspapers were forever spreading rumour and fact about what was going on, and the hint of strikes was never out of some of the more lurid accounts.

'Why would Harold be worried about it? He's not down the pits, is he?' she said at last.

'No, but he reads a lot about it, and if the miners' leader, Arthur Cook, whips up all the unions into an all-out strike, it could affect the whole country if they all rally behind him. You'd be all right, of course. Captain Lance doesn't have a proper job, does he? Sorry, I mean his Lordship!'

For the first time, Cherry heard the resentment in Paula's voice, and it dawned on her how far their friendship could be stretched if what she was suggesting came to pass. But it was all nonsense. Surely it was. There had been so much going on in the Melchoirs' lives these past couple of months that she had been only fleetingly aware of any such problems. Domestic and family issues had kept her as blinkered as one of Lance's horses. She was certain he would have been fully aware of it all though, since he read the newspapers avidly, and he had never mentioned any of it to her. So it couldn't be too serious, and she refused to let it blight this sunny afternoon.

'Well, let's not think about it, Paula, and it will probably never happen. I'm dying to see what you've got prepared for the baby by now, and I can promise you I'll have your shawl finished in good time,' she said determinedly.

Nine

C herry wasted no time. As soon as she left Paula's house she walked swiftly through the back streets to where Brian's seedy lodgings were. She had vowed never to come here again, but after what Paula had told her about Brian sniffing around, then if he had any ideas of getting in touch with herself or Lance again, she intended to nip it in the bud.

The back streets were filthy and smelled rank, and she wrinkled her nose as she walked through them, aware of the glances and snide comments of some of the layabouts hanging about in door-ways. She was very conscious that the last time she had come here, hammering and hollering on Brian's door to demand that he stop threatening the Melchoirs with his dirty blackmail schemes, she had been wearing her kitchen-maid's usual garb, and now she was dressed like a lady in the finer clothes she had become accustomed to.

After two years of marriage to Lance and sharing his way of life, they had become perfectly normal everyday attire, but with a sudden rush of blood to the head she could see exactly why Paula and the kitchen staff eyed her differently than of old. *Things were different now* – and so was she.

She stuck her chin in the air, ignoring the taunts from a couple of grubby urchins playing football in the street. She found the stained door of Brian's lodgings, and banged on it with her gloved hand, smothering a guilty sense of relief that she didn't have to touch it with her bare fingers. She tried to look through the window but it was so grimy that she couldn't see anything inside, and then she jumped as a voice sounded right behind her.

'He ain't here, lady. He's been gone this coupla weeks and he owes me plenty of rent money. If you're another of his creditors you'll have a hard time catching up with the bugger, and if I ever find him sneaking back here again I'll have him round to the Bridewell so fast you won't see his arse for dust.'

Cherry flinched at the landlord's crude words. It was no more than she'd half expected, but the fact that Brian had slithered away and denied her the chance to tell him exactly what she thought of him once more was as infuriating and mortifying as realizing that he must have plenty more debtors after him.

'Thank you,' she said in a choked voice, and half turned away.

'Here, hold on a minute. Ain't you that sister of his who came round here before?' the landlord said suspiciously. 'You look as if you've come up in the world, but anybody would remember that bright hair, and if you're a relative then I reckon you could pay up what he owes me in rent money.'

'Don't be ridiculous,' Cherry snapped in the most imperious voice she could muster that would do Lady Elspeth proud. 'If you think I'm acquainted in any way with the kind of riff-raff who lives here you're sadly mistaken.'

'What you doing here then?' the landlord snapped.

Cherry thought quickly. 'It's a charity mission,' she said, remembering one of Lady Elspeth's occasional forays into the city. Although Lance's mother would never have been so foolish as to venture here alone, Cherry thought with rising panic, risking the curiosity of the small crowd who were edging nearer at the small rumpus going on around Brian 'Knuckles' O'Neill's lodgings. A crowd who looked none too pleased at seeing somebody better off than themselves, and could easily be set on robbing her. She felt sick to her stomach.

'Oh, a charity mission, is it?' the landlord said, his lips curling disdainfully. 'You're one of them bloody do-gooders, are you? I might have known it. Well, we don't like your sort around here, lady, so get back to your own kind, and be quick about it if you know what's good for you.'

Without waiting for anything more, Cherry turned and almost fled away from the man, ignoring her dignity. She pushed through the small crowd, her cheeks flaming. She still felt positively ill, and she knew she had done no good at all in coming here so impulsively. She hadn't been able to confront Brian ... and despite her intention a good part of her was thankful that she hadn't been able to see him. But the worst and most shameful thing of all was that she had denied being his sister. How would her mother ever have felt about that? She felt a sob rising in her throat, knowing how far apart they had actually grown.

But as she walked back through the crowded city and towards

the blissful green area and fragrant fresh air of the Downs, she felt her heart harden against her brother. She had done nothing wrong except marry the man she loved, and Brian had brought everything on himself. His life had gone in the wrong direction, and if a man turned bad, then nobody could be blamed for it but himself.

By the time she reached the Downs she had calmed down a little, and forced herself to forget Brian and think of other things. Worrying things. After seeing Paula, she was determined to find out from Lance just how far this miners' business had gone. It was obvious that Paula was anxious about it, but in Cherry's secluded world, she couldn't see how it would affect her and Lance in any way. And that too, indicated how far she had come from her old life, she thought bitterly. In the old days, news like this would have been thrashed out in the Melchoir kitchen, with Mr Gerard and Cook having their say as they pored over the newspapers with the most glaring headlines, and the rest of them putting in their two-penn'orths.

Like his father, Lance always said that such gutter reporting was not for ladies to bother their pretty heads about. Cherry bristled at the very thought that a woman was thought to be so feeble. Was this what the suffragettes had fought for, to continue being seen as second-class citizens?

As if she had conjured him up out of her imagination, she caught sight of a horse and rider coming towards her and recognized her husband at once. Forgetting everything else for the moment, her heart soared with a surge of pride and admiration at seeing how easily and upright he sat on the horse as if he and the animal were a part of one another. She raised her hand, knowing he must have seen her, and minutes later he had arrived at her side and slid off Noble's back to walk beside her.

'Where have you been to look all hot and flustered?' he greeted her with a smile. 'If you wanted to go into the city for a shopping expedition, you know you could always ask Gerard to take you. But from the look of you I gather it wasn't too successful,' he added indulgently.

She looked at him dumbly, momentarily aghast at the thought of asking Gerard to take her shopping in the limousine, and he laughed.

'Well, I'm not a mind-reader, but I don't see any bags of shopping, you goose, so what else have you been doing?'

'I've been to see Paula,' she stuttered. 'You don't mind, do you?'

'Why should I mind?' he said, holding on loosely to Noble's reins as the horse trotted along beside them. 'She's your friend, and you'll naturally want to keep in touch with her. So what did she have to say?'

He spoke casually. She was sure he wasn't really interested and was just being polite. She certainly wasn't going to mention her brother to him, so instead she blurted out the other news that Paula had told her.

'Paula seems to be worried about all this miners' business. I don't know why. How could it possibly affect them? Her husband works on the railway, not down a coal pit.'

He was silent for a minute and Cherry looked at him sharply.

'Is it something to be worried about, Lance? What business is it of anybody's other than the miners themselves?'

'It could be everybody's business if things escalate,' he said. 'But this is not the time or place to talk about it. Have you ever ridden a horse before?'

The question startled her, and he had changed the conversation so quickly she had no time to wonder why.

'You know I haven't,' she exclaimed with a nervous little laugh.

'Then there's no time like the present. We'll ride home together like the knight and his lady coming home in triumph from the battlefield,' he said, more lightly. 'You'll be my Guinevere and I'll be your Lancelot.'

Before she had any idea what he was talking about, he had lifted her on to the back of the horse, leapt up behind her and grabbed the reins. Her heart pounded as she sat side-saddle the way ladies did while he sat astride Noble behind her, and urged the horse gently forward.

'How do you like it, my lady?' he whispered into her ear as they jogged along amiably, gathering smiling glances from walkers on the Downs.

'It's a bit scary, but rather nice,' she admitted, aware of the strength of the horse beneath her, and even more, the heat of Lance's body holding her close.

She had never realized the horse was so big and powerful, or that they would be so far off the ground, but it was thrilling in a way she had never experienced before. It put them in a special world of their own, and when she felt Lance's lips nuzzle daringly into her neck when they were out of public view, no thoughts of unknown miners and their problems or a bare-knuckle fighter's disappearance occupied her mind.

'So are you going to tell me?' Cherry said that evening when they went to bed and she snuggled up to him.

After they had returned to the house, he had been busy for the rest of the day, and his mother had declined to join them for dinner, complaining of a headache, so this was the first time she had really had a chance for a proper conversation with him.

'Tell you what?' he said lazily. 'I thought we could find more interesting things to do than indulge in chit-chat.'

As his hands slid down her body she felt the familiar shiver that he could always stir in her. But she still wanted to *know* . . .

'You know what I'm talking about, Lance. All this miners' stuff!'

He gave an impatient sigh. 'For pity's sake, Cherry, you should leave men's business to men and not worry your sweet head about things you don't understand.'

If she wasn't in bed, she would have stamped her feet in frustration. It wasn't often he came over all masculine and superior, and she hated it when he did. She wasn't some little idiot incapable of understanding things. She had controlled her own life for years now, and she had no intention of being treated like a fool — or a plaything. She stilled his hand on her breast and spoke carefully.

'Lance, darling, I may have a sweet head, and I thank you for saying so, but I do have a brain inside it. Paula's worried and that makes me worried too. Please tell me what you know — or do I have to spend tomorrow in the library looking through the newspapers?'

He was silent for a moment and then spoke more sharply. 'I didn't know I'd married such an inquisitive woman. What will it be next? Taking up arms in their defence?'

'Hardly, since I don't know what it's all about,' she replied. 'In any case, I'd leave the soldiering to you. Women are usually left to pick up the pieces, aren't they?'

She hardly knew why she was goading him like this. She hadn't meant to do so. It had just been an innocent question.

He gathered her into him so suddenly that it made her gasp.

'Tomorrow, Cherry-ripe,' he said, his voice dropping seductively. 'We'll talk about it tomorrow, I promise. Will that satisfy you?'

Well, something was, the wicked little voice said inside her head . . . And she abandoned any more idea of discussing miners or Paula or anything else, to the far more delightful sensations of being cherished and loved.

She awoke feeling relaxed the next morning, stretching her limbs in a lazy, feline manner and reaching out her hand to touch Lance's body next to hers. But the bed was cold and she realized he was already up and gone. The memory of the unfinished discussion last night immediately filled her mind and wiped away any feeling of indolence. Was this his way of avoiding the issue, thinking her too much of a flibbertigibbet to take any interest in serious matters? If so, he really didn't know her at all, she thought in annoyance. She flung off the bedcovers, washed and dressed, and made herself presentable before going down to the dining room, hoping to find him still having his breakfast. There was no one there but one of the maids, and she spoke crossly in her disappointment.

'Where is everybody? Have my husband and his mother both eaten?'

She was aware that she spoke in a more imperious way than she had intended, and that the girl's eyes flashed at her before she lowered them.

'Lord Melchoir had an early breakfast and went out riding, my lady,' she said. 'Lady Elspeth hasn't come down yet.'

And I'll be standing here like a flipping lemon until she does, with all this good food going cold, and me perishing feet are throbbing already . . . and I'll end up getting tongue pie from Cook, telling me I've been time-wasting when it's no fault of mine . . .

As if she could hear it out loud, Cherry imagined just what

was going through the girl's mind and gave her a sympathetic smile. Didn't she know all about Cook's tongue-lashing!

'I'll just have some eggs and toast then, Mavis, and you can go back to the kitchen and wait until Lady Elspeth rings the bell for you. Tell Cook I said so.'

'Thank you, Madam,' the girl said with a gulp. She served the food quickly, scuttling away with a little bob when she was done, to report to Cook that the new m'lady wasn't too bad really when she wasn't putting on her airs and graces.

Cook snorted. 'You mind what you say about her ladyship, my girl, and get on with your work.'

'Cook won't hear nothing bad said about her, Mavis,' one of the other maids confided in her. 'She was always her favourite even before she struck lucky and married his lordship. I think Cook fancies herself as being a bit of a matchmaker as far as the two of them were concerned. Even though we all know it was nothing to do with her, and more to do with what his lordship's got in his trousers, if you know what I mean.'

The other girl went off in a burst of giggling as Cook bustled about and demanded to know what they were gossiping about.

'Nothing, Cook,' Mavis said airily and made a rude sign behind her back which got the other girl stuffing a tea towel in her mouth to stop herself laughing out loud as Cook went about her business, muttering suspiciously at the cheek of young girls nowadays.

Cherry finished her breakfast, thankful that Lady Elspeth didn't put in an appearance while she was there alone. They may have acquired a slightly more tolerant relationship of late, but it was better managed when Lance was there to act as a buffer between them. Cherry knew that in her mother-in-law's eyes, she would never be anything more than the upstart kitchen-maid who had ensnared her son. When in truth, it had been Lance who had ensnared *her* – if that was the right word to describe that one glorious encounter in the stables all that time ago when he had made love to her for the first time. Love, or lust . . . whatever it had been then, it was love now, she thought with a little glow in her heart, and remembering how passionately he had proved it to her last night.

Anyway, she couldn't spend any more time lingering over the breakfast table and daydreaming. There was still the little matter of the discussion she and Lance had never had. And if he was reluctant to talk to her about it, there were other ways to find out what she wanted to know. There was always a nip down to the kitchen for a chinwag with Cook and Mr Gerard, who would know everything there was to know about any miners' problems.

But with a little sigh, she knew that wasn't the cleverest thing she could do. Cook might be happy enough to chat to her, but the other skivvies would think it very odd that the lady of the house preferred to talk to servants than with her own kind. She gave a small snort. Her own kind, indeed! It was going to take a lifetime for her to feel she was at one with the likes of Lady Elspeth and her circle of toffee-nosed friends.

She went out of the dining room before she began to get maudlin, and sped up the stairs and along the corridor to the book-lined library, with its mingled aromas of old books and leather chairs. It was very definitely a gentleman's room, and she wondered if Lady Elspeth had ever deigned to come in here at all. Since she considered herself well-read, Cherry supposed she must have done at some point, unless she merely ordered someone to bring a suitable volume to her.

For a moment Cherry felt oddly sad for her, remembering the times she and Paula had pored over the well-thumbed books at the free library in the middle of town, and decided which of them was worthy of reading beneath the bedcovers of a night – especially if they could find one that was a bit saucy!

There were various newspapers spread out on the surface of the large central table in the Melchoir library. None of the more salacious ones that reported scandalous goings-on, of course, only the very best . . . but no doubt they were all interested in this dispute that according to Paula had been going on for years, as the miners quibbled over low wages and threatened drastic action when their pitiful wages were lowered even more. Cherry wondered how any decent boss could do such a thing without expecting a revolt. She turned the pages quickly, and hardly had time to find what she was looking for when a voice from the door made her jump.

'Can I help you, Lady Melchoir?'

She turned around quickly.

'Mr Gerard, did you know about all this miners' business?' she exclaimed, seeing the butler at the door. 'If I'm reading this correctly it seems that they're expected to accept pay cuts when they already get so little for all the horrible work they do. That's not fair, is it? I think they should be paid more, not less!'

She saw a faint smile crack his normally stern features. If he thought it ironic that someone who just a couple of years ago was earning less than a pittance herself, was now talking so indignantly on behalf of the coal miners, his feelings were overcome by the sincerity of her voice.

'Nothing's fair for the workers in this life,' he conceded, coming farther into the room. 'It's a bad business and no mistake, and the Lord knows where it will all lead, with the Trades Union Congress taking up the cudgels. They do say that if a strike begins, others will come out in support and it could bring the whole country to a standstill.'

'Could it? How? I don't understand,' Cherry said.

Gerard shrugged, but his natural inclination to show off his knowledge in such matters was quickly overcoming the fact that he shouldn't be talking like this at all, as if Lady Cherry Melchoir, née Cherry O'Neill, kitchen-maid, was his equal. She had been his underling before, and now she was anything but that. But she had always been an inquisitive little thing with a thirst for knowledge, and her eyes were full of eagerness now.

'There's talk of a general strike,' he said at last.

'But what does that actually *mean*?' she persisted. 'Who will take part in a general strike? Will it include the gardeners and stable boys and you and Cook and the kitchen staff? Are you suggesting that we'll get no dinner just because the coal miners refuse to go to work? It sounds a bit far-fetched to me.'

She had begun to smile at the very thought until she saw the flash of anger on his face. She wished at once that she hadn't put them all into their separate compartments, the lower classes and those born with privileges who had no need to work at all, and she knew she had to make amends.

'I'm sorry, Mr Gerard. I didn't mean to make it sound so trivial when I'm sure it's not,' she said clumsily.

'That it's not, and it's best left to those who know what they're doing,' he said stiffly. 'Now if you'll excuse me, I'll get about my business.'

He was excusing himself, yet Cherry was the one feeling as though she had been dismissed. She had never realized before how skilful he was at doing just that. But she quickly forgot him and turned again to the newspapers. It was the end of April now, and most of the papers carried a scathing report on a rebel rouser called Mr Arthur Cook, who seemed to be urging the miners and their supporters to hold the government up to ransom until they backed down. But anyone with any sense knew that no country could do without its workers. The gentry might think they ruled over everything, but it was the ordinary workers who kept things going. And if they all went on strike . . .

Cherry frowned. Surely it didn't truly mean that bus drivers and bakers and labourers would all down tools at the same time. How could it happen? Her eyes were drawn to one person's eyewitness account.

> From his position on the platform in Trafalgar Square, Mr Cook sounded like a bombastic preacher, but he didn't seem to have any idea about how to administer a strike if that was his intention. He was just an agitator, and seemed in a bit of a muddle about it all, but there's no doubt that he stirred up plenty of fight in his listeners. Everyone has sympathy for the miners, but none of them knows the right way to go about getting justice for them. Arthur Cook will have plenty to answer for if this gathers momentum. A general strike will be disastrous for the country, but there's no doubt there's plenty of support for it.

Cherry sat down on one of the leather chairs and tried to think what this could all mean. Every house in the country relied on so many things, for food, for heating, for transport simply to get from one place to the next. Would it all come to a halt if this blessed strike happened? If there was no work, there would be no wages, and what good would that do to anybody. The miners themselves may get poor wages now, but poor wages were better than none at all. And what about Paula and Harold if the trains stopped running and no wages were coming in there, with a new baby on the way?

She shivered, unwilling to think how lucky she was in being Lance's wife, when so many people seemed destined to face hardship. It brought it all closer to home when she realized how it might affect her best friend, and how different their circumstances had become.

She was hardly aware of footsteps on the landing outside the library, or the door being opened until she heard Lance's voice behind her.

'What the devil are you doing in here, Cherry?' he said, seeing the spread of the newspapers in front of her.

'Why didn't you tell me about all this?' she burst out. 'Didn't you ever think how it might affect Harold?'

He looked at her as if she was stupid, and she thought at once that he probably couldn't think immediately who Harold was. He would know Paula's name, and remembered her visit to Ireland, but as far as he was concerned, she was just another skivvy who had got married and left his employ.

'Harold is Paula's husband,' she went on deliberately. 'He works on the railway, and if all the transport workers go on strike in support of the miners as the newspapers seem to imply, it could spell disaster for them with a house to rent and a baby on the way. You really have no idea how other people live, do you, Lance?'

She was bristling with anger by the time she finished. Maybe it had taken this to make her realize how she had been cocooned all this time. After his parents had sent them off to Ireland rather than face such an ill-matched marriage she and Lance had been living in an idyllic world of their own making. It had brought this situation that had nothing to do with them, to make her fully realize how different they really were, and that her loyalties would always lie with her friends.

'I think you're being quite ridiculous,' Lance said coldly. 'I'm quite aware of the situation and hope that everyone will come to their senses. But there's nothing that I can do about it, and certainly not you. There will always be fanatics who whip up public opinion and make things worse.'

'That may be, but they have to have someone who will stand up for them, don't they?'

'Whose side are you on now? This man is dangerous. If it was all left alone, it would all get ironed out eventually.'

'I can't believe you think any group of workers should accept pay cuts. Or perhaps I can. After all, you've never had to work for a wage packet in your life, have you?'

She made to storm out of the library, but he caught hold of her arm so hard that she cried out.

'You're a fool if you think I spent years in the army without expecting and deserving a proper salary. It may have been considerably more than your railway worker gets, but it wasn't a life of roses and honey, either,' he snapped. 'And I won't have my wife turning into some kind of political animal. It's not feminine and it's not seemly.'

Cherry gasped at the way he was turning on her and for no good reason that she could see. All she had wanted was to have a bit of information so that they could discuss things like rational human beings, not to have him sounding so superior and bloody-minded!

'Do you think I don't have any sense in my head then?' she demanded. 'Even when I was skivvying for your family I was able to think for myself, and I'm not going to stop doing it now.'

She was breathing heavily, knowing how he hated to be reminded of her skivvying days. As if he was ashamed of them. As if he was ashamed of *her*. Her resolve suddenly crumbled and her stomach felt hollow with nerves.

'Are you sorry you married me, Lance?' she asked in a choked voice.

He was still holding her arm but less cruelly now. She wanted desperately to rub the soreness, but she felt too frozen to move a muscle, wondering what he was going to say, and wishing she hadn't provoked him with such a question.

'If you think that, then you don't have as much sense as you think you do,' he said at last. 'Of course I'm not sorry I married you. I just want you to realize that things have changed for both of us now, Cherry.'

Hadn't she been thinking that for ages now? But somehow they had never faced up to it together before.

'When my father died, our lives changed for ever, and there's nothing we can do about it,' he went on. 'But all I ever wanted was to make you happy.'

'And so you do,' she said in a rush, feeling her eyes smart. 'I want to be everything you want me to be, Lance, but in the end I can only be myself.'

She had no idea how the conversation had got around to this, but perhaps it was something that needed to be said. She was always going to be herself, Cherry O'Neill, no matter what outer trappings her new position gave her.

She saw him give a rueful smile, and then he leaned forward and kissed her cheek.

'Well, it's yourself that I fell in love with, isn't it? Look, let's get out of this room and take a walk in the garden to clear the air between us.'

'And you'll explain a little more about what's going on with these miners? Just so I can understand it all on account of Paula and Harold,' she added quickly, knowing she was pushing her luck, but still not prepared to give in completely.

He sighed, and put his arm around her waist, squeezing her tight.

'If I must, you persistent little madam,' he said.

Ten

A few days later Lady Elspeth took to her bed with a severe chill. She had been slow to take any interest in her old social gatherings or intimate little afternoon soirées or any of her charity work since her husband died. The doctor told Lance and Cherry that all this was quite normal, and everything would work out in its own good time. No two individuals were the same, and where one person might bounce back quickly, a period of mourning was far more desirable, in his expert opinion, to give both the mind and the body time to heal from their loss.

'He's such a pompous old fool,' Cherry muttered when he had gone. 'He never talks like that to ordinary patients, only to those who can pay plenty for his services. The longer words he uses, the more he thinks people will think he's so clever.'

'He's right though,' Lance said, ignoring the barb. 'No one can recover from a bereavement in a day or a week or a month. It takes time to adjust to being without someone dear to us. You must have felt the same when your parents died, Cherry.'

'I can't even remember my dad, but yes, I felt ill and anxious for weeks after Mum died, but that was partly because there was only Brian and me left then. He was never the most caring of brothers, and I didn't know how long he was likely to be around.'

She bit her lip, knowing she shouldn't have mentioned her brother at all. It was like holding up the proverbial red rag to a bull, but thankfully Lance ignored it. He clearly had something else on his mind.

'How would you feel about sitting with Mother for a little while today?'

Cherry gulped. 'Do you think she'd want me to? It would be more likely to set her back than make her feel any better!'

'I think it would be the right thing for a daughter-in-law to do, but if you don't feel up to it you only have to say so.'

He spoke blandly enough but she could see the challenge in his eyes. Of course he thought she would back down. *Of course* he knew she'd rather be doing anything else on earth than have to sit at his mother's bedside and pretend a concern she didn't feel for a woman who detested her.

'I wouldn't know what to say to her,' she muttered.

'You probably wouldn't have to say anything. Since the doctor has given her a sedative she'll be sleeping most of the day, anyway. Take that knitting you're forever grumbling about and just be there when she wakes up. Or you could read to her if you fancied it. And if she wants a hot or cold drink you could ring the bell for someone to bring it to her. She'd appreciate that.'

To Cherry it sounded like the very worst way to spend a day, and one that she was sure neither woman would enjoy. But supposing it was her own little mother, frail and ill, and wanting company? Just knowing someone was there was the best thing of all when you were sick. She swallowed her pride and her nerves and agreed to do it.

Her reward was a lingering kiss from Lance. 'Thank you, sweetheart. We all have to try to mend bridges where we can.'

It seemed an odd remark to make. As if his mother being sick was the ideal way for her unwanted daughter-in-law to be seen to be concerned for her. But if that's what he thought, Cherry wasn't going to argue with it. Despite his apparent disinterest in the varied newspaper reports about the miners' problems, she knew he was worried about something – and it was something more than his mother's illness, however anxious he might be about that.

But it was only a little chill after all . . . and Lady Elspeth had always seemed to have a pretty robust constitution. And those in less privileged positions would have simply coughed and snorted a bit and never bothered to take to their beds. They couldn't afford to lose any wages through illness, anyway. There was many a time when one or other of the downstairs workers had dragged their feet down to the kitchen and been told smartly by Cook to get on with it and not make such a fuss over a little sniffle.

Cherry supposed that if she herself got a chill now, she too would be allowed to stay in bed for a while and be pampered with hot and cold drinks and doctors' visits. It was a strange old world all right, when one person was just as sick as the next. But if Lady whatsit needed something from the kitchen, Cherry determined that she would run down and fetch it for her herself. She could just imagine Cook's face if it was Cherry O'Neill's voice asking for service upstairs!

She waited as long as she could before making the tentative visit to her mother-in-law's bedroom early that afternoon. She had never been in here before, and it smelled of camphor and violets and a slight mustiness. They were old-lady smells that made her wrinkle her nose for a moment before she tiptoed over to the bed. To her relief Lance's mother was asleep, and she was struck by an unexpected sense of compassion as she looked at her.

With her face relaxed and without the tight-lipped look she so often wore, and her hair unpinned, there was nothing to mask the signs of age. She was an old woman who had recently lost her husband, and who had had to bear the shame of her only son marrying a kitchen-maid in the belief that it was the only way to stave off the greater shame of the girl bearing his illegitimate child. Cherry could suddenly see everything through this woman's eyes, almost as if she was looking at her through a mirror.

'Have you come to torment me with things I don't need?'

The voice from the bed spoke in a slurred and drowsy way because of the sedative. Her eyes were still closed, and she probably thought it was one of the maids fussing about according to the doctor's orders.

Cherry came nearer to the bed and spoke softly.

'I hope not, Lady Elspeth. It's me, Cherry, and I've come to sit with you if you'd like a bit of company. If you want anything, you just tell me, otherwise I won't disturb you and I'll just sit and do my knitting.'

For a moment she thought the woman was asleep again. She still lay exactly as before, and then very slowly she turned her head towards Cherry and opened her eyes a fraction.

'Has my son sent you to do this?'

Cherry gave a half smile. 'It's miserable to feel ill and all alone, and he did suggest that I might like to sit with you, and of course I said I would.'

There was the barest tug of a half smile in return. 'I'm sure we both know you'd rather be doing something else. Stay if you must, but my head aches so don't clack those knitting needles for too long.'

'I'll sit by the window so that they don't annoy you,' Cherry said hastily, but by then Lady Elspeth had turned away. The small amount of talking had exhausted her and she had drifted back to sleep again.

Cherry was glad to move across to the window seat where she could look out at the fine spring day as an alternative to knitting. But she needed to get on with it for Paula now. The baby would be here soon and she wanted the shawl ready for when it arrived. She felt her heart turn over every time she thought of it, wondering what it would be like, and if it would be a boy or a girl. There was always a little twist of envy too, that Paula would be the one to hold a baby in her arms before she did.

There had been a time long ago when they were very young girls with their eyes full of dreams – which seemed like another lifetime – when they had fondly imagined walking out with their babies together – after a suitable time of being married to the *men* of their dreams, of course. At least they had both done that, Cherry thought with a little glow. Paula had Harold, and no matter what the circumstances were that had brought them together, she had Lance, whom she had adored for so long and never thought would give her a second glance.

She realized she was sitting idly, gazing unseeingly out of the window with her knitting lying loosely on her lap. This was not the way to get it done, she told herself briskly, and set about continuing with the stitches Lady Elspeth had helped her with. Folk tended to think the toffs knew nothing about ordinary occupations, but Lady Elspeth knew how to knit, and probably a good few other things as well. But now she had to really concentrate on the intricate lacy pattern and had been doing so for nearly an hour when she heard the hoarse voice speak to her again.

'My throat is very dry. Ring for a cold drink, please.'

Cherry let the knitting slip to the floor and moved quickly over to the bed. If anything, her mother-in-law looked more feverish than before, and she felt a stab of anxiety.

'It will be quicker if I fetch it myself, Lady Elspeth.'

Without waiting for any objection, she sped out of the room

and down the stairs to the kitchen, where several faces looked up at this unexpected intrusion. She spoke quickly before she lost her nerve.

'I need a tray for Lady Elspeth, please Cook. I want a jug of barley water and a glass, a small bowl of water and a face cloth.'

'See to it, Maisie, and be quick about it,' Cook said after a moment's startled silence as the girls stood gawping. 'She'll take it up to her ladyship's bedroom directly, Lady Melchoir. We heard that the lady was poorly.'

'No, I'll take it myself,' Cherry said firmly. 'There's no need for anyone else to bother.'

'Well, if you think so,' Cook said, clearly outraged.

'I do think so, thank you,' Cherry said, her eyes unwavering. 'I'm sure you'll understand that her ladyship prefers to be private when she is so unwell.'

'Not prepared to show herself to servants when she's not so starchy as usual is what she means,' Cook said angrily to Gerard later. 'I never thought young Cherry would get so uppity, either, but I daresay mixing with toffs is all rubbing off on her.'

'You can hardly blame her, can you? She has a position to keep up now.'

Cook glared at him. 'Well, you've changed your tune, haven't you? I thought you was against mixing the breeds as you might say.'

Gerard gave a faint smile. 'Maybe so, but I speak as I find, and I think the girl has deported herself with dignity at all times since her marriage. As for getting uppity – well, she came downstairs for her ladyship's tray herself, didn't she? She could easily have rung the bell and sent for what was needed. She's not forgotten her old friends.'

Cook sniffed, none too pleased at being taken to task when the younger maids were giggling in the background. She rounded on them instead.

'Get on about your work, you skivvies,' she shouted, 'and stop listening to other people's conversations. If you haven't got enough to do I can soon find you some more.'

Cherry was unaware of the small discussion going on downstairs, but knowing them all so well, she could easily imagine it.

Cook was annoyed with her for counter-minding her decision, and would no doubt be complaining to Mr Gerard. While he . . . her eyes softened. She was sure he had become less stiff towards her of late and had accepted her new position at last. It would have been hard for them, she conceded. Almost as hard as it had been for Lady Elspeth and the late Lord Melchoir to learn that their son had brought disgrace to their family.

She lifted her head up high as she negotiated the kitchen stairs and made her way to the wider upper landings. She had vowed when she and Lance married that she would never let him down, and she passionately believed that she had been true to that vow, every bit as much as she had been true to their wedding vows.

She entered Lady Elspeth's room carefully balancing the tray in the crook of one arm, which wasn't difficult, since she had been used to carrying far larger and bulkier items of kitchen ware in the past. She thought her ladyship had fallen asleep again, but her eyes opened as she heard Cherry approach. She was very flushed now, even more than before, and Cherry felt another stab of alarm. She quickly put the tray on a side table and poured out a glass of barley water.

'Let me help you to sit up a little,' she said at once, putting one arm behind the lady's shoulders as she made the effort to move up in the bed. Then she tentatively put a hand behind her head and held the glass to her lips.

'Not too fast, Lady Elspeth,' she murmured. 'Small sips are best. Little and often is what I was always told, and when you've had enough I'll soothe your forehead with a cold flannel. My mother used to call it our magic flannel when I was a little girl, and it always did the trick.'

She carried on talking as if she was talking to a sick child, which was what the lady resembled at that moment. Cherry had a growing sense of pity for her, knowing her pride, and how she would hate to feel so beholden to other people, especially her daughter-in-law. But sickness took no account of pride. Prince or pauper, it could strike anyone at any time.

'Thank you. I'm so very hot,' she heard the weak voice say as she sank back on the pillows. 'Your mother sounds like a caring woman.'

Cherry came to another decision, but she knew she had to

tread very carefully as she kept her tone dispassionate. 'Many years ago I saw my mother nurse a friend through a similar illness, and I think it might help even more if you had a sponge down, plus a change of nightdress and bed-sheets. I will willingly help you if you will allow me, but I realize that you may not. Forgive me if it sounds too intrusive, and if you would prefer to have a professional nurse to attend you, I'm sure Lance will arrange it.'

Cherry lowered her eyes in the silence that followed, guessing that she had gone too far. Why would this autocratic and very private lady ever agree to a chit of a serving girl doing such intimate things for her? It wasn't the way things were done in upper-class families. But this serving girl was also her son's wife, and as close to a daughter as she would ever have.

'If you think it would help,' Lady Elspeth said at last.

Cherry wasted no more time. She rang the bell at the side of the bed and ordered what she needed to be brought to Lady Elspeth's room at once – a fresh nightdress, clean sheets, a bowl of tepid water, soap, flannel and towels. A short time later two maids knocked on the door and brought everything into the room, leaving with wide eyes at the sight of the young Lady Melchoir with her sleeves rolled up and preparing to do whatever menial task was needed for her ladyship and ready to report everything downstairs.

Lance didn't return home until early evening, having spent part of the day at his club, and the rest of it in meetings with some of the town's bigwigs discussing the likely outcome of the miners' situation if a strike came to pass and how it might affect the city. He was more worried about it than he cared to divulge to Cherry, but right now, he was more concerned about finding out how his mother had fared during the day. He went straight along to his mother's bedroom.

'Well, you're looking much better that you were this morning,' he said at once, ready to cheer the invalid, but relieved to see her half-sitting up in the bed with her hair tidied and wearing a different nightdress from the one he'd seen her in earlier. There was a jug of barley water and some fruit on her bedside table.

'Don't be fooled by appearances,' Elspeth said in a tired voice. 'I'm exhausted if you must know.'

'What have you been doing to tire yourself out then?' Lance said, preparing to indulge her.

'Not me! It's that girl.'

She closed her eyes, as if even this small amount of talking was truly tiring. Lance had meant it when he said she looked better, but he could see now it was only because she had had her personal needs attended to. And just who had done it all . . . ?

'You mean Cherry?' he exclaimed. 'I asked her to sit with you and to read to you if you wanted her to, so how has she worn you out?'

He overlooked the fact that she had referred to his wife as *that girl*. Now was not the time to take offence until he learned what had been going on. Before he could get any reply the door opened and he turned around to see Cherry enter with a tray, and the delicious aroma of chicken soup wafted into the room.

'Ah, so you're back,' she said unnecessarily.

'What are you doing?' Lance said.

'I'm bringing your mother some chicken soup since she doesn't feel like anything more substantial for dinner,' she said steadily, aware of the annoyance in his voice.

'I mean why are *you* doing it, instead of one of the servants? This is not your job, Cherry.'

'I'm doing it because when someone who's ill says they feel like eating, they should be pampered straight away, and it was quicker to fetch it myself than to wait for someone else to bring it.'

She dumped the tray on the bedside table and glared at him. She had done everything he had asked of her that day, and more, and she didn't deserve to be spoken to this way. She ignored him and spoke directly to Lady Elspeth.

'Do you think you can manage it yourself, or would you like me to help you? It's not too hot, but it might be a little awkward for you.'

Lady Elspeth gave a small nod. 'I'd be grateful for some help, though I'm not sure how much of it I can eat.'

Cherry didn't look at Lance as she spoke to him. 'Lance, why don't you just leave us to it? I'm sure your mother will be glad to see you later when she's a little more rested, and I'll join you for dinner in a little while.'

He looked furious at being more or less dismissed from his own mother's bedroom, and by the person he had expected her to least want to see. He had no idea what had been going on here today, but by thunder, he intended to find out. Cherry was behaving like the bloody lady of the manor now . . . and as he strode out of the room he paused at his own thoughts. Because that was exactly what she was, and he had put her there. For the first time, he found himself questioning his own choice of wife, and hated himself for doing so, but the nagging thought wouldn't leave him now, and he stormed into his study, forcing himself to cool down and not be so bloody resentful of something that couldn't be changed.

By the time he and Cherry met again it was in the dining room for dinner. She looked at him warily, knowing she had done the unforgivable in reverting to her servant duties, but hardly seeing what all the fuss was about. Any daughter or daughter-in-law would have done what she had done, and it was only the toffee-nosed twerps who thought otherwise and expected to be waited on hand and foot. Supposing Lady Elspeth had taken a turn for the worse?

Was she expected to stand by and see her suffer until a doctor was called, when she was perfectly capable of fetching some sal volatile and sprinkling her handkerchief with the stuff so that she wouldn't have to sniff the pungent stuff in and splutter herself to death? She knew all about caring for an older woman, even though she had been so young when her own mother died. But if she was aware of his annoyance, it was very obvious that he was aware that she was bristling too.

'So you've been acting as nursemaid today, have you?' Lance said, once they had eaten the main course in silence, dessert had been served, and the maid had left them alone.

'Isn't it what you asked me to do?'

'I didn't expect you to take on the duties that belong to other people. You have a position to maintain now, Cherry.'

Her blood suddenly boiled. 'Good God, I don't know what it is you want of me, Lance. I can never seem to please you lately. I sat with your mother and read to her, and fetched her a drink rather than let her wait for it. When she looked so hot and bothered I helped her into a clean nightdress to make her more comfortable. Was that beyond the call of duty?' she added sarcastically. 'I'm starting to think that your mother's beginning to look more kindly towards me than my own husband!'

When he didn't answer immediately, she blinked away the angry tears that threatened. She wouldn't let him see her cry, she wouldn't! She was Lady bloody Melchoir now, and nothing could change that.

'Or is there something more serious behind all this? Are you regretting that you married me, Lance? Is that it? A kitchen-maid was never fit to be the wife of a lord, was she? And no doubt some of your lah-de-lah friends are still laughing at the way you were taken in. Maybe we should have stayed in Ireland after all, where none of your nasty little secret was ever going to come out.'

She was visibly shaking now, and she clasped her hands tightly together rather than let him see. They had drifted so far apart in these few minutes that she was shocked and hurt, even by her own bitter words that had been milling about in her mind ever since he had come to his mother's bedroom and seen her delivering a tray. How ludicrous it was to get so upset by an act of kindness.

'Stop being melodramatic,' he snapped. 'And keep your voice down. Do you want the servants to hear a slanging match between us? It may be the way they behave in the kitchen, but I expect a bit more decorum from my wife.'

He stopped speaking abruptly as he saw the flash of temper in her eyes.

'How dare you,' she said hoarsely. 'Have you forgotten that these people are my friends and that I spent half my life working with them? You shame me and you insult them with your hateful words.'

She got up from the table, leaving her dessert half-finished. She intended to go to her room and to blazes with him. But before she could move very far he had reached out and grabbed hold of her arm, hurting her as he had done once before, his fingers digging into her flesh.

'For God's sake, sit down, Cherry, and stop all this nonsense.'

'It's not nonsense to me! You're ashamed of me and you wish

you'd never married me,' she said shrilly, feeling as though her world was falling apart in front of her. It was the biggest irony that his mother seemed to be softening towards her, when Lance, her dearest, darling, infuriating Lance, was glaring at her as if he hated her.

'I do not wish I'd never married you,' he said, his voice so cold it might as well have belied every word. 'I loved you then and I love you now, strange as it may seem, since you make it so difficult for me sometimes.'

All she heard was he loved her now, and all the fight went out of her.

'I love you too, Lance,' she said shakily. 'I always have.'

In the long moment that they seemed to be simply staring at one another, she registered that the grip on her arm had become more gentle, almost caressing. *Thank God*, she thought, unable to bear it if they were at constant loggerheads – and over something so petty – at least to her. She smothered the lingering thought that there was no way she was going to abandon her old workmates, but at the same time acknowledging that Lance had elevated her to the comfortable life she now led, and she owed him her loyalty.

Whatever either of them intended to say was interrupted by the arrival of a maid to clear the table. In any case, any more thought of food was farthest from either of their minds. There was already a certain look on Lance's face that Cherry recognized all too well. She hoped it was true what someone had once told her. That no matter how bitter the row, the making-up was all the sweeter. But there were formalities to go through first.

'I must see if Mother needs anything before we turn in, and then perhaps we can have an early night,' he said, with a promise in his eyes.

'Why don't we go and see her together?' Cherry said, and immediately wondered if she was being too bold. Would he think this was breaking into the special relationship between mother and son? To her relief he nodded.

'I expect she would welcome it after all the help you've given her today. It's good for her to have your companionship, Cherry. I haven't given much thought to how lonely she must feel after Father's death. Another woman is probably more understanding of those feelings than a man can ever be, and you do have the gentle touch, Cherry-ripe.'

It was an unexpected compliment that sent the blood rushing to her face. For all the kind words, though, she wasn't sure that that stiff and starchy woman really welcomed her companionship. She had been vulnerable in her sickbed today, but there was no telling how she would be once she was up and about and back to normal again.

But this wasn't the time to fret over something that may or may not happen. It was enough that they were visiting his mother together, the son and his wife, the way things should be. And amazingly, the first weak smile from Lady Elspeth as they entered her bedroom, was directed towards Cherry.

'Is there anything you need tonight, Mother?' Lance said at once.

She shook her head. 'I shall ring for a maid if necessary, but I have been so well looked after today I am starting to feel better already but now I'm ready for sleep. Don't fuss, Lance.'

He gave a small smile. It was a typical remark, and she was obviously on the mend, and in no small way thanks to Cherry.

'Then we'll say goodnight and not disturb you any further,' he went on.

He kissed her lightly on the forehead, and after a moment's hesitation, Cherry did the same. It seemed churlish to stand by and not give her a gesture of affection, even though she wasn't sure it would be appreciated.

'Come and see me again tomorrow,' she heard Lady Elspeth say sleepily.

'I promise,' she said.

Outside the bedroom she felt a moment's apprehension, hoping again that Lance wouldn't think she had gone too far, or that she was worming her way into his mother's affection. It was what he wanted, but he had been the favoured and only son for all these years, and she prayed there wasn't a faint hint of jealousy.

As he brought her hand to his lips, she knew her fears were mistaken.

'I think it's bed for us too, Cherry-ripe. It's been an eventful day. Not that sleeping was what I had in mind.'

As he squeezed her hand she felt her nerves begin to tingle

in anticipation. It was as though they had weathered a storm and come through it safely, and now was the time for celebration.

Then they were opening the door of their own bedroom and he was speaking again, almost guardedly, as if only just realizing she had a mind of her own and wasn't afraid to use it.

'Of course I don't know how tired you are after your busy day.'

Her heart was beating fast, and this was no time for false modesty. She closed the door behind them and leaned up to kiss him.

'Not too tired,' she whispered. 'Never too tired for you, my love.'

Eleven

'Your brother's back in town,' Paula said flatly.

It was a few days later and Cherry had gone to visit her friend now that Lady Elspeth had more or less recovered from her chill and was insisting that she didn't need any more molly-coddling, even though she didn't get up until mid-morning, and then retired to her room again for a sleep during the afternoon. Cherry wouldn't say they were exactly friends, but at least they were on speaking terms, and there wasn't the palpable sense of animosity on the older lady's part as there had been before.

But now her heart gave a jolt at Paula's words. 'Are you sure? I went to his lodgings very recently, and the landlord was bleating over non-payment of rent and how much Brian owed him. I thought I'd got rid of him this time,' she added bitterly.

Paula's face was uneasy. 'I'm quite sure, Cherry. I caught sight of him myself, and last night Harold was meeting some of his railway pals at the Smuggler's Inn to discuss what the outcome might be for them if the miners' strike went ahead, and your Brian was there, bragging as usual about some fight he'd won. Harold kept well out of sight in case he recognized him, but he couldn't help hearing some of the things he was saying, and you're not going to like it.'

'Well, if he's mocking Lance and his family, I'll have the law on him, brother or not,' Cherry said furiously.

'It's worse than that.'

She stared at her friend, a feeling of dread starting to steal over her. 'How can it be worse than that? You'd better tell me what you know, Paula, and for goodness' sake stop dithering as usual. It's not good for the baby.'

She tried to make a small joke of it, but Paula's face was so serious she knew it was nothing to be taken lightly, and her heart was already beating too fast for comfort.

'Well, he was only talking to a few of his cronies, and they were all rolling drunk like pigs in muck, according to Harold, so maybe none of them will have remembered anything by morning. But Harold said he was sniggering over the fact that his sister had got herself in the family way and that the new lord of the manor had installed her at Melchoir House, letting everyone think they were married. Those were Harold's exact words to me, Cherry.'

'Well, of course we're married. You know that!'

'Yes, I know it! But according to Brian's nasty little rumour, you just went off to Ireland until the fuss of Captain Lance associating with a kitchen-maid died down. He's saying that you never got married at all and you're just living in sin. I never thought he'd say such wicked things about his own sister, Cherry, but what I'm telling you is the truth.'

Cherry never doubted it. Paula couldn't tell a lie and keep her face from colouring up if her life depended on it. The fact that she was flushed and looked so desperately miserable now, was mere proof of how badly she felt for her friend and having to report such things.

Cherry's mouth was dry. 'God, I can hardly believe it, even of him. I came here to see how you are, not to hear of such degrading things coming from my own brother. How could he be so cruel?'

'I'm really sorry I had to tell you, but Harold said I should. Your Brian was only saying it to a few blokes last night and he swore they were all out of their heads with drink, but Harold said it was better for you to know what was going on, and to be forewarned if you should see him again.'

'Oh, I'll see him all right. I daresay he's gone back to his old lodgings, and if not, I'll go to the Smuggler's Inn myself,' Cherry said furiously. 'He's not going to get away with this.'

'Be careful, Cherry,' Paula pleaded. 'You know what an awful dive that place can be. The street girls sometimes go there to pick up sailors, and the last thing you want is any more gossip.'

It was obvious what she meant. But if the place was good enough for Harold and his mates to meet, which Cherry declined to comment on, then she wasn't going to baulk on it.

'I'll try his lodgings again first,' she compromised. 'Though I doubt that he's gone back there now. He's probably holed up in some other horrible dump, and I wish he'd never come back here at all.'

She ended on a vicious note. It was a terrible thing to wish your own flesh and blood somewhere else – *anywhere else* – but she never wanted to see him again after all the trouble he'd brought her and Lance. And now this! How could her dear father and her sweet little mother ever have produced such a monster?

She smothered a sob, hardly knowing how she continued sitting in Paula's tidy house, making small talk about the baby and the fact that she had nearly finished knitting her shawl and it would probably need a good wash before Paula wrapped the baby in it, because of the many times she had had to unpick a row or two. On and on she babbled, listening to herself and wondering how soon she could decently get out of there and do what she had to do.

Finally, she stood up to go. 'I'll come and see you again, Paula, but right now I've got some urgent business to attend to and if I leave it much longer I shall explode.'

'Wouldn't it be better to let Lance deal with it, Cherry?' Paula said nervously, realizing what she had stirred up.

'I'm not telling him unless I have to! Brian's my brother, more's the pity,' Cherry said. 'But don't worry about me. You know I can handle him.'

It was said in a spirit of bravado, but she wasn't too sure about it herself as she retraced her steps towards the part of the city where Brian had lodged for so long. She prayed she wouldn't encounter the landlord again. By now he might have twigged who she was, and demand that she paid whatever Brian owed him in rent. And if he also realized she was now Lady Melchoir, who knew what kind of money he might try to extort out of her?

She left the main streets, crowded with pedestrians and bicycles, horses and carts and the occasional tooting small cars, her heart thudding even more painfully as she walked nervously down the narrow, dank alleyways that didn't see much light of day between the tall buildings. It was a horrible place to live.

Poor as her own family had been when she was a child, they had never lived in such squalid places as these. Her mother had always kept a clean house, and studiously taught her children that cleanliness was next to godliness. At least one of them still lived by the values she had instilled in them, she thought fervently. Even as a kitchen-maid, and without the luxuries that marriage to Lance had brought her, she had always kept herself clean.

To her relief there weren't too many people in the alley that morning, other than a road sweeper and a few urchins kicking a ball about. It was a blustery day, with a lingering nod to the tradition of March winds and April showers, even though they were on the brink of May. And then she stopped abruptly as she faced the normally grimy windows of Brian's lodgings.

They were grimy no longer, and there were fresh curtains hanging there, where before there had been just a ragged piece of sacking dragged across the windows to hide the mess inside. Had he come into money or something? Or moved some wretched street girl in to live with him and clean for him, which was more likely. The thought of any young girl choosing to live in such surroundings was enough to make her stomach curdle.

She was still undecided what to do next when a middle-aged, motherly-looking woman wearing a flowered overall that completely covered her, opened the door and looked curiously at Cherry, now standing motionless outside. The appearance of anyone in such fine clothes was clearly an unusual sight here.

'Did you want something, my dear?' she was asked.

'I was just wondering about the person who lives here,' she said evasively.

The woman nodded and sniffed. 'Well, whoever he was, he don't live here no more. Got his marching orders, and not before time. The state the place was in, the landlord was losing money hand over fist. I've been hired to clean it up for a new tenant, and I'm earning my money, I can tell you. The whole place needs fumigating. What are you – a social worker?'

As she paused for breath Cherry found herself backing away.

'No, but thank you for the information.'

She turned and walked away quickly before the woman could start asking any more probing questions. It wasn't hard to see even more curiosity in her eyes, the same way the landlord had looked on seeing her in this disreputable part of the city in her smart clothes and trying to speculate on what she was doing here.

So Brian had already gone from here, but according to Paula he was still in the city, and the only other place she knew she was likely to find him was the Smuggler's Inn. She hated the thought of going there again, but this shameful thing that Brian was doing had to be nipped in the bud before it reached Lance's ears – and those of his acquaintances too, she thought in horror.

It hadn't occurred to her before, but it would be doubly humiliating for him if he had to defend himself against such untrue allegations. She felt so protective on Lance's behalf that it overcame any last feeling of hesitation about going to the waterside pub.

She had left the alleyways and walked towards the busy Centre where she could breath fresher air when she became aware of a motor car slowing down alongside her. She had no intention of turning around, but having heard no more than a purring engine sound, she knew it must be a limousine, and such expensive machines were still enough of a novelty in the city to make people turn and stare.

This particular sound reminded her vividly of a night long ago. She hadn't thought of that night in ages, when she and Paula had been scurrying away from some ruffians at a dance hall, and a certain limousine had cruised along beside them offering them a lift.

They had been kitchen-maids in the Melchoirs' employ then, and it wasn't seemly for them to be offered a lift by the son of the house, or for them to accept it. But accept it they had, and drowsy with cider, Paula had fallen asleep in the back seat long before they reached Melchoir House. While she had been seduced by the rich, velvety sound of Captain Lance's voice and her attraction to him. She had been lured by her own desires to join him in the hayloft, losing both her innocence and her heart to him . . . and in doing so, starting a chain reaction that had led her here . . .

'I was asking if I can drive you back to the house before it starts to rain, Lady Melchoir?'

Startled, Cherry realized she had been momentarily dreaming, caught up in the past and forgetting the ugliness of the present. She blinked as she saw that the limousine had stopped beside her and that the familiar figure of Mr Gerard in his chauffeur's garb had wound down the window and was waiting expectantly for her reply. The sky had indeed begun to darken and she was still a long way from home. She was not obliged to wear deepest mourning for Lance's father, and her navy-blue dress and matching jacket in a light spring fabric would do nothing to save her from a soaking if it poured. She could hardly refuse the offer of a lift. Finding and confronting her brother would have to wait.

'Thank you, Mr Gerard,' she muttered, as he came round and opened the door for her, waiting until she sank down into its luxurious leather interior before returning to the driver's seat.

'I thought you were looking a little troubled, Lady Melchoir,' he went on as the car smoothly gathered momentum. 'Sometimes when you're deep in thought it's easy to lose your footing on these uneven footpaths, especially when the streets are so crowded.'

In other words, she had been walking along in a dream . . .

Before she could stop herself, she had forgotten her position and was blurting out something that should have been kept strictly to herself, at least for now. But having known him all these years, she was confident that he had never been anything else than discretion itself.

'I *am* troubled, Mr Gerard, and I have to tell someone or I'll burst. It's about my brother. You know how Cook always made a fuss of him, thinking him no more than a lovable rogue, even a bit glamorous with his so-called boxing occupation. But he's up to no good as usual, and I've just had proof of it. Paula's not a girl for making up wicked stories.'

Her tongue was running away with her again, and she paused for breath when he didn't reply to her ranting. Had she gone too far? He was of the old school that kept people in their respectful places, and gone were the days when she could have gone to him or to Cook as a kind of older confidant. She should have remembered that. She was mistress of the house now, and he wouldn't welcome such intimacy. Her eyes blurred for a moment, with a sudden burst of nostalgia for the days when she and Paula had run laughingly over the Downs, or gone to the pictures or a dance-hall of a Saturday night, free and easy of responsibilities other than their kitchen duties. And good God, she was starting to sound like a blessed matriarch now, instead of a young bride.

She realized that the car had already climbed the steep city streets and had approached the open spaces of the Downs. And before she knew what was happening, Gerard had brought it to a stop in one of the narrow roadways that criss-crossed the refreshing green acres, and turned off the engine.

'You can tell me to mind my own business, my dear, but I've known you too long not to see that something's badly wrong. If I can help, then I will, and you can be sure it will go no farther. Whatever your brother's done I'm sure it can't be too terrible.'

She swallowed hard. Should she tell him, or would it be breaking Paula's confidence? She should be able to sort this out by herself . . . but she knew she couldn't, and she felt more helpless than she had ever done before.

'It's the worst thing, Mr Gerard,' she whispered. 'If it was just to blacken my name I wouldn't care so much, but he'll hurt Lance and Lady Elspeth, and it will bring shame on the whole house, and I couldn't bear it.'

She guessed that his continued silence was some kind of clever waiting game to make her say more. And why not? She had gone this far, and if she didn't come out with it all, he would be bound to speculate on the rest.

'Paula's husband, Harold, heard him bragging at the Smuggler's Inn last night about some fight he'd won. He was also saying that Lance and I weren't really married and we'd gone to Ireland until the fuss died down and then come back as husband and wife. You know that's not true, don't you, Mr Gerard? But how many people might start to believe it if such rumours got around?'

Her eyes were frantic with worry as she looked at him, and she could see the flash of fury and outrage on his face. He had his pride too. He had worked for the Melchoirs for years, long before she and Paula came there, and in his way he was as much a part of the family as any of them.

'If you'll take my advice you'll say nothing to Lord Melchoir about this,' he said, his voice crisp. 'I'll see that the matter is dealt with.'

'You?' she echoed, her eyes growing even larger.

He gave a short laugh and the car began to move slowly again.

'Being in my position has its advantages, my dear, both with the upper classes and the lower ones. I have my contacts, and I promise you these rumours will be squashed before they get any farther. Now, let's get you home, Lady Melchoir, so that you can compose yourself before you next see your husband.'

She had no idea what he meant or what he could do, but she gave him a tremulous smile as he reverted to addressing her more formally, feeling marginally more relieved than before. The kitchen-maids had always looked on his stern persona with some awe, and yet also as a kind of pseudo father figure. And Cherry had never thought of him in that way more than she did right now. She knew it was a way she could never have considered Lance's father. Her own father had died many years ago and it was an oddly comforting thought to realize that this man was the nearest thing to a father figure than she had known for years. They reached the house without saying anything more, and before she got out of the car, he put a hand on her arm.

'Put it out of your mind, Lady Melchoir, and I give you my word that you'll hear no more about it.'

'Thank you, Mr Gerard,' she said awkwardly, already half wishing she had kept her mouth shut after all, but it was too late for that now. It was also impossible to put it out of her mind completely, and Lance couldn't fail to notice she was fretting over something that evening.

'It's just that I saw Paula today, and she's getting increasingly worried about the likelihood of this strike that Harold is sure is coming, and what it will mean for them,' she invented quickly.

'It's not just a likelihood, it's a certainty,' Lance told her.

'But it's only the miners who will be on strike, isn't it? Why would it affect Harold? He's a maintenance worker on the railway, not a miner.'

'Because, my dear sweet innocent,' Lance went on patiently, infuriating her with his condescending words, 'if you had half an inkling of reading between the lines of the newspapers you were supposedly studying a few days ago, you'd realize that other unions will come out in support of their cause. If they strike, or rather, *when* they strike, it will affect transport around the country, which in turn will affect food supplies and other commodities as well. We'll all be involved in one way or another.'

She ignored the fact that he was treating her like an imbecile now and felt a sliver of fear at his last words.

'I still don't see why it should,' Cherry said stubbornly. 'How will it affect us, anyway?'

Lance gave a heavy sigh. 'Wait and see. If there's trouble in the

city, the police may not be able to cope, and in extreme circumstances they may well call on the army or civilians to control any
riots or unruly rallies. It's happened in the past, and as an ex-
Captain, I would feel it my duty to offer my services in any way
I could, even as a special constable if the need arose.'

'Surely it wouldn't come to that?' Cherry said, feeling her heart
pound uncomfortably.

'It might well do so. I don't want to anticipate trouble until
it happens, but only a fool sticks his head in the sand and closes
his eyes to reality.'

He changed the conversation, and she knew she wouldn't get
any more out of him regarding any strike. But it had been enough
to take her thoughts away from her brother and his spitefulness,
and on to the more immediate danger that could affect the whole
city. She had never realized that what affected one branch of
society could have the kind of far-reaching effects that Lance
implied. But she knew from the seriousness in his voice that he
meant every word.

But how could it affect the family here, safe in their cocooned
world of affluence? Nor even the other family below stairs,
Mr Gerard and Cook, the maids and the gardeners and grooms.
The pantries and wine cellars were always full, and life would
carry on more as before . . . unless fresh food became in short
supply and Cook had to put all her ingenuity to the test.

No, it would be people like Paula and Harold who would feel
the pinch the quickest. If he had no work to go to, there would
be no money coming in to pay the rent, and with the coming
baby as well, they could soon be in real hardship. It was a disaster
that could be repeated in small houses like theirs all over the city.
All over the country, perhaps, and all because the rotten government wanted to slash the wages of the miners. Cherry doubted
that many government men, sitting on their fat backsides up in
London, would care to do the filthy, back-breaking jobs that the
miners did for a pittance! For a moment, she wished she could
close her eyes and ears to all of it, but she couldn't, not while it
might affect her friend so deeply.

Meanwhile, she had other things on her mind that were more
personal than worrying about a possible strike. There was Brian,
and what Gerard may or may not be able to do about his evil

rumours. After the first sense of relief that the man was going to help, she was having less and less confidence about it. Brian was a vicious bare-knuckle fighter, and for all Gerard's fine physique and his so-called contacts, she had no idea what he might be able to achieve, or what danger he might be putting himself in on her account.

But it wasn't just on her account, she remembered. It was for the honour of the Melchoir family that he had served for so many years and his loyalty to them. That loyalty was proven a day or so later when she received a carefully worded note on her breakfast tray.

'The matter has been resolved, Madam,' was all it said, and the rare sight of Gerard with a suspiciously darkening eye and scraped knuckles told her all she needed to know. She should find out more, and show her gratitude in a more realistic way, but instinct told her it was best to leave things as they were. The less she knew, the less she could blurt out to Lance. She trusted Gerard, and if he said the matter was resolved, then so it was.

After weeks of uncertainty and unease the miners' situation finally erupted, and with just as much ferocity and solidarity as Lance had anticipated. The government subsidy for the coal industry ended on the last day of April, and the shrieking newspaper head-lines and more sombre wireless announcements told the country that from midnight on May the third, not only the workers in iron and coal, but those in transport, printing, metal and building industries, electricity and gas suppliers would all come out on strike in support of the miners.

'I'm going down into the city with Gerard,' Lance informed her soon after breakfast on the first day of the strike. 'We're going to offer our services where we can.'

'Please be careful, Lance,' Cherry said.

He leaned over and kissed her. 'I'm always careful. The main source of any trouble will be in London and the other big cities, but Bristol will probably get its share of unofficial rallies and even riots, and if that happens the police will be glad of all the support they can get. You and Mother keep each other company and don't worry.'

Well, that put her neatly in her place, Cherry thought with a stab of resentment. The little women keeping one another company while the masterful men did whatever men did on such occasions. It was on the tip of her tongue to make some sarcastic remark, but one look at his tense face and she bit back the words and promised to do as he said and keep his mother company.

Thankfully, Lady Elspeth was nearly back to her normal self now, and there had emerged an uneasy truce between them. Cherry wasn't sure that they would ever be truly friends, let alone think of one another as part of a family, but for Lance's sake, there seemed to be an unspoken agreement to try. His mother always had a breakfast tray sent up to her room, but about mid-morning Cherry decided she couldn't put off the moment any longer and went along to the lady's bedroom to tap gently on the door.

'Come in,' she heard, and from the testy response she sensed that her mother-in-law was truly recovered after her illness. She was greeted by the kind of restlessness that told of someone who was tired of illness and was anxious not to put up with any more fussing.

'Please help me with this necklace, Cherry,' she was commanded. 'I'm having difficulty with the clasp. And then you can tell me what's been happening to Gerard. I saw him out of my window this morning, and he looks the worse for wear. Has the man been in a fight?'

Cherry's hands shook slightly as she fastened the necklace for Lady Elspeth, giving her a moment to get her thoughts together.

'I really don't know, Ma'am. I thought he looked a little shaken myself, and I thought perhaps he'd had a fall,' she said cagily.

'Fiddlesticks! He might be a stiff-necked butler, but he's a man for all that. My guess is that he's got into some kind of ruckus. And for goodness' sake stop calling me Ma'am. You're not my servant.'

In the small silence that followed, Cherry drew in her breath. It was the first time since that dreadful day when she had been summoned to join Lance in the drawing room where they would confront his parents with the news that he wanted to marry her, that such words had been uttered. Cherry was no longer a servant, even though, according to Paula, it would see hell freeze before Lady Elspeth ever acknowledged as much. But amazingly, here was that day.

'I'm sorry, Lady Elspeth,' she choked.

The lady didn't answer for a few seconds. It was as though her own words had taken her by surprise as much as they had Cherry.

'It seems we both have some adjustments to make,' she said at last. 'I have to confess that I never thought this ill-matched marriage between you and my son would last, and God knows I never approved of it, but during my illness I've seen something in you that's to be admired, and perhaps my disapproval was not altogether deserved.'

'Oh please, Lady Elspeth, there's no need to say as much,' Cherry began, hot with embarrassment at this admission, but she was waved aside.

'No, I will speak out, girl. You may have attended to my recent needs to please my son, but it takes more than that to spend so many hours with a cantankerous, sick old woman. I had plenty of time to think while I was confined to my bed, and there's a goodness in you that I never recognized before. I began to see something of what my son saw in you.'

Such outspokenness was making Cherry squirm. She almost preferred the old autocratic *shrew* to this almost-humble woman. Neither was to her taste, but at least this attitude couldn't possibly last, she thought hopefully.

'Thank you for that, Lady Elspeth,' she murmured, not looking at her.

She felt a bony hand grasp hers.

'So for my son's sake,' the voice was almost detached now, as if she was rehearsing something in a play, 'and for the sake of society, to which I must shortly return after the period of mourning for my husband is over, I would prefer it if you could bring yourself to call me Mother. I realize it will be difficult for you to say and for me to hear, but we must observe the proprieties.'

Seeing the way she avoided looking at her, Cherry's thoughts whirled.

Good God almighty! She really wants this, and not just for Lance's sake either, but she's too bloody proud to say so. And I'm too bloody proud to let her think I'm grateful for the honour.

'Then I will do my best to do as you say,' she said with as much dignity as she could muster, continuing with her own part in the charade. 'It will show unity in the family, and I know Lance will be pleased – Mother.'

Lady Elspeth inclined her head and looked away again. 'Then that's settled. Now we'll go down to the library together and look through the newspapers to see what's happening in the world. I've been so out of touch with things this last week and I know there's something afoot with these wretched miners, isn't there? One must always keep up with the times, however distasteful.'

She was almost laughable, Cherry thought, switching her thoughts as quickly as she could from anything that was too personal. And yet it was a little sad too. However serious the miners' struggle, and however awful their working lives, this woman could have no real concept of it all. But against all that, she would always give generously to whatever cause asked it of her. She was never lax in her charity donations, and for whatever reason, she had just offered a real hand of family loyalty to a girl who had once been nothing more than a lowly kitchen-maid in her employ.

Before she had time to think about it, Cherry put her arms around her and gave her a hug.

'You'll still be feeling a little weak after your time in bed, so give me your arm before we go to the library, Mother,' she said huskily, and was rewarded with the smallest of smiles.

Twelve

The telephone rang in Lance's study late that afternoon and since he wasn't there to answer it himself, Cherry went inside the room and nervously picked up the receiver. She wasn't used to taking messages from any of his well-heeled acquaintances, but she was relieved to hear Lance's voice at the other end of the line. It also gave her heart a jolt. It was an odd sensation to hear him so near, and yet so far away.

'I'm calling to let you and Mother know I'm staying at my club, Cherry. Gerard will be staying with some friends until we see how things are going down here. There's trouble brewing, but there's no need for you to worry. Just let the staff know that we'll both be away from the house for a few nights.'

'What kind of trouble?' she said at once, hardly taking in anything else.

'It's just a lot of rowdiness so far, but we've both signed on as special constables so it's best that we're close at hand should anything more serious occur. If the groups can just get themselves organized into proper rallies, no matter what the protest, it will be all the better for them.'

'And what if they don't?'

She heard the impatience in his voice now. 'Then they'll have to be brought under control until they do. Look, don't worry, and I'll be in touch again when I can.'

Before she could ask for any more details the line had gone dead, and she replaced the receiver slowly. It was just typical, she thought, fuming. Leaving her with half a tale, having to let Cook know that Gerard wouldn't be back, and that there would be one less for dinner upstairs. She shivered, wondering just what Lance had meant by there being trouble brewing. Here in Melchoir House, far from feeling secure from anything that might be happening in the city, she began to feel isolated and alone.

Lady Melchoir had retired to her bed for her afternoon sleep, and right now she felt a sudden longing for the camaraderie she had always known below stairs. She missed Cook's ranting at her and Paula for idling and gossiping and giggling when they should be getting on with scraping and cleaning and scrubbing until their hands were red raw.

Well, there was none of that now. She found herself gazing at her hands that no longer needed to do any menial tasks. They were white and slim now, a lady's hands, leaving others to do the servile tasks she had been born to do.

She shook herself angrily. What kind of an idiot was she being, when she had everything she had ever desired, a husband who loved and cherished her, and a home fit for a queen. Was nothing ever good enough?

Without thinking any more, she left the study and ran down the flights of stairs to the kitchens, where Cook and the skivvies looked up in surprise at her flustered face. They were all drinking mugs of tea, and scrambled to their feet in embarrassment at her appearance.

'For goodness' sake, sit down again, all of you,' she said in annoyance. 'If there's another cup of tea in that pot, Cook, I'd be glad of one.'

'Of course there is, Lady Melchoir,' the woman said quickly. 'One of the girls can take it up to the drawing room for you right away.'

'Don't be silly,' Cherry snapped. 'I want it now and want it here.'

It was hard to know who was more surprised – Cherry herself for snapping at Cook in a way she had never done before, or the woman herself, outraged at being addressed so in front of the sniggering skivvies.

'I'm sorry, that was rude of me,' she forced herself to say. 'Just pour me the tea, please Cook, and I'll tell you what I've come to say. And if you've got a slice of your best Madeira cake to go with it, I wouldn't say no.'

There was always cake. She had never known a time when there wasn't cake. They might be servants below stairs, but they always ate well. For a moment she wondered how it would be if food supplies dwindled to nothing because of this strike, and there was no longer the basics to feed a family and their servants.

But it was nonsense to think that way, and she brushed aside the uneasy thought.

She hardly noticed Cook ordering the skivvies out of the kitchen to get on with their work, until the mug of tea was placed in front of her, together with a large slice of Madeira cake.

'Now then, I don't think you've come down here just to pass the time of day,' Cook said shrewdly when they were alone. 'And from the flush on your face I'd guess that either the madam upstairs has been getting on your nerves or there's something up.'

Cherry gave a small laugh. 'You know me too well, Cook. As a matter of fact, it's not her ladyship. We've been getting along surprisingly well in these last few days. I wouldn't say we're bosom pals, but things are improving.'

'I wouldn't say she's got too much of a stringy bosom to be pals with,' Cook said drily. 'So if it's not her, what is it? You and your man aren't having matrimonial problems, are you?'

If it seemed incongruous for Cook to be asking her these intimate questions, neither of them seemed to notice it. They had known one another too long to stand on ceremony.

'It's this strike,' Cherry said. 'You know all about it, of course.'

'Well, unless a body's been walking around with their eyes shut for the last few months, everybody knows all about it. Mr Gerard went off to see what's what early this morning.'

'That's what I've come to see you about. Captain Lance just telephoned me to say that he and Mr Gerard have signed on as special constables and won't be coming back to the house for a few days. Captain Lance is staying at his club, and I don't know where Mr Gerard has gone.'

It seemed so natural for her to refer to Lance as Captain Lance, the way she had always done in the old days when this kitchen was her domain.

'Good for them,' Cook said with relish. 'The captain – I should say Lord Melchoir, of course – will soon deal with any rebels, and Gerard can be a tough nut when he wants to be. He got caught up in some scuffle or other a few days ago. He wouldn't say what it was all about, only that he came off the better.'

Cherry kept her eyes lowered, knowing only too well what

kind of scuffle Gerard would have got caught up in on her account.

'But doesn't it worry you that there might be fighting in the city? What good is it going to do? People might get hurt, and it's not going to give the miners any more money, is it?'

'Maybe not, but they'll know they've got the support of the rest of the community. They're not alone in their fight.'

Cherry felt exasperated by her words. Cook was a hefty woman, and there was a steely light in her eyes that said if it was seemly for a woman of her years to raise banners on the miners' behalf, she'd be marching through the streets with the rest of them.

Cherry finished her tea and slammed the mug down on the scrubbed table. 'Well, I just hope it will all get settled quickly before ordinary people get hurt. Paula's not as complacent as you seem to be about it. She's more concerned about Harold having to go on strike and with no money coming in to pay their rent. And them with a baby due to arrive at any minute.'

'No, that's not good news,' Cook agreed thoughtfully.

'Anyway, there'll be one less for dinner upstairs this evening and until I tell you any different, Cook,' Cherry said, undoubtedly ruffled now.

'I'll make a note of it, Lady Melchoir,' she was told coolly.

Cherry went out into the gardens, hoping her hot cheeks would calm down before she returned to the drawing room, feeling more unsettled than before she spoke with Cook. She had hoped for some sympathy, some support for her worries over Lance and Gerard, and for Paula and Harold too.

And instead of that, all she had felt was the divide that now existed between her and the cosy relationship she had known for years. She might have been under Cook's thumb for all that time, and more often than not got the rough edge of her tongue, but there had been a fondness there all the same. She was sad not to feel that any more.

Before she knew it she had reached the stables, where the sweet smell of hay filled her nostrils. An older groom was going about his business, nodding to her as she passed, and she glimpsed Lance's favourite horse, Noble, inside one of the stalls. He hadn't ridden into the city then, nor been driven in the limousine, which she had seen in the garage. Was this a prudent choice, in case of trouble among any roughneck rioters?

She caught her breath as the words came into her mind. What kind of person had she become, that she could think of the people in her own city in such a way? She stroked Noble's elegant head, breathing in the pungent scent of his body, and wondered where it was all going to end.

'Were you wanting something, Lady Melchoir?' the groom said, hovering behind her.

'You live near the river, don't you?' she said, not answering his question. 'What was it like down there this morning?'

The man shrugged. 'There was plenty of shouting and arguments breaking out among rival gangs armed with placards and the like, getting ready to march into Queen's Square and the Centre. They didn't seem to know what they were doing, if you ask me. I daresay there were a few other things as well as placards ready to be chucked about in case things get rough. Some of them will use any excuse to have a bit of a fight. It's best to keep away if you ask me, Ma'am.'

'What about transport? Has it all stopped?'

'I didn't hear no trains, but there's still buses running, and I heard that some chap was setting up a ferry service across the river for passengers and cars for them who've still got things to do.'

'Are you the only groom here today?' Cherry said suddenly, alarmed by all he was telling her.

'Oh, the young bucks have gone to join the rallies. You can't blame 'em for joining in a bit of excitement, but I daresay it'll all fizzle out as quickly as it's begun.'

'I hope you're right.'

Cherry left him, more uneasy than before. She had no doubt that with his military skills Lance would be in the thick of it all, organizing and trying to keep the rallies in order. Gerard would be flexing his muscles too . . . and another name flashed into her mind. Brian wouldn't miss the opportunity to get into a fight, for whatever reason, and she prayed that their paths wouldn't cross.

By the time she went back indoors it was to find Lady Elspeth in the drawing room, a look of annoyance on her face.

'Have you seen the state of this newspaper?' she began. 'There are barely enough pages in it to warrant its publication, and it tells you nothing.'

'I think we're lucky to get a newspaper at all, since it's possible that production may stop altogether until this strike is over – and with no trains to bring the nationals from London,' Cherry added. 'We'll have to rely on the wireless for news, and only then, with what they're allowed to tell us.'

'Well, that's just an added nuisance, isn't it? It's bad enough that we're told very little of what's going on, without putting half the country's businesses out of action. And the wireless announcements are always evasive. Really, don't they think we have a right to know what's happening in our own country?'

Cherry just managed to hold her tongue at this regal outburst. Since when did the likes of her ladyship ever take such an interest in the country's business? Come to that when did she last go on a train – if ever?

'And where's Lance?' his mother went on irritably. 'I haven't seen him all day, and I thought he might have spent a little time with his mother, since I've only recently recovered from my chill.'

Oh Lord, this was it now. Cherry spoke as lightly as she could, feeling as though she seemed to be forever repeating the same words.

'He went out quite early today, and he telephoned while you were having your rest to say he would be spending a few nights at his club.'

'What on earth for? Have you two been having words?'

'No, it's nothing like that, Mother.' She forced herself to say the word as naturally as she could as she smiled. 'He and Gerard have gone down to the city to see what's happening, and they've signed on as special constables until any trouble has been settled.'

The lady's face was a picture, and she almost spluttered in her outrage.

'*Special constables?* I never heard of such a thing. It may be all right for the lower orders to join such an organization, but it's out of the question for a gentleman in my son's position. It's so undignified!'

Cherry wanted to laugh out loud at the absurdity of her remark until she saw that Lady Elspeth really believed every word she said. She was so out of touch with everything that wasn't taken care of for her, that she had no idea how the rest of the world lived.

'I'm sure they'll be grateful to have someone with Lance's experience in the military in case there's a need for crowd control,' she said. 'I'm proud of him for volunteering, and Gerard too.'

Lady Elspeth looked away for a moment.

'You don't really think there's any danger in all this, do you?'

'Oh, I shouldn't think so,' Cherry said hastily. 'I'm sure there will simply be orderly demonstrations, that's all.'

She kept her fingers crossed as she spoke, since she had no idea at all just how ugly the scenes might become. And the thought of Lance in the middle of it sent a wave of fear running through her for the first time.

'Anyway, it's London where the biggest marches will be,' she went on. 'The protesters will be badgering the government to help the poor miners, not deprive them of their livelihood, and there's not much we can do in the provinces except give them what support we can.'

'I didn't realize you were such an anarchist, Cherry.'

'I'm not sure what that means, but I believe in standing up for your rights and helping folk who are worse off than yourself.'

She wasn't sure if she was being censured, either, but apparently not when her mother-in-law leaned over and patted her hand.

'Then you and I are in agreement about that, at least. I have my own charities that I support, but I have never seen the need to go out and march for them. Now then, why don't we forget all about it and send down for some tea? I'm parched after my afternoon sleep.'

Cherry felt as though she would be awash with tea soon, but it was a ritual the lady liked to observe, and she felt obliged to go along with it. Only this time, she rang the bell and a girl arrived a short while later with a tray containing a silver teapot, milk jug and sugar basin, two china cups and saucers and a plate of biscuits. Very civilized, she couldn't help thinking, and a world away from the heavy mug of tea she had drunk with Cook earlier.

It was going to be a long evening without Lance being at

home, and over dinner the conversation was somehow stilted and forced between the two ladies, until Lady Elspeth said she was going to retire early as she had a headache.

'Then I shall have a walk around the gardens before bedtime,' Cherry told her, relieved to be alone.

But once outside, wearing a light coat against the early evening chill, she was aware of an eerie silence over the city. There would be buses running, according to the groom, but not that many, and there were no trains. From this high over the city, the sounds of cars were muted unless they were coming this way. It was as though the entire city was holding its breath . . . but who knew what it might be like down below, where the rioters might be in full flow and bringing danger and mayhem to those who tried to control them?

She wouldn't think of that. It did no good to let her imagination run away with her, but nor could she think about turning in. Her mind was too active, too restless, and after a little hesitation, she strode away from the estate to the edge of the Downs, where she could look over the railings at the silver thread of the river far below, where some enterprising man was apparently starting up a ferry service for those needing to get from one side to the other.

She wondered where Lance was right now, where Gerard was, and where her brother was too. She wondered if Paula's husband had joined some of the marchers and if they would all somehow be caught up in whatever conflagration occurred. She wondered just how long this strike would go on, and whether it would be days, weeks, months . . .

The sound of men's voices told her she was no longer alone. It was getting dark, and it wasn't wise for a lady to be out alone at night. Once, she and Paula would have had no such fears, but things were different now, and it wasn't right for Lady Melchoir to be wandering out alone at night. She wrapped her coat around her more securely and made her way back to the house, but she had made up her mind about something.

Tomorrow she would walk down to Paula's house and see that she was all right. If Harold was doing what he thought of as his patriotic duty she might even suggest that Paula came back to Melchoir House for safety, and to stay there until the strike was over. She shouldn't be in that little house alone with the baby's birth imminent.

Once she had made that decision, she went indoors with a lighter heart.

But it was impossible to sleep. Since their marriage, she had never spent a night without Lance's arms around her. She missed his warmth and the familiar feel of his body. She missed feeling his rhythmic breath on her neck as they slept snuggled together like spoons in a box as she had once told him to his amusement. She reached out her hand to feel the cold side of the bed where he usually lay, and cuddled his pillow into her until she finally slept.

Next morning, she left a note for Lady Elspeth in the drawing room to say she would be out for a while, knowing the lady wouldn't see it until much later. By then, Cherry would have walked through the city to Paula's house, and hopefully, persuaded her to come back with her. It had seemed such a good idea last night, but now she realized how far it was for Paula to walk in her condition. They would have to make several stops at a couple of tearooms, to give her friend time to rest.

She decided to wear something more drab and ordinary than her normal attire. Somewhere in the back of her wardrobe was one of her work dresses that she hadn't quite been able to throw away, and she donned it now. It fitted a little more snugly than of old, but there was no sense in stirring up more trouble among folk who might very well see her as a do-gooder in her fine clothes when they were bent on rebel-rousing on account of the miners' pay.

She looked at herself in her bedroom mirror, and apart from the burnished shine on her hair that told of regular attendance, and her pale hands, she could easily have passed for the kitchen-maid she once was. She rammed a hat on her head, satisfied with her changed appearance, and slipped quietly out of the house without anyone seeing her.

The nearer she got to the city centre, the noisier it became. Not with the normal noise of traffic and tooting car horns, although there were still a few of those, but with bellowing and shouting and in some cases, raucous singing. There were

occasional buses trying to get through the crowds, but no trams
or taxis that she could see, and people were pushing and jostling
one another in their efforts to make their voices heard. And
this was only the beginning, Cherry thought fearfully. Who
knew how long it was going to last, or what damage it was
going to do to people and property? She kept her head down
as she hurried through the side streets until she reached Paula's
road, hammering on the door until it opened, and she almost
fell inside.

'Good God, you frightened me half to death. What are you
doing here?' Paula said, startled. 'And why are you dressed like
that?'

'It's hell out there,' Cherry gasped. 'Everybody seems to have
gone mad, and you'd be hard put to make sense of what any of
them are shouting. I came to see if you're all right.'

She paused abruptly, since it seemed that of the two of them,
Paula was the calmest. But Paula hadn't had to force her way
through shrieking hotheads.

'Of course I'm all right. You're the one who looks as if she's
been pulled through a hedge backwards.'

'Well, if that's all the thanks I'm going to get, I wish I'd never
bothered,' Cherry said angrily. 'Aren't you anxious at being here
all alone?'

'I'm not alone. Harold's upstairs having a wash, but he's
going out shortly to join his workmates in a rally. They've
arranged to start it at midday when they can all get lined up
together. Harold says there's safety in numbers, and they'll
continue rallying until they get the result they want. All night,
if need be.'

And how pointless would that be? Harold was still organizing her life as well as his own, thought Cherry. But lucky for
her that he took such good care of her. As for the result they
wanted, it wasn't up to a bunch of railway workers, or any of
the other crackpots storming through the streets just to make
their voices heard. It was up to the bloody government as always.
And despite Paula's brave words, Cherry could see the anxiety
in her eyes, and from the size of her now, she was almost ready
to pop.

'Look, why don't you come back to Melchoir House with me,

Paula? Stay for a few days. At least until all this fuss is over,' she said persuasively.

'Good God Almighty, what would I do there?' Paula said, starting to laugh. 'Cook won't want me cluttering up her kitchen in my state of health! She'll say I'm making the place look untidy.'

'I wasn't suggesting that you spend your time in the kitchen. Come back to my rooms and have a bit of comfort.'

She wasn't sure if this was the right thing to say, or if Paula might think she was implying that Harold couldn't provide for her and the coming baby. But she had said it now, and this was no time to stand on her high horse.

'Please, Paula,' she went on, catching hold of her hand. 'I'm thinking of your welfare and the baby's too. What will you do if it starts to arrive and Harold's not around, especially if he's out all night?'

'The same as I'd do if he was at work, of course,' Paula said tartly. 'I don't know much, but I do know that babies don't get born in five minutes, and I'd go down the road to fetch the midwife.'

Cherry resisted the urge to stamp her feet, recognizing that other tactics were going to be needed.

'Do you remember when we were young girls, and we hoped we would have our babies together? That's never going to happen now, but at least I could be by your side when yours is born. I could take care of you, Paula, and you'd have your baby in comfort. It would be just you and me, anyway, as Lance is away at his club.'

She didn't add that he was also a special constable, but as if to add weight to her words, they heard the sound of shouting in the street outside, and through the window they could see a gang of men marching with banners on their way to the Centre. Paula visibly shivered, and while she was still dithering, Harold came down the stairs, clearly having heard what was going on. He took his wife's hand in his and brought it to his lips.

'There's a lot of sense in what Cherry says, sweetheart. Why don't you do as she suggests? I'll keep the home fires burning here, and I daresay there'll be no problem in me coming to see how you are whenever I can?'

'Of course not,' Cherry said quickly. 'You'd be very welcome.'

Lance wouldn't be there for the time being, and she was deliberately blotting out the fact that Lady Elspeth would. But she was the lady of the house now, and if she wanted a friend to visit, then she would bally well invite her.

'Well, the midwife did say she thought I was never going to last out my time,' Paula said weakly. 'But what do you really think about it, Harold? You know I wanted to have our baby in our own house.'

'I think it will be far better if the baby comes where you can be properly looked after,' he said.

Paula gave a sudden gasp. 'We're forgetting something else, aren't we? What about her high-and-mighty ladyship? She might have come round to the fact that you're installed as Lance's wife now, but she won't take kindly to another kitchen-maid muscling in on her territory.'

'But you're not a kitchen-maid now, you ninny. You're a respectable married woman with a home of her own, same as me, and you'll be there as my guest. Besides,' she added, with her chin in the air, 'what I say goes.'

Paula gave a nervous giggle. 'Blimey, Cherry, you can put on airs with the best of them now, can't you?'

Harold gave a low chuckle, shrugging into his coat and clearly wanting to get away. 'You always said as much, didn't you, love? Now, you just go and put a few things together and don't worry about me, and I'll see you when I can.'

He kissed her soundly and then he was gone.

'He's just like all of them. He can't wait to get into the fray,' Paula said. 'And I don't really want to be alone here fretting over him every minute he's gone. So all right then. If you're sure.'

Cherry wasted no more time, bundling her upstairs and putting clothes into a bag, including the small bag of things that were ready for the baby's arrival. And then they closed the door behind them and began the long walk through the city and up the hills to Melchoir House. After a very short while it was clear it was becoming a struggle for Paula and then they saw the welcome sight of a bus trundling their way.

'Quick,' Cherry said. 'It'll take us part of the way at least.'

'Don't tell me to be quick! I'm waddling like a duck now, in
case you hadn't noticed, and I'm not sure the blooming bus is
going to stop, anyway.'

The crowds that were milling about the streets had the same
idea. It wasn't clear if any of them wanted to get on, or if they
were trying to stop it going about its business. But Cherry wasn't
going to be deterred. She pushed through the militant men, and
almost dragged Paula along behind her.

'Make way for a lady in a delicate condition, unless any of
you men fancy acting like midwives here and now,' she shouted,
ignoring Paula's choking embarrassment.

Those nearest to the bus parted hastily, and she almost flung
Paula on to it and climbed on behind her with the bags, to flop
down beside her.

'This will take us up to the Downs, and we can walk from
there. There are plenty of benches about where we can have
a few stops on the way, and there's no hurry now that we're
this far.'

She eyed Paula warily. She was quiet now, and she had
gone very pale, and it probably wasn't a very good idea to haul
a woman about who was so near to giving birth. But neither
would it have been a good idea to leave her in that little house
all alone.

'Here, are you all right, duck?' A middle-aged woman peered
down at her. 'You should be indoors in your condition.'

'That's where we're going,' Cherry snapped.

The woman raised her eyebrows, looking them both up and
down in a manner that said they were probably no better than
they should be in their working clothes, and with one of them
who'd got herself in the family way. Cherry glared at her and
she went away muttering to the front of the bus.

'*Are* you all right, Paula?' she said urgently.

'I think so. My back aches something awful and I feel as if
I've wet myself with all that rushing about.'

'Oh my God, you know what that means, don't you?'

Paula began to laugh hysterically. 'Don't be daft. Whoever heard
of a baby being born on the seat of a bus? I told you, it takes
more than five minutes!'

But the look in her eyes was young and scared now, and they

both knew that the sooner they got to Melchoir House, the better it was going to be. And how was Lady fusspot Elspeth going to react when it was highly likely that it probably wasn't just going to be one visitor taking up residence in her pristine mansion, but two?

Thirteen

The bus had several stops to make before it got anywhere near the Downs, and by then Paula was babbling that her back had stopped aching, and she thought it was all the excitement that had made her feel as if she'd wet herself. She'd also begun fretting over the things she should be doing at home that day.

'I think it was a false alarm,' she muttered now. 'The midwife said I may get a few twinges and odd feelings in the last weeks before the baby's due, like a sort of practice run.'

'I flipping well hope that's what it was then,' Cherry said. 'Imagine having to give the place of birth as on the back seat of a bus!'

'You worry too much,' Paula said with a grin.

She was starting to annoy Cherry with her apparent control of the situation. 'Well, somebody's got to worry about you,' she snapped.

'I've got Harold for that.'

Cherry stared ahead out of the bus window, resisting the urge to snap back. Good God, before long they'd be in the middle of a headlong squabble, and that wasn't what she had gone through crowds of protesters to do. She'd seen herself as a bit of a heroine, if the truth were told, rescuing the downtrodden friend and taking her to a place of safety. But seeing the steely look in Paula's eyes now, she knew she had better get rid of that notion pretty fast, or Paula would be just as likely to get on the next bus back home again.

She heard a soft giggle come from the other seat.

'This is a bit more like it, isn't it, kid? You and me having a barney before we get back to the house for a bit more tongue pie from Cook for larking about instead of getting on with our work and bringing home the bacon.'

Cherry laughed too, her brief resentment fizzling out.

'Instead of that, we'll be facing disapproval from her glorious ladyship when she sees what I'm bringing home.'

'You mean she doesn't know?' Paula squeaked.

'She doesn't get up very early since she had her chill. I left her a note to say I was going out, but I didn't say where I was going.'

'Well, that's just dandy, isn't it? I knew this was all a big mistake!'

'Oh, don't get your knickers in a tangle. She spends her days in her own rooms, and me and Lance have our own. There's no need for us to even see one another if we don't want to. Except that I shall have to check that she's all right, of course, as a dutiful daughter-in-law should.'

It sounded such a clinical way for a family to live, and nothing like the rough and tumble of the family life she had once known long ago, in the little house with her mother and father, her brother and herself. She swallowed, blotting out those images, and she kept her voice bland, aware of Paula's growing unease.

'You won't be doing yourself much good with her when she sees me, will you?' she muttered. 'You shouldn't have done this, Cherry.'

'Don't be so blooming daft,' Cherry said roughly. 'The day when I can't help an old friend will be the day when I've really turned into one of them. And I'm not ready for that yet!'

'And I'm not sure I'm ready for Lady high-and-mighty to see me as another charity case either!'

Once off the bus, they were practically trudging along now, she realized, as Paula's steps dragged more and more. This was really exhausting her, she realized, and neither temper was improving as they took another rest on the nearest bench. They didn't have that much farther to go, but every step seemed an effort for Paula. At least there were no marchers or protesters in this part of the city, and not too many people around either. Except one, walking elegantly in their direction with a little dog that minced its feet as prettily as its owner.

'Oh no,' Cherry groaned.

'What is it?' Paula said without much interest.

Before she could reply the stranger had reached them. Except that she was no stranger to Cherry, who sat with her head bent low with her hat shielding her face in the hope that she wouldn't be recognized. With any luck the young lady wouldn't give the time of day to two young women dressed as servants. But she was forgetting Paula's obvious late stages of pregnancy.

'Are you in some kind of trouble?' they heard the young lady say awkwardly. 'Do you need any assistance?'

There was no option now but to look up.

'Good Lord, Cherry! What on earth are you doing?'

'Good afternoon, Cynthia,' she said, as coolly as she could, considering how sickly her heart was hammering. 'This is my friend, Paula, and she's coming to stay at Melchoir House for a few days until the disturbances die down.'

It was highly unlikely that the Honourable Cynthia Hetherington would recognize Paula as a previous kitchen-maid from Melchoir House. The toffs didn't usually recognize servants. They were simply there to wait on them and to give them a comfortable life. But whether she guessed the truth or not, Cynthia was nothing if not diplomatic, and she had also developed a strange fondness for Cherry, and had championed their cause when Lance fell for her.

'You look as if you could do with a bit more help,' she went on, not pursuing the fact that Cherry was dressed in the most extraordinary outfit for the wife of a Lord. But that didn't matter now. The other girl looked in a distressed way, and not likely to turn away another helping hand.

Without waiting for an answer she offered her arm to help Paula, who struggled up, hot with embarrassment, and making the slightly hysterical comment that she never thought whales lived on land until now. The minute she had said it, her face turned scarlet, but Cynthia laughed out loud, and between them and the obediently mincing dog, she and Cherry guided the pregnant girl the last part of the way to Melchoir House.

'Shall I see you inside, or will you be able to manage now?' she said.

'We'll manage fine, thank you, Cynthia,' Cherry told her, just as awkward as Paula now and praying that she would go before Lady Elspeth happened to look out of an upstairs window and saw the three of them turning up like a group of mismatched *Three Musketeers.*

'Good luck with the new arrival when it comes,' she said to Paula.

'Well, that's a relief,' Paula said, blowing out her cheeks the minute Cynthia had gone. 'She made me feel all fingers and thumbs, and I don't know how you could talk to her so naturally, with her being an Honourable and all.'

'She's just a person, same as you and me, that's why. Now, come on, let's get you indoors and I'll show you which room you can have.'

'I don't want anywhere posh. If I've got to stay I'd far rather have something near our old rooms. I mean it, Cherry.'

Cherry was exasperated. 'Good God, Paula, I can't put you in one of the attic rooms in the servants' quarters, can I?'

'Well, I'm not going to be anywhere near her Ladyship and that's flat. I'd rather go home again. In fact I wish I'd stuck to my guns and stayed there.'

Cherry could see she was near to tears, but she was also worn out, and then, to her wild relief as they neared the house, a motherly figure appeared from one of the side doors to throw some crumbs out for the birds, standing with her mouth open and gaping at them both.

'Bless my soul, I thought I was seeing a couple of ghosts for a minute,' Cook exclaimed. 'Except that one of you's a bit large for a ghost, if I may say so. What are you doing here, Paula, and you wearing such an unsuitable outfit, your ladyship?'

Cherry wasn't sure whether she wanted to laugh or cry. It was concern and censure all at the same time. But before either of them could answer, Cook had taken charge, as always.

'Well, don't just stand there. Come inside and sit down and have a cup of tea or a drop of brandy if you feel the need. My girls have gone down to the market to see what's what, so we can talk in private.'

'I'd love a cup of tea, Cook,' Paula said weakly.

The woman didn't ask any more questions until the three of them were sitting at the scrubbed kitchen table as they had done so many times before, and steaming mugs of tea were put in front of them. And then the questions and answers came flooding out.

'And you really think you'll be better staying here in case the babby comes while your man is out patrolling the streets, do you?' Cook said finally.

'Don't you, Cook?' Cherry demanded, not expecting this implied criticism.

Cook shrugged. 'It's not for me to interfere, but I'd say a body's always better in her own home than in somebody else's, with all her own things around her and with her man always somewhere on hand.'

'That's what I think, and it's an awful long way for Harold to have to keep coming up to Clifton to check up on me,' Paula admitted.

'Well, if that's all the thanks I'm going to wish I hadn't bothered,' Cherry began indignantly.

Cook turned on her. 'Wouldn't you always rather be in your own bed when you were feeling poorly? And this poor dab looks as though that's where she should be. I bet you've got plenty of neighbourly help there.'

'The midwife only lives along the road from us, and she was going to look in on me every couple of days, and so were my neighbours,' Paula told her, as if Cherry wasn't there. 'I haven't even told any of them where I've gone.'

'If you'll take my advice, my girl, you'll get a few hours' kip upstairs, and then think about going back home. Home's best, when all's said and done.'

Cherry leapt to her feet, eyes blazing, her voice oozing sarcasm. 'Thank you for your opinion, Cook. I was going to suggest that Paula takes a rest myself, and we'll have some hot soup sent up to my rooms in an hour, please. Then I'm sure Paula can make up her own mind what she wants to do.'

'Well, when she's made it up, I daresay one of the grooms will walk her back to a bus stop, or even take her all the way,' Cook said, not giving an inch. 'I've seen a few babbies come into the world in my time, and I don't reckon this one's due just yet, for all the way things look. How long is it meant to be, duck?'

'About three weeks,' Paula mumbled.

'And there's no hurrying nature. It'll come when it's ready and not before.'

Cherry almost bundled Paula up the stairs to her own quarters, fuming at the way Cook had seemed to undermine her. Treating them almost the way she used to when they were skivvies. But catching sight of her dishevelled appearance in the long mirrors in one of the guest bedrooms, her face flushed and angry, and still wearing her old working clothes, she could hardly blame her.

'Paula, you have a lie down,' she told her. 'I must look in on Lady Elspeth before I do anything else, but I'd better change my clothes first, or she'll have a fit if she sees me looking like this.'

To her added fury, Paula was giggling now.

'Blimey, Cherry, I never heard you go on at Cook like that before. You were really the lady of the manor. The Honourable Cynthia-whatsit would have been proud of you.'

Cherry bit her lip. 'I don't normally pull rank, but she annoyed me, telling you you'd be better off at home, when you and Harold both agreed you should come here.'

She paused when the other girl didn't answer. By now she had sunk down on the bed on her back, her hands protectively over the mound of her belly, and looking as though she'd never be able to get off the bed again.

'She was right though, Cherry,' Paula said, not looking at her. 'I don't belong here any more. All these fripperies and soft living – well, it's very nice, and I'm sure you're used to it now, but it's not for me. It's not the home that me and Harold have made together. And that's where I should be. That's where I *want* to be,' she finished, catching her breath. 'So thank you for all you've done, Cherry, but when we've had our soup, I'm going home where I belong, with or without one of the grooms to take me.'

'I think you're mad!'

'And I think you're my best friend, and you'll do as I ask.'

Cherry stared down at her for a long moment, seeing the determination in her eyes, no longer the eyes of the scared little kitchen-maid but a married woman who knew what she wanted. She was no longer the pliable young friend hanging on to Cherry's coat-tails either. She had a mind and a will of her own.

'Have a kip then, Paula, and I'll see you in a little while,' she said in a choked voice, and left her to it.

'Are you sure Lance won't be joining us for dinner?' Lady Elspeth asked her a short time later, when she had reverted to looking her usual self, and had visited her mother-in-law in her sitting room.

'Quite sure. I don't know how long this strike will continue, but I went for a walk this morning out of curiosity,' she said, 'and there are plenty of marchers and protesters in the city. I'm sure he and Gerard will attend to their duties as they said, and Lance will be staying at his club.'

'Then let us hope it will all be resolved very soon.'

She had no idea, Cherry thought. Providing everything continued as usual in her own little circle, the way the rest of the world lived was no concern of hers. And yet that was not altogether fair. Like most ladies of her ilk, Lady Elspeth did what she could for her own charities – as long as she didn't have to come into contact with any of them.

'You're looking a little out of sorts today, Cherry. I hope you're not sickening for something,' she went on.

'I don't think so. It's probably just being anxious about Lance.'

She could hardly say it was more likely from rushing about trying to get Paula settled, and having a bit of a set-to with Cook about it!

'Is there nothing else on your mind? A healthy young married woman can often have other anxieties, and I'm always ready to listen to them, my dear, however delicate they may be.'

It suddenly dawned on Cherry what she was getting at. Good God! Her mother-in-law was actually hinting that she might be in the family way! But was that faint flush on the lady's parchment cheeks because the thought might be pleasing – or because she still had reservations about an ex-kitchen-maid being the mother of her grandchild?

'I'm perfectly fine, thank you,' she muttered. 'Now, is there anything I can get you, Mother?'

It was still an effort to say the word, but she forced herself to do so.

'Nothing at all. Lady Hetherington is calling on me this afternoon, and you're welcome to join us for afternoon tea if you wish.'

'Thank you, but I'll probably leave you two ladies to your own conversation. I still have a shawl to finish knitting, and the time for Paula's confinement is getting nearer,' Cherry said hastily.

Cynthia was always amiable, but her mother was a different matter. She was courteous enough, but Cherry was quite sure that none of the older members of Lady Elspeth's circle had quite come to terms with Lance's choice of wife.

She immediately realized she shouldn't have mentioned Paula's shawl.

'Ah yes, your little friend,' Lady Elspeth said. 'She must be nearing her time now.'

'A few weeks more,' Cherry muttered.

And please don't ask if I've seen her lately . . .

To her wild relief one of the maids appeared with a query for her mother-in-law, and she quickly excused herself before she could be quizzed any further. It was ridiculous how a little act of kindness could descend into the need for little white lies. Not that she had said anything that wasn't true, she had simply avoided adding to it.

She looked in on Paula who was sleeping peacefully, and she couldn't resist a grin as she saw how the great belly moved up and down with her deep breathing. What must it be like, she wondered, to have that extra weight to lug around, and know that it was a living, breathing being inside you? For a few seconds, she stood without moving, feeling the most enormous sense of envy for the future that Paula and Harold were going to have with their baby.

Paula stirred slightly, and Cherry turned and tiptoed out of the room, her throat closing, and a slight sense of panic taking over. She and Lance had been married for two years now, with no sign of a baby. They were passionate lovers, and somewhere in the back of her mind was the nagging thought that maybe they had displeased whatever gods were looking down on them by their earlier deceit.

It was a sin to have let his parents think she was expecting, when she wasn't, in order to get their consent to their marriage. It was a sin to have lied about something so fundamental. Who knew whether their punishment was for her to remain barren? It wasn't the first time she had thought of it, and seeing Paula so eagerly awaiting her own baby only brought it home to her more. But then common sense rushed in. Paula hadn't fallen for a baby at the drop of a hat, either. She and Harold had been married for quite a while before it happened, so why should she and Lance be any different?

Contrary to her eagerness to get Paula to Melchoir House to look after her she was just as anxious now for Paula to wake up, for the soup to arrive that she had ordered, and then to get Paula out of here. Before any of that could happen, she went down to the stables to see about one of the grooms escorting her safely home. One of the younger ones was almost too ready to do it.

'You will come back, won't you, Jed?' she said suspiciously. 'You're not going to use this as an excuse to join in any of the rallies, are you? You've got work to do here, and Lord Melchoir won't be pleased if he finds you're neglecting the horses.'

'Oh, I'll be back, Ma'am, don't you worry. I might take the long way round,' he added cheekily, 'but I won't let you down.'

'Then be ready when I bring the young lady out here,' she said.

He was new, so he wouldn't recognize Paula from her previous employment here, and the head groom would be discreet enough not to say anything, she was sure. Anyway, what did it matter if he did? Paula was her friend, and as such, she deserved every consideration.

She was already awake when Cherry went back to the guest room, having somehow rolled herself off the bed, and was standing at the window, gazing out.

'Everything looks different from up here, doesn't it?' she said in greeting. 'Our attic window was so high up you couldn't see much out of it, anyway, but you can see for miles from here. We don't have a view from our house, and we get a lot of smuts and noise from the railway, but I wouldn't change it,' she added with a smile.

'I can tell,' Cherry said. 'Come along to the sitting room then, and I'll ring down for Cook to send up that hot soup. I daresay you're ready for it after all that walking.'

'I'm starving and I could eat a horse. I'm eating for two, you know,' she said, patting her stomach.

'Are you sure there's only one in there? It looks more like a football team! And by the way,' she went on, as casually as she could, 'Jed, one of the grooms, is going to walk you home whenever you're ready. If you're sure.'

'Quite sure. And I don't mean to sound ungrateful, Cherry, but I know this is the right thing for me.'

She linked her arm through Cherry's and as they walked along the corridor to the sitting room, they were perfectly at ease with one another again. Ten minutes later, a tray of soup and bread was brought up and when they had eaten, it was clear that Paula was anxious to leave.

'I don't want to risk her ladyship seeing me and causing you any trouble,' she said, and they both knew it was the feeblest of excuses.

'All right, we'll go down to the stables and find Jed. I'll come and see you again in a few days, Paula, but promise me you'll take care of yourself, and the minute anything starts to happen, you let me know.'

'Of course I will. You're going to be an honorary auntie, aren't you?'

They gave each other an involuntary hug, then broke away awkwardly, to bustle about getting Paula's bags together again.

In no time at all, it seemed she was ready to go, and Cherry watched her leave with the young groom, who promised to take good care of her, to get her on to a bus as far as it went, and then take her right to her door.

And then she was alone, in what suddenly seemed like a great mausoleum of a house, without Lance, and with time on her hands. For a while she had been busy, the way she had always been busy in her past life, and now she had nothing to do. Getting Paula here had taken up a major part of the day and now it was all so quiet, when down in the city there would be chaos and rioting – and Lance was somewhere in the middle of it all. She feared for him, and she wandered about for what seemed like hours, but in reality was less than one, trying to find something to do to take her mind off what might be happening elsewhere. She tried to continue knitting Paula's shawl, but had to give it up in despair, completely unable to concentrate.

She jumped as she heard a tap on her sitting-room door a little later, and she looked up to see Lady Elspeth standing there.

'Has your friend gone?' she said.

Cherry's tongue seemed to stick to the roof of her mouth as her mother-in-law came into the room and gave a wry smile.

'My dear, I wasn't born yesterday. I could see that something was troubling you, and when I saw Cook to request something light

for my dinner menu this evening, it all came out about your bringing
your friend here for safety for a while, and how she changed her
mind. It must have been a blow to you.'

To her horror, Cherry burst into tears. The last thing she
expected was Lady Elspeth's understanding, but for the second
time that day she found herself clasped to someone's bosom.

'I wanted to care for her, but she had her own ideas,' she
sobbed. 'She wanted to be in her own home with her husband.'

'Well, that's perfectly natural, but it's nothing for you to feel
upset about, Cherry, and you shouldn't feel slighted. You did what
you thought was a kindness, but we all have to do what we think
is right in the end, don't we?'

'I suppose so,' Cherry sniffed, wondering how she could
decently extricate herself from this embarrassing embrace. But
Lady Elspeth did it for her.

'Now dry your eyes, and you're to come along and say hello
to Lady Hetherington and take tea with us, and I won't take no
for an answer. In half an hour, Cherry.'

She was her old imperial self again, but there was a softness
in her eyes that she couldn't quite disguise. It was almost – almost
as if she *wanted* to welcome this upstart daughter-in-law into her
circle of friends. How odd.

But with an insight she had never acknowledged before, Cherry
realized that for all her starchy exterior maybe she was lonely
too, and in her autocratic way, she had difficulty in showing it,
or even admitting it. But her husband was dead, and she was
probably having a hard time readjusting herself to the life of
widowhood. She needed friends, even though she rarely opened
her heart to those who weren't already close to her. Maybe she
needed a daughter-in-law too.

'I'll be there,' Cherry said gently.

And after all, it wasn't the ordeal she had expected it to be.
Cherry wondered suspiciously if Lady Hetherington had had a
talking-to from her forthright and progressive daughter, and
accepted that this was the daughter-in-law of her dear friend, so
she might as well accept it. Whatever the reason, the afternoon
passed off amicably, and when later Cherry went anxiously down
to the stables to find Jed, it was to hear that Paula had got home

safely. A bus had taken them most of the way until it was blocked by the crowds, and they walked the rest of the way without incident.

'What was the mood like in the city then? Did you see any trouble?'

The lad shrugged, clearly disappointed at not being able to report anything dramatic. 'Not much. There were a few rallies and various marching bodies, but they were all kept in order by the police. It was a bit like a carnival atmosphere, except down by the waterfront, of course. Things always get more heated there, with the seamen and the roughnecks about. There were a good few scuffles and fights going on, but I didn't stay there long enough to find out.'

He'd obviously taken the long way home, as he'd hinted before, but she couldn't blame him for that. He was young and keen, but the waterfront was probably where they would send the special constables, thought Cherry, while the regular police did their job among the crowds in the Centre and Queen's Square. That was probably where Lance would be sent, and Gerard too. And where Brian 'Knuckles' O'Neill would be sure to be in the thick of it, if he was around at all. She prayed to God that he wasn't, and that he'd had the sense to keep well away from trouble and out of Bristol altogether. But when did the words Brian and good sense ever go together?

It was late that evening when the telephone rang in Lance's study. Thankfully her mother-in-law's rooms were well away from theirs, and she knew Lady Elspeth wouldn't have heard it as she sped along to answer it, closing the door behind her. She gripped the receiver tightly as she heard Lance's voice, sending up a quick prayer of thanks that he sounded the same as usual.

'I just wanted you to know that all's well, Cherry. I'm having supper at my club before turning in for a few hours, then I'm on duty again in the early hours. We've got a shift duty organized, but with any luck there won't be any trouble then. But how about you? Are you all right? And Mother?'

'Of course we are. It's you I'm worried about!'

'There's no need. Everything's under control, and we don't have the kind of disruption they're having in London where the army's been called in. There was some fighting earlier on, but nothing that we couldn't control. The usual gangs are out and about taking advantage of the situation and there's been some looting in empty houses as might be expected and a few shop windows broken.'

Cherry had a sinking feeling in her stomach. It might have been expected to Lance, but this was something that hadn't occurred to her.

'You will be careful, won't you, Lance?'

'With you to come home to, I'm always careful, Cherry-ripe,' he said, his voice softening. 'Now, go to bed and don't worry about me, and I'll be in touch again when I can.'

The line went dead, and she put down the receiver with shaking fingers. She did as he said and went to bed, knowing she wouldn't sleep. How could she, wondering just what and who was out there, and just how much danger Lance was in? But she couldn't ignore the fact that just like all men, including Jed the young groom, there had been a certain excitement in his voice, she thought bitterly. They all thrived on danger, while it was the women left at home who bore all the anxiety.

Fourteen

Several days later, after his regular nightly phone call home, Lance was well aware that he hadn't told Cherry everything, and nor was there really any need for him to remain at his club. He hadn't told her that that very night he'd come across her brother and a gang of roughnecks at the waterfront, and that he'd been one of the authority figures to break up the group with batons and fists. He hadn't told her that he'd seen pure hatred in the thug's eyes as he recognized Cherry's husband – or that it wasn't the first time their eyes had met.

He flexed his bruised knuckles now as he ate his cold supper at the club. Knowing he would be hardly looking his best in the exclusive environment, he'd asked for the meal to be sent to his room each night. He preferred to eat in private without curious stares from the few contemporaries who were still using the club in these troubled times. Or even worse, having to deal with questions he wasn't prepared to answer. Besides which, he could turn on the wireless while he ate, and hear whatever information was being sent out. It was always guarded and not very forthcoming, and anyone with any sense had to listen hard to get the real meaning of any news that was broadcast.

The newspapers weren't any better. You got flimsy news at best, and melodramatic, ghoulish accounts from overzealous newshounds at worst. He guessed that the government had put out orders to keep the seriousness of the situation under wraps at all costs. As if the general public didn't have a right to know what was going on in their own country, on account of those poor devils, the miners and their families. People like himself, privileged from birth, didn't know the half of it, and Lance freely admitted as much. It didn't mean that he didn't sympathize with them though, and was prepared to do what he could.

But he knew he had better turn in and get a bit of sleep while he could. He was on duty again at 2 a.m., and he turned off the wireless and settled down, well aware of the shouting and rumpus still going on outside, plus the occasional sound of splintered glass, and knew it would probably continue into the night. He wondered briefly how Gerard was faring. He had no idea where he was, nor where he was staying, and he had only glimpsed him on one occasion since the first day of the strike, but he hoped he was having a better night than he looked like getting.

He sighed heavily and tried to sleep. But even when he slept, it was to have disturbing dreams intruding. They were bad dreams, where he saw Cherry receding away from him in some kind of ghostlike state, with her brother leering and towering over her as he lured her away from him. Always the victor, dragging her down to his level, while Lance was impotent and powerless to save her from his evil clutches.

The dreams caused him to wake up in a cold sweat, as if they were some kind of omen. But he didn't believe in such things. He left that to gullible fools who saw signs in everything, while he was the hard-headed soldier who believed in logic above all things.

He had just emerged from one of those dreams, jerking awake with his hands clenched so tightly together that he had made his palms raw, when he realized the hammering was not only in his head as the result of the brandy he'd drunk to help him sleep, but on his bedroom door.

'I'm coming,' he yelled angrily, wondering why a chap couldn't get a decent bit of rest in a respectable club any more. He yanked open his door, to find Gerard standing there, fully dressed. He was only ever admitted in case of necessity on account of his status in the Melchoir household. For a moment Lance's heart leapt, and since she had figured so prominently in his dream, his thought flew at once to Cherry.

'I'm sorry, your lordship, but there's big trouble in Queen's Square, and they're asking for all hands on deck. I said I knew where to find you.'

'I'm coming,' Lance said, alert at once. Despite what might be happening in the city, his immediate feeling was relief that nothing had happened to Cherry, and he was more than thankful to get out of bed and be rid of the bizarre dreams, at least for a while.

Gerard had already gone on ahead while he shrugged into his clothes, and minutes later he was out of the club and into a chilly and starless night with dark clouds overhead and the heavy mist that shrouded the street lights turning people into ghostly shapes. He strode off towards Queen's Square, where the evidence of Gerard's words was ugly. There was hand to hand fighting now as the police tried to control an angry mob, and Lance felt the full force of a fist on his cheek as he gave punch for punch.

How long it would have continued, or how bad the outcome might have been was anybody's guess, but there was a sudden almighty crash of thunder right overhead. The heavens opened in a torrential downpour of rain, and the mob scattered. Police whistles pierced the air, and in minutes, it seemed, the Square was empty of rioters. The rain continued unabated with no semblance of stopping, and finally the patrols were told to stand down. Lance looked around for Gerard, and grabbed hold of his arm as he saw him sway.

'Are you hurt, man?'

'Just winded,' Gerard grunted. 'I'll be all right after an hour's sleep.'

'Come back to the club with me,' Lance ordered. 'At least have a comfortable bed for the night.'

The butler shook his head. 'No thank you, Sir. It wouldn't be right. A friend is putting me up until this is all over, and I'm quite comfortable there.'

'Good God man, you don't need to stand on ceremony now.'

They were both soaked to the skin as the rain hammered down, although it had become a saving grace, since it seemed the rioters had no stomach to continue their fight in such discomfort. But there was no persuading Gerard, and in the end they went their separate ways, with Lance wondering just how much longer this could go on. And if these scuffles were a sample of what was happening in London, then God help them all.

Each night he telephoned Cherry and reassured her that all was well, and that he would be home soon. But that one night seemed to be the climax of much of the local trouble, and things had definitely quietened down locally by the time the strike had gone on for more than a week. Nothing could be done here to help the plight of the miners, and some of the earlier rallying groups had simply got bored and disbanded. So much for loyalty. But by now, cars and taxis were on the roads again and food supplies hadn't really dwindled, especially with so much locally produced food in the surrounding countryside, and farmers ready and willing to do what they could.

After nine days, it was announced that the General Strike had been called off, and the country collectively breathed a sigh of relief. Nothing had been resolved, but at least the miners were no longer holding the country to ransom.

'Poor devils,' Cook observed to nobody in particular in the late afternoon. 'It's all very well for the government to say they've got everything under control now, sitting up there in London on their fat backsides, but the miners will still go hungry, and they'll still be getting a pittance in their wage packets. They should have a woman ruling the country, then you'd soon see a difference!'

The young skivvies giggled, knowing it was best not to inter-rupt her when she got up steam. But one of them couldn't resist it.

'When do you think that will be, Cook? Are you hoping for the job?'

Cook glared at her. 'You get on with your work, my girl, and don't ask such soppy questions. All I'm saying is that it's women who hold the purse strings in any household. Women know how to make the money go around, and how much is needed for the essentials, that's all. Make the head of government a woman, and you'd soon see fair play for all, and none of these strikes, neither. When did we ever go on strike in this kitchen, I'd like to know? There'd soon be uproar upstairs if we did! Now stop idling about with your mouths open and catching flies, and get on with your work.'

She turned with a start as she heard a man's voice, and put her hands to her ample bosom as Gerard came inside the kitchen.

'Well, you're a sight for sore eyes and no mistake, Mr Gerard,' she exclaimed. 'Come and sit down and let me make you a drink. You're looking a bit peaky. Are you unwell?'

'It's nothing to prevent me doing my work,' he said, brushing her concern aside. 'I'm back now, Cook, and I'm not going to waste my time telling you what's been going on for the past nine days, so don't ask. Suffice it to say there was a lot of noise and fighting, as I'm sure you know if you've sent your girls down there for supplies and for sniffing out the details. So let's just get back to some peace and normality.'

It was just the same after the war, thought Cook, when none of the returning heroes ever spoke about what had happened to them. Gerard might not consider himself a hero, but in her eyes, he was certainly that to leave his comfortable post and take up the cudgels to restrain the louts that always took advantage of such situations.

'Has his lordship returned home too?' she said instead. 'I only ask, as I'll need to know what to do about dinner this evening.'

'I'm sure you'll be informed in good time, Cook. Now, if you'll excuse me I need to wash some of the city grime from my skin and change into my usual clothes. I'll see you in a while, and then I'll have that drink.'

It was only later that she realized he hadn't told her anything of Lord Melchoir's whereabouts. It was just as well she didn't know, any more than the two women waiting anxiously for his return.

Thankful that the skirmishes were all over with no heads broken as far as he knew, Lance had left his club before returning home, and walked along the waterfront for a breath of fresh air, if that wasn't a contradictory term. The air was never too savoury here, especially later in the day, with the many ships and fishing boats jostling against one another, the aroma of seamen who had been at sea for weeks on end, and the stench of the river at low tide, when the banks were high and thick with stinking mud. But it was part of the city that he loved, and it was good to know that all was serene again.

As if to mock his own thoughts, there was a sudden uproar coming from inside one of the waterfront pubs, followed by the sounds of breaking furniture. He walked on grimly, keeping his eyes on the distant suspension bridge that spanned this river. His time as a special constable was over, and he had no wish to get involved in any minor problems between a landlord and his clients.

The next minute it was as though all hell had broken loose as a tangle of men burst through the pub doors, landing almost at his feet, so much so that it was all he could do to keep his balance. He grabbed at the pub's signpost to steady himself, not wanting to be concerned with what was going on here. But common humanity wouldn't let him ignore what the thugs were doing to the poor wretch being kicked and punched to the ground.

'Get off him,' he shouted. 'Can't you see you're killing him?'

'It's no more than the toe-rag deserves,' one of the thugs yelled back. 'He's a bloody thief and we don't want his kind around here.'

The victim had already been punched to a pulp and there was so much blood around his face now he was virtually unrecognizable. But he was still groaning so he was clearly still alive despite the pummelling, and from the way he clutched his stomach, it was clear he was more hurt by the vicious kicking.

'You don't want to concern yourself with the likes of him, young sir, and you'd do best to keep away,' a portly man shouted, who was obviously the landlord. 'If a man can't pay his way and resorts to thieving, he should be locked up. And with what he owes from previous occasions, there's not many pubs around here that'll let him through their doors. He's in debt all over the city and we're doing his debtors a favour if you ask me.'

'That's no reason to kick a man half to death,' Lance snapped. 'You should let the law deal with him.'

The word seemed to incense the thugs, who let out a stream of expletives at Lance and began kicking their victim again. For a moment he found himself wishing he hadn't handed in his baton and still wore his special constable's armband. He immediately squashed the thought. The last thing he wanted was to turn into the kind of thug he was confronted with now. In any case, it was obvious these people had no truck with the law.

'All the same, I'd say you've done enough, unless you want to have a murder on your hands,' he snapped.

Seeing that the wretch on the ground had gone quiet now, the landlord's eyes narrowed, and he put a restraining hand on one of the attackers.

'All right, that's enough. I think we've made our point, boys. Let's leave him to stew in his own juice.'

One of the thugs gave the man a last kick before they all went back inside the pub, slamming the door closed behind them. And leaving Lance wondering what the hell he was supposed to do now. He'd come down here for a breather, not to turn into a Good Samaritan. He wanted to go home, to his fragrant wife and clean sheets and his orderly life, and to forget all about the last nine days.

Then he heard a low groan, and he looked down at the bundle of rags on the ground, revulsion turning to pity that any human being could be reduced to this.

'Can you stand?' he asked.

The groan deepened. 'I can barely bloody breathe,' came a strangled mutter. 'Bugger off and leave me alone.'

'I'm trying to help you, you ungrateful wretch!'

'I don't want your help. I want nothing from you.'

Lance stared down at him, noticing the slight emphasis on the last word. It was an odd thing to say. It was as though he knew who his saviour was. And with a sudden sense of horror, Lance knew immediately who he was attempting to help.

'Good God. *O'Neill.*'

But as if those few angry words had been enough for him, Brian O'Neill sank back into a stupor again. Lance felt his heart thundering in his chest, wrestling with what the devil he should do now. His hatred for this man and all that he stood for was paramount in his brain, and yet, for all that, he was Cherry's brother and he couldn't just abandon him.

He was aware that there were a few onlookers now, keeping their distance, but curious to know what was going on, and clearly thinking he must be some kind of do-gooder. Well, he was anything but that, he thought viciously, but he couldn't do otherwise than get the man to a place of safety. He obviously needed medical attention and a hospital would know how to deal with him.

He called to the group of people edging nearer, ignoring the fact that they looked almost as disreputable as O'Neill himself. He spoke authoritatively.

'Would one of you see if there's a taxi on the street? This man needs to go to a hospital as soon as possible.'

They snorted. 'You won't find no taxi driver willing to put that lump of nothing into a cab, mister. They won't want him bleeding all over their seats.'

'They will if they're paid enough,' Lance blazed back. 'Now

will you do as I ask, before the man bleeds to death here and now? If that happens, you'll all be partly responsible.'

'You bloody fool,' Lance heard the husky voice from the ground. 'Get back to your wife and leave me alone.'

'I wouldn't leave a dog in this condition, so shut up and save your strength until a doctor can take a look at you,' Lance said coldly.

If he was honest, he knew he'd rather be anywhere but in this predicament. But the sooner he could get rid of O'Neill and hand him over to a hospital department the better. The next second he found his arm being clutched in a surprisingly hard grip.

'No hospital,' Brian croaked savagely. 'People go there to die. If you take me there, I swear I'll crawl out of it on my hands and knees.'

He slumped back, exhausted. The next minute, the small crowd of onlookers was back with a taxi driver among them, who began backing away at once when he saw what was awaiting him.

'That thing ain't getting in my cab,' he said with an added curse.

Lance was furious after all his efforts. 'I'll double your fare, treble it if you insist, and I'll pay for your cleaning, but this man needs help, and you're his best chance. Now, are you going to help me, or not?'

'I'll see your money up front first,' he hedged.

'You'll see it when you get this man inside the cab and not before,' Lance said, well aware that once he handed it over, it was probably the last he would see of the driver or his cab.

The man shrugged and called for assistance, and between them, the group manhandled the groaning and sometimes shrieking Brian, and got him into the back seat of the cab parked in the street behind the pub.

'Where to then, mister? I ain't got all day to waste on the likes of him.'

'I mean it,' Brian said hoarsely. 'No hospital or I walk.'

It was doubtful that he'd ever walk again unless he had proper medical care, thought Lance grimly. In those few seconds he made up his mind.

'Melchoir House,' he snapped.

★　★　★

Cherry was becoming increasingly eager for Lance to come home. The news was everywhere now. Thankfully, the strike was over, and even though it hadn't touched Bristol the way it had London and some other cities, if it had been enough to keep her husband away for all these nights, she knew it would have been serious enough. She didn't want to hear the details. She might be burying her head in the sand, but all she wanted now was for him to come home. She had missed him so much, more than she had imagined she would. It had surprised her how much she longed for him.

Their whole marriage had been built on a brief passionate affair and continued on a lie, but through it all, she had never wavered in her love for him. Yet, there was always some little devil inside her that wondered if it was the same for him. If, deep down, he really regretted tying his life to a former servant when he could have had the pick of fashionable society. The Honourable Cynthia Hetherington, for one, even though he always professed that he and Cyn were just good friends. To Cherry, even the way Lance called her Cyn was embarrassingly intimate, and could hint at something closer than friendship.

She sat by her sitting-room window late that afternoon, putting what were almost the last touches to Paula's shawl, thank God. Gerard had come home, and surely there was no reason why Lance shouldn't be here too. Unless he didn't want to come home. Unless these nine days away from her had made him wonder if she was the person he really wanted to come home to. She wished she could dismiss this little devil of doubt, but somehow she never could.

She watched without much interest as a taxicab trundled along the road beyond the grounds of Melchoir House and then turned towards the house. She had no idea who it might be, and she didn't much care. It stopped outside the side doors leading to the kitchens and away from the front of the house. But she was just able to see Lance step out of it and begin shouting for Gerard to come and help him. Her heart leapt. She couldn't see too clearly from here, but oh God, was he hurt? Surely that wasn't blood on his clothes!

She found herself flying down the stairs and through the kitchen to the side doors where the taxi had stopped. Gerard had already been alerted and was at the open door, and Cook and the kitchen-maids were crowding round.

'Let me through,' she gasped. 'I need to see if my husband is hurt.'

'I don't think it's his lordship,' Cook began uneasily, and then she put a restraining hand on Cherry's arm. 'Oh, good God Almighty, you'd better come and sit down.'

'Don't be stupid. I want to know what's going on,' Cherry snapped, and then she gasped as she saw the pathetic figure supported by her husband and Gerard, his face a pulpy mess, his clothes torn and bloodied.

'*Brian!*' she croaked.

'Cherry, we need to get him upstairs and into one of the guest rooms, but we've brought him this way so as not to alarm Mother,' Lance snapped warningly. 'He needs a doctor, so will you telephone for him to come as soon as possible, please? And Cook, prepare a bowl of hot water and a stiff drink of brandy. I'll ring down as soon as we're ready for it.'

'I told you, no doctor,' Brian snarled in a weak voice.

'Shut up man, and do as you're told.'

Cherry recognized Lance's army training. Issue the orders and keep people busy, and let those who were most involved get on with the job. She almost felt as if she should salute. But then her feet began to move and she fled back upstairs and into Lance's study, to pick up the telephone with shaking hands and ask the operator for the doctor's number.

She felt sick. After all he had done to ruin her and Lance, how could she bear to have her brother staying here in one of their pristine guest rooms and bleeding all over their perfectly laundered cotton sheets . . . Almost at once, she felt ashamed of her thoughts. What kind of a sister was she, when he was obviously hurt, even if it had been due to one of his disgraceful bare knuckle fights? But instinct told her it was something worse than that.

And this was one time when she felt glad of her status in this house, because the doctor said he would be there directly. Minutes later Lance was in the study beside her, and closing the door behind him.

'What's happened?' she said tremulously. 'And why bring him here? It's surely the last thing you wanted to do, Lance.'

'He's been kicked half to death and I wouldn't leave a dog to die like that.' He repeated what he had told Brian earlier. 'He's got nowhere else to go, and he's your brother. Does that answer it?'

She swallowed hard. Brian was a rat and he didn't deserve such compassion, especially from Lance. 'So was he in a fight?'

Lance turned away. 'You might as well hear all of it, since it all came out while we were in the taxi, and I've had to pay the damn driver handsomely for the cleaning of his cab and to keep his mouth shut. Your precious brother is in massive debt for gambling and his manager has washed his hands of him. He'll get no more work here, and he dare not advertise his name for fear of reprisals.'

Cherry was shocked. Bad as her brother was, she had never thought it would come to this. He had always come up smelling of violets in the past. But no more, it seemed.

'So what's going to happen to him?' She caught her breath raggedly. 'Lance, you're not thinking of employing him here, are you? Please don't even consider it! I couldn't bear it. You don't know what he's like. Once he gets over all this, he'll be bragging over how soft you've been and he'll be back to his old ways in no time.'

He caught hold of her hands and held them tightly.

'*If* he gets over this, I'll see that he's out of our lives for good. But first of all, we have to see what the doctor says. I'd have preferred to put him in hospital but he was having none of it, and at least while he's here I've got my eye on him.'

She had to respect him for that, even though she still thought it a bad idea to bring her brother here. Cook would be talking nineteen to the dozen to the kitchen-maids by now, letting them know who the injured man was, and what connection he had with the mistress of the house. But then she rejected the thought. Even though Cook had always had a soft spot for Brian, thinking him no more than a colourful rogue, she knew the woman would be loyal to the family, and Cherry was part of that family now. Even so, she had to be sure.

'Is Gerard with him now?' she said quickly.

'He'll stay with him until the doctor arrives.'

'Then can I inform Cook that we'll need hot water and that brandy now?'

She guessed that he was about to say that she would do best to keep out of the way for now, and in any case she never wanted to see her disreputable brother in such a state. But it was also important for her to do something, and he nodded, saying he would go back to the patient.

She went quickly back down to the kitchen, where the women were all in a huddle like a bunch of chattering magpies. They sprang apart as they saw her enter the room.

'I'd like a few words with you in private, please, Cook,' she said imperiously, and Cook shooed the younger ones away. When they were alone, she told Cherry smartly to sit down before she fell down.

'It's not me who's the patient. I don't know what's happened yet, Cook, but you know who's been brought here, and I hope I can rely on your discretion.'

She could almost feel a change in the temperature of the room as Cook's mouth tightened and she pulled herself up to her full, buxom stature.

'And I hope you're not suggesting that after all the years I've served this family that I'd ever go talking out of turn to the young skivvies, Lady Melchoir. Not me, nor Mr Gerard, I can assure you of that, and if ever our loyalty was put in question, I'd say it was time for us to leave.'

Cherry wilted at once.

'I wouldn't dream of questioning your loyalty, Cook. I just needed a word of reassurance because I'm so flummoxed by it all.'

The woman softened. 'Of course you are, my dear, and you'll be upset as well. But remember this. No matter what, he's still your brother.'

Cherry didn't want to hear this, but it was just as she thought. Love him or hate him, there was no getting away from it. When it came to blood ties, there was an obligation that could never be denied.

'Then I'd better go and see what's happening,' she said shakily. 'And please see that our requirements are sent up directly. And thank you, Cook.'

She ran back up the stairs, hesitating for a long moment outside the guest room where her brother was now installed. How could this ever happen, she thought, in a last moment of rage? After all her need to disassociate herself from ever being part of his family, he was here, in her home, and she loathed the very thought.

She hadn't heard the footsteps along the carpeted corridor until she heard a voice right behind her. She whirled around, her heart leaping, to face Lance's mother, her eyes full of suspicion and disapproval.

'What on earth is going on here, Cherry? I've been hearing such noises and disruption, and you're looking quite flushed and out of sorts. Has Lance returned home yet?'

Fifteen

Without pausing to think, Cherry caught hold of her mother-in-law's hand and pulled her along the corridor and into her sitting room. She didn't dare to try to explain anything until they were in private, and she couldn't risk Lady Elspeth either having an attack on hearing that Brian O'Neill had been badly injured and brought to the house, or walking into the guest room and seeing her brother.

'Please sit down, Lady Elspeth,' Cherry said tremblingly, wondering how delicately she could say what she had to say, and completely forgetting to address her as Mother. But perhaps after this, she would prefer not to hear that word from Cherry's lips again.

'My dear girl, what on earth has happened?' There was real concern in the lady's face now, and then her expression changed. 'It's not Lance, is it? Has something happened to him?'

'No, Lance is perfectly well,' Cherry said. She bit her lip. 'I'm really, really sorry to have to tell you this, but it's my brother who's hurt. From the look of him he's been badly beaten up, and Lance has brought him here and is expecting the doctor to arrive very soon. I'm so sorry. I know it's the last thing any of us would have wanted.'

She held her breath, awaiting a tirade of anger from Lady Elspeth. When it didn't come, she looked at her quickly. Her ladyship's face was white. She wasn't a young woman, and this news could have a bad effect on her.

'This has been a shock. Can I get you something? May I send down for some brandy?' Cherry said quickly.

Then, to her horror she burst into noisy tears. Her body seemed to go limp and hardly knowing what was happening, she felt Lady Elspeth's arms go around her, holding her tight. Without their support, she was sure she would have fallen down. The tears gradually subsided into helpless weeping, and hugely embarrassed now, she extricated herself from the embrace.

'I'm truly sorry,' she gasped. 'I didn't mean that to happen, but it just all came over me.'

'Come and sit down, Cherry, and take some deep breaths,' she was instructed, and she allowed herself to be led to an armchair. She hardly dared look at the lady sitting beside her now, offering her a dainty linen hanky to dry her tears. It was all surreal, and she wished she could turn back the clock . . . but to when, exactly? Her head was buzzing and it was hard to think straight at all.

'Do you feel a little better, my dear?' Lady Elspeth was saying, in a surprisingly gentle voice.

'I think so. But what must you think of me – and my family? We've let you down so badly,' she said abjectly.

But dear Lord, this wasn't how she wanted to be! She wanted to be strong and self-assured, the way she had always been, but all the stuffing seemed to have gone out of her, and she could only sit here, holding the hand of the woman who should truly despise her.

'We're not responsible for our families, Cherry.'

'But we are! Aren't I supposed to be my brother's keeper – or something?'

She felt herself blush scarlet. Why the dickens she should start spouting the Bible now, she had no idea. She felt as if she was in the grip of some kind of madness when words she didn't mean to say kept erupting from her mouth.

'I'm sending for some strong sweet tea to help you calm down, Cherry.'

'Why are you being so kind to me?' she asked huskily after a moment.

'Because you're my son's wife,' came the unexpected reply.

It was turning into such a bizarre day, Cherry thought. She dearly wished she knew what was happening in the guest room now, but it was best to wait for Lance to tell her what the doctor had said. Facing Lance was something else that was making her heart pound. The fact that his mother had become astonishingly understanding was odd enough, but how was he going to feel towards her, knowing her brother was presumably obliged to stay in the house for a while? Would he turn against her for bringing this madness into his ordered life? No matter how illogical the thoughts, she simply couldn't get them out of her head.

She had calmed down a little by the time the strong sweet tea was delivered by a maid, and Lady Elspeth stayed with her until at last Lance appeared. If he was surprised to see his two ladies apparently companionable together, he made no comment on it, and spoke briskly.

'Your brother's not seriously hurt, Cherry. He has facial bruising and considerably more bruising to his body, but he has a strong constitution because of his profession, so no bones were broken. The pain is quite severe, and he will be kept sedated for twenty-four hours. Gerard is tending to him now, but tomorrow morning the doctor will send a nurse while he remains in bed for at least a week. She will stay in the adjoining dressing room and meals will be sent up to them both.'

In other words, there was no chance of Brian O'Neill becoming part of the family. It was obvious that the less Lance had to see of him the better, and Cherry couldn't blame him for that.

'And afterwards?' she said, as he paused. 'I suppose you will allow me to see my own brother now and then?' she couldn't resist adding sarcastically.

'Of course you may see him, my love, but before you do, you should know that he and I have exchanged some harsh words and come to a mutual decision regarding his future.'

She stared at him. He couldn't mean he was going to hand him over to the police or contact his debtors, or he would surely have done so by now.

'What are your plans, Lance?' his mother said, since Cherry seemed momentarily to have been struck dumb.

'While he is here I am going to see the shipping agent at the docks to see what cargo ships are shortly bound for Australia. Your brother will be signed on as a crew member on a one-way journey as soon as possible. I will supply him with a set of clothes and enough money to send him on his way, and that will be the last we shall see of him.'

His voice was distant now, and he didn't look at Cherry while he spoke as if expecting indignation at the very least. But as she gave a choking sound, he looked at her sharply.

'It's for the best, Cherry, and he's in total agreement.'

'I know, and I'm grateful,' she said with a strangled gasp. 'It's just that it all seems so final – and such a *relief*!'

If it was wicked to think that way about her brother, she didn't care. The relief was so great she almost felt like fainting, and her head swam.

'My dear girl, this has all been a shock for you, so why don't you go and lie down?' Lady Elspeth said gently, and this whole day seemed to be so topsy-turvy now she could only nod and let herself be led away to her bedroom.

'I won't forget this,' she murmured to no one in particular as she finally lay on her bed, but by then she was alone. She closed her eyes tightly, blocking out the entire world.

Next morning she stood outside the guest room door with her heart beating rapidly, knowing she had to go in, and not knowing what she would find. Lance had gone when she awoke that morning and she felt oddly bereft. But Gerard was already in the guest room with a tray of tea and porridge, and her brother was half-sitting up in the bed, wincing with every movement. His face was swollen, his eyes black, and she allowed herself a moment of pity, even though she knew he brought everything on himself, and always had.

'Morning,' he grunted. 'This is a rum do, isn't it?'

'You could call it that,' Cherry said, hardly knowing what to do next. It was embarrassing to talk with Gerard still in the room, but he was as discreet as ever, seeming to fade into the background as soon as he had delivered Brian's breakfast and arranged a bed table over him.

'I'll be back for the tray in half an hour, Ma'am,' he said, addressing Cherry. 'And I understand the doctor will be calling with the nurse shortly.'

'Thank you, Gerard,' she murmured, well aware that he preferred to talk to her than her objectionable brother.

Once they were alone, Brian snorted. 'Did you see the way he looked at me? He thinks I'm the scum of the earth, and he's nothing but a bloody servant. I don't need a bloody nurse fussing over me neither.'

Cherry's brief sympathy fizzled away.

'You should be thankful you're here at all,' she snapped. 'Lance should have left you in the gutter where you belong.'

'Well, that's a fine way to talk to your brother,' he growled. 'And take this muck away. I can't eat slops.'

'You'd have a job to eat anything else with that swollen face. Can't you be grateful for once and realize that people are trying to help you?'

'By sending me off to Australia and out of your way for good?'

'I thought it was what you wanted. And for goodness' sake eat something. You look like a scarecrow.'

He grimaced as he spooned some of the porridge noisily into his mouth.

'Yes, I do want to get out of this bloody hell-hole for good. There's nothing here for me any more,' he said at last.

For a second Cherry's eyes prickled to think they had come to this. He was her older brother and their mother had left her in his care. Instead of which he had always been a thorn in her flesh. She blinked the tears away.

'I'll leave you to your breakfast,' she said. 'I'm sure the doctor will be here soon, but if you need anything, you just have to ring the bell.'

'And will you come running?' he couldn't resist taunting her.

'No. I'm not one of the servants here,' she retorted, and then she turned and walked stiffly out of the room before either of them could say anything more.

She was shaking, but it was more with the realization of the distance between them now, that nothing could ever cross. Their lives had gone much too far in different directions.

To her surprise Lady Elspeth was in the dining room when she went down for breakfast. She hadn't been up this early for weeks, but it gradually dawned on Cherry that this latest incident was giving her a strange sense of vitality.

'Lance has gone to see the shipping agent, my dear,' she said matter-of-factly, as if this was a normal occurrence.

'Thank you,' Cherry said, swallowing. It was all going to happen then, but she had had no doubt of that. Lance had influence and money, and he would send her brother away as surely as the sun rose every morning.

'It's for the best, Cherry,' Elspeth said sharply.

'I know. It's just that he's the only person in the world who's my flesh and blood, and it's hard to accept that he's such a rotter.'

She turned away from the sympathetic eyes and helped herself to the food on the side table, even though she didn't have much appetite. Her innards seemed to be constantly churning lately, and if it wasn't that she felt obliged to stay in the house at least until the nurse arrived, she would dearly love to go and see Paula and spill out all her emotions. But she couldn't do that, and nor was it fair on Paula when she was so near her time.

'I'm sorry but I can't eat this,' she said finally, when she had only picked at the scrambled egg, and the fried bacon threatened to make her stomach revolt. 'I need some fresh air. Do you mind if I take a walk around the grounds?'

'Some fresh air will do you good, dear. You do look a little pale.'

She escaped as soon as she could, knowing that the mere smell of the food was making her want to throw up. Outside, she took in long gulps of air, and walked slowly through the fragrant gardens in the direction of the stables. She guessed that Lance would have gone to the docks on Noble, and she strained her eyes, wishing that he would come back and give her some news. She glimpsed the doctor's car arriving and kept well back, not wanting to get into conversation with him, or to meet the matronly and starchy-looking woman with him. Gerard would see that they were taken to Brian's room, and she hid a smile. If her brother expected to see some pretty young nurse he was in for a shock. This one looked as if she would stand no nonsense from a prickly patient.

A short while later she forgot them as she saw a rider approaching the stables and recognized Lance's stance on the horse. As always her heart skipped a beat at the upright way he sat, and his control of his mount. But today such things were not as important as wanting news of his plans for her brother.

As he dismounted and handed over Noble's reins to one of the grooms, she found herself clasping her hands together. She had brought this family such turmoil, and she could never forget it. What if they were never going to rid themselves of Brian O'Neill? Immediately, coupled with that thought was one of guilt that she could be thinking so badly of her brother. Despite all, he was still her brother, she thought bitterly.

Lance saw her standing motionless and as he reached her she began to speak nervously. Her voice was stilted and awkward, and for a moment she felt she didn't know this hard-faced man at all.

'I was worried when I didn't see you this morning. Your mother told me where you'd gone.'

'I don't want to talk here,' he replied. 'Let's go into the shrubbery.'

She followed him almost meekly, wondering if something had gone wrong, but once they were in the seclusion of the shrubbery he caught hold of her hands and held them tightly.

'After a considerable amount of persuasion I've managed to secure a post for your brother on a cargo ship to Australia in ten days' time,' he said guardedly.

'Persuasion, and bribery?' she couldn't help saying.

'A bit of that too. So how do you really feel about it?'

She looked at him in bewilderment, hearing the anxiety he couldn't quite hide, and realizing for the first time that he might think she was going to turn against him for doing this. And he couldn't be more wrong!

'I'm more relieved than I can say,' she told him shakily. 'For far too long I've always dreaded when he's going to turn up again like a bad penny.'

Lance replied grimly. 'There'll be no danger of that when we've got half a world between us and him.'

He pulled her into his arms, and she gave a soft sigh as she leaned against him, wondering if this was truly the end of all their worries.

'Let's go and see him together and tell him the good news,' Lance went on, his face breaking into a smile for the first time that morning.

Feeling more relaxed now, Cherry went indoors with him and they tapped on the guest-room door, preparing to let Brian know what was to become of him. The door was immediately opened, and the middle-aged woman in a sensible nursing uniform barred their way.

'Good morning. I'm Nurse Jenkins, and my patient is resting. Am I addressing Lord and Lady Melchoir?'

Cherry resisted the wild urge to giggle at her starchy manner. Heaven help Brian, she thought mischievously. He had undoubtedly met his match with this one. She felt Lance squeeze her arm and she composed her face.

'That is correct,' he said smoothly. 'And if the patient is awake, then we will see him now.'

She was clearly no match for Lance, and she backed down at once and stood aside to let them in, muttering about getting on with her work in her room.

'Good for you,' Cherry whispered. 'And how are you today, Brian?' she asked her brother quickly, before Lance could tell him the news.

Her sympathy faded as she saw the scowl on his face, just visible among the bruises. She wasn't sure if he was going to like what he was about to hear, either, but he was going to hear it anyway.

'I'm as you see,' he growled, 'and I'd be a damn sight better without the old dragon breathing fire on me all the time.'

'The old dragon isn't hard of hearing,' came a voice from the adjoining dressing room, making Cherry smother an outright laugh.

But they were here for a reason that didn't need eavesdroppers.

'Would you please leave us for half an hour, Nurse Jenkins?' Lance called to her, and the woman left stiffly.

He sat on a bedside chair and pulled out a sheaf of papers from his inside pocket, and spoke coolly to Brian.

'These are your papers to join a Captain Doyle on the cargo ship Alliance, bound for Sydney, Australia, in ten days' time. You have been signed on as a deck-hand and you will be suitably attired before you leave, and given sufficient money for your immediate needs. Once you arrive in Australia it is up to you what you do with the opportunity. Is that clear?'

'Perfectly,' Brian said. 'Am I expected to thank you?'

Cherry felt sick with shame at such ill manners, but Lance put a hand on her arm to restrain her from saying anything.

'The only thanks I want is that you get out of our lives for good and never come back. If I get one sniff of you revealing anything at all about me or my family, I will have you behind bars so quickly you won't see it coming.'

'Oh really? And how will you do that?' Brian sneered.

'By revealing where you are to a number of interested parties, and by showing the police certain blackmailing letters I still have in my possession.'

It was his trump card. Cherry could see it by the way her brother seemed to shrink down in the bed. Her heart thumped wildly as he slowly nodded.

'All right. You have my word, if it means anything to you.'

'Good. Then I'll send your nurse back to you. I'm sure she'll be gentle giving you a bed bath.'

'I bet she won't be!' Cherry almost exploded when they were finally out of the room.

'I'm counting on it,' Lance told her.

The days before Brian left seemed to pass in a daze for Cherry. She visited him every day, despite his grumblings about his dragon nurse. He was physically strong, but under Lance and the doctor's orders, Nurse Jenkins remained in the house and in control until the day he was to depart on the cargo ship for Australia. Only then did the enormity of it all hit Cherry. She was really getting rid of the person who had betrayed his own sister so wickedly in trying to extort money out of Lance and his father. But through it all, that one small sliver of regret for what was happening to him remained in her mind. Because he was still her brother, her only living blood relative.

She found it impossible to relay such thoughts to Lance, sure that he wouldn't understand. And although she and Lady Elspeth had found a new respect for one another now, she could hardly confide in her. She felt oddly isolated from both of them. They ate together, they conversed, and she slept in her husband's arms, but there was a restraint between them now that she knew wouldn't be finally resolved until Brian O'Neill was out of this house for ever. She kept tight-lipped about her feelings, and very often she felt sick with worry that it could still drive her and Lance apart.

It didn't occur to her that Lance was being extra wary too, because even now, he wasn't sure of her real feelings about all this. It could so easily end in her resenting him to the point of hatred for sending her brother to the other side of the world where they were hardly ever likely to meet again.

But all these thoughts were put aside when the day finally came, and Gerard drove them and her brother down to the docks. By now, his bruises and scars had faded and he looked rugged and respectable in the new clothes that would be suitable for a deck-hand on a cargo ship – they were nothing fancy, but better than he had worn in ages, Cherry suspected.

She sat in the back of the limousine with him, not knowing what to say to the virtual stranger who sat beside her. Until the moment when the docks came into view and the whiffs of the river enveloped them, he too had said nothing, and then she felt his hand grip hers.

'I won't forget what you and your man have done for me, Cherry,' he said gruffly. 'I know damn well I don't deserve it, but if it means anything at all to you, I'll do my best to make good in Australia. I'll probably never see you again, but I'd like to think I could make you proud of me in the end.'

She looked away, biting her lip. Australia was so far away, and whatever became of him after this, she could have no way of knowing.

'I could send you a postcard now and then,' he added almost desperately, as if reading her thoughts.

'Well, I know if Mum were here, she'd want us to know how you were getting on,' she muttered, transferring her own feelings to that of their mother.

It seemed to satisfy Brian, and he gave one last squeeze of her hand as the car slid smoothly to a halt in the road behind the docks.

'We'll see you on to the ship. Make sure you've got all the necessary papers I obtained for you,' Lance told him briskly.

'Making sure you've really seen the back of me, eh?' he said with a grin.

'Something like that,' Lance agreed.

They walked to where the cargo ship was anchored. It looked grim and forbidding, and nothing like the lively pleasure boats that cruised up and down the river in the summer months. This was a businesslike, working ship, and from the look of some of the hands already on board, Brian was going to have to pull his weight. And a good thing too, Cherry thought savagely. He shouldn't think all this was being made too easy for him.

'So this is finally goodbye, sis,' he said, turning to her.

'Goodbye, and good luck,' she said, unable to stop her voice choking.

The next moment, whether she wanted it or not, he had put

his arms around her and hugged her tight. Then Lance pulled her away and they returned to the car without a backward glance. She found it hard to hide the tears, knowing this was truly the end of an era, and that the last part of her old life was gone for ever. Lance spoke gently now.

'He'll be all right, you know. His sort always fall on their feet.'

'His sort?' she asked bitterly.

'He's a fighter, isn't he? They always know how to fall.'

Cherry supposed he was trying to vindicate his harsh words, but they did nothing to lessen the empty feelings inside her now. She was sending her brother out of her life, and it felt as if she was abandoning him for ever. And to add to her misery, she and Lance were as far apart as if they too had half a world between them.

'Can we just get home? I have a splitting headache and I feel sick. I need to lie down for a while,' she mumbled, suddenly exhausted, and feeling more like an old crone than a happy young married woman.

As soon as they arrived back at Melchoir House she went to their bedroom, drawing the bedroom curtains and trying to blot out all her thoughts as she lay on the bed. But it was futile, because the thoughts kept crowding her mind, and none of them was pleasant. She had no idea where Lance went, but no doubt to celebrate with his horses, having got rid of an irritating burr in his life. Perhaps he thought of his wife in the same way now. Perhaps he regretted ever marrying her, since she had brought him nothing but trouble. The tears trickled down her cheeks, wondering if there was any real future for them at all.

When she could think more sensibly, it horrified her that she could even imagine such a thing. Where was the excitement and the passion that had filled her with so much happiness in those first heady days of being Lance's wife? Where had it all gone? Where had that carefree girl gone? She turned into her pillow and sobbed, wishing for one mad moment that she could truly turn back the clock and still be that girl, the one who had always confided her deepest secrets to her best friend, whispering them long into the night in the small attic bedroom they shared.

With such memories came thoughts of Paula, whom she had

barely thought about at all during these last few frantic weeks. Her time must be imminent now, and she must think Cherry had forgotten her. Her last conscious thought before she drifted into an uneasy sleep was that she would definitely go and see her tomorrow.

The urgent tapping on her bedroom door awoke her with a start. She had no idea how long she had been asleep and at first she thought it must be night because the room was so dark. Then she realized the curtains were drawn, and the recent memories came flooding back. She dismissed them at once, and called out to whoever it was to come in. One of the maids stood there, excitement in her eyes, her voice flustered and high-pitched.

'There's someone come to see you, Ma'am, but Cook says he's to stay in the kitchen, and asks you to come down if you will, begging your pardon.'

As she turned tail, Cherry sat up at once and followed the girl downstairs. Her heart thumped, wondering if something dreadful had happened – even if Brian had done the unthinkable and jumped ship almost before it sailed, and turned up here again for more handouts.

Before she reached the kitchen she could hear the sounds of merriment. Cook had always had a soft spot for her brother, so the noise could have signified anything or nothing. She opened the door quickly, to the sight of Cook and Gerard handing round glasses of cider to the giggling kitchen-maids. In the middle of them all was Harold, Paula's husband, his scarlet face as round and beaming as a full moon. Everyone was jabbering at once, but the minute he saw Cherry he pumped her hands up and down and shouted out his news.

'Paula's had the baby, Cherry, I mean your ladyship, and I was told to come up here and tell you as soon as possible, since you had to be the first to know. But Cook prised it out of me before I got the chance, so I hope you'll forgive me for that, and come to see Paula as soon as you can.'

As he paused for breath, still laughing like a maniac, Cherry yelled back at him above the din. 'But what is it? A boy or a girl?'

'Eh? Blimey, I nearly forgot to tell you, didn't I? It's a boy, and a real little bouncer according to the midwife, with a pair of lungs on him that would do credit to a town crier. We're calling him Thomas, after my old dad.'

Cook laughed, and thrust a glass of cider into Cherry's hands.

'And he's obviously the best baby that ever lived, like they all are,' she added with a wink. 'I daresay Paula will be bringing the little tyke to see us when she's out of her confinement.'

'Of course she will,' Harold said. 'And now I've delivered the message I've got to get back to them, so I'll say goodbye to you all. You won't forget to come, will you, Che . . . your ladyship?' he said directly to Cherry.

'Tell her I'll be there tomorrow. I was going to come and see her then anyway, so now I'll have two of them to see, won't I? And give her my love.'

She escaped out of the kitchen as soon as she could. She should have been there to support Paula in these last days, she thought distractedly. She should have known when the baby was about to be born, and instead of that, she had been caught up in her brother's reckless life as usual. But no more.

She told Lance and his mother about the new arrival at dinner that evening, and could see that Lady Elspeth was more interested than Lance. Babies weren't of much interest to men unless they were their own sons and heirs, she supposed, and the way things were going between them now, such an event seemed as far off as, well, Australia. But when she said she would be going to see Paula and the baby tomorrow, Lance said at once that Gerard could drive her there.

'I'd rather walk, thank you,' she said. 'Walking is always a good time for thinking. I've done plenty of walking into the city and back from this house over the years, and it hasn't killed me yet.'

If he took it as a deliberate snub to his offer, and a stark reminder of her past role in Melchoir House, she no longer cared. After the excitement of Paula's news, she felt deflated and out of sorts. It was envy, of course, she thought with total honesty. Paula now had everything she had ever wanted . . . while she felt as though she had nothing. No pot of gold at the end of this rainbow after all.

She could barely control her impatience until early afternoon the next day, by which time she hoped Paula would be rested and eager to see her. She brought out the knitted shawl it had taken her so many frustrating hours to finish, and she wrapped it in some gift paper, all the time imagining how it was going to look holding his warm little body. And then she was on her way, her heart beating fast, because Paula was no longer the same girl she had always been. She was a mother now, a million miles away from being simply Cherry's girlhood friend.

She knocked on the door of the house anxiously, and it was opened by a motherly woman who introduced herself as Mrs Bond, the midwife.

'I can guess who you are by your smart clothes, my dear. You'll be Lady Melchoir, if I'm not mistaken,' she said cheerfully.

'That's right,' Cherry murmured. And she was also the visitor, while this woman, with her sleeves rolled up, looked as if she was part of Paula's life.

'Well, you go on upstairs and see the two beauties while I put the kettle on, and I'll bring you both up a nice cup of tea. Paula's been singing your praises for I don't know how long, and I know she can't wait to see you.'

To say she was nervous as she climbed the stairs was an understatement. It was absurd, but she felt as though she was about to see a new and different Paula from the one she had always known. Instead of which, she looked exactly the same, sitting on the side of the bed with her hair tumbling about her face as she leaned over the crib and crooned softly. When she looked up her face broke into a delighted smile.

'I thought you were never coming, Cherry, and I've been so impatient to see you. Come and look at him. Isn't he the most beautiful little thing you ever saw? And to think that me and Harold managed to make him between us!'

She was suddenly laughing and crying at the same time, and Cherry crossed the room, feeling as though she crossed far more than that. Whatever enormous divide she had imagined between them was gone in an instant, and they hugged one another as if they had never been apart.

But then it was time to do her duty and admire the pink-faced infant lying peacefully in the crib, his mouth blowing tiny bubbles in his sleep, his shock of dark hair just like Harold's. She told Paula how wonderful and perfect he was, and handed over the shawl with great ceremony.

'It's lovely, and I'll always treasure it because I know what a hard time you had making it,' Paula told her solemnly and then they were laughing again.

By the time Mrs Bond had brought the tea they had calmed down. The baby had woken up and Cherry was allowed to hold him, breathing in the special scent of him and falling instantly in love.

'That's right, my dear, start getting your hand in for when your own bab arrives,' the midwife commented.

Cherry grimaced. 'Heaven knows when that will be!'

Mrs Bond scrutinized her steadily. 'Oh, I'd say in about six or seven months at most. I'm never wrong about these things, and you've got that certain pinched look around your nose, and maybe your clothes have been feeling a bit tight lately, as well as missing certain other natural functions and feeling off your food. But I'll leave you ladies to enjoy your tea while I get on downstairs.'

When she had left them, Paula almost squealed.

'Is she right, Cherry? Are you expecting?'

'I don't know! I don't think so,' she said, completely taken aback by the woman's words, and too shocked to know what to think. 'I have been feeling off colour for days, but I thought that was because of Brian. But I'm not going to tell you about that right now, except to say that he's gone for good.'

'Well, if Mrs Bond says you're in the family way I bet you are! Some say she's a bit of a witch in that department,' Paula said in a hushed voice. 'Oh, I hope it's true, Cherry, just like we always wanted it to be!'

She prattled on and on, but Cherry couldn't remember a thing that they talked about after that. She went home in a daze, her footsteps quickening the nearer she got to the house. She should dismiss Mrs Bond's complacent words as being no more than old wives' tales, and yet it was all beginning to make sense. The feelings of queasiness and being off her food; the tightness in the bodices of her clothes; and the absence of her monthlies once or twice recently which she had merely put down to anxiety. But maybe it was more than that. And if Mrs Bond was a bit of a witch, and never wrong . . .

She was desperate to talk to Lance now. Would this be the one thing that would bring them together again, even though they had never really been apart? People always said it was wrong to think of a child holding a marriage together, but she knew it was something he had dearly wanted for a long time, and so had she. So where would he be on this lovely spring afternoon when she needed him so much?

Her steps took her unerringly towards the earthy scents of the stables where she saw him rubbing down his horse after their gallop across the Downs. They looked so good together, the man and the horse. For a moment she was jealous of their companionship, and she wanted that closeness for herself. She called his name, and as he turned, he smiled, and then she was running, running towards him, back to the place where it had all begun, when she had believed she was simply chasing rainbows in falling so hopelessly in love with a man she could never hope to love her in return.

As he looked at her excited face he could see there was something special she wanted to tell him, and he held out his arms to her, enfolding her inside them. Knowing she had been to see Paula, he nuzzled his lips into her cheek.

'Let me guess. This is going to be all about babies from now on, isn't it, Cherry-ripe?' he said teasingly.

'You know, I think you could just be right,' she said, the laughter catching in her throat.

NEATH PORT TALBOT LIBRARY AND INFORMATION SERVICES

1		25		49		73	
2		26		50		74	
3		27		51		75	
4		28		52		76	
5		29		53		77	
6		30		54		78	
7		31		55		79	
8		32		56		80	
9		33		57		81	
10	.	34		58		82	
11		35		59		83	
12		36		60		84	
13		37		61		85	
14		38		62		86	
15		39		63		87	
16		40		64		88	
17		41		65		89	
18		42		66		90	
19		43		67		91	
20		44		68		92	
21		45		69		COMMUNITY SERVICES	
22		46		70			
23		47		71		NPT/111	
24		48		72		.	

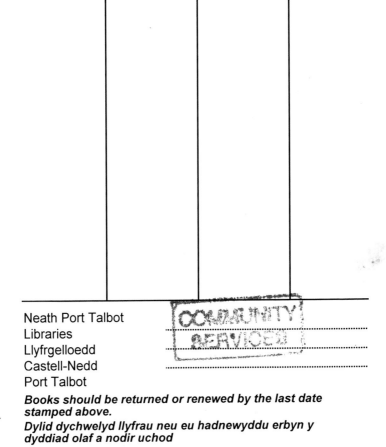

Neath Port Talbot
Libraries
Llyfrgelloedd
Castell-Nedd
Port Talbot

*Books should be returned or renewed by the last date
stamped above.*
*Dylid dychwelyd llyfrau neu eu hadnewyddu erbyn y
dyddiad olaf a nodir uchod*

COMMUNITY
SERVICES

NEATH PORT TALBOT LIBRARIES

2300004171